ENCLAVE

ALSO BY
CLAIRE G. COLEMAN

Terra Nullius
The Old Lie

ENCLAVE

CLAIRE G. COLEMAN

hachette
AUSTRALIA

This project has been assisted by the Australian Government through the Australia Council for the Arts, its arts funding and advisory body.

Published in Australia and New Zealand in 2022
by Hachette Australia
(an imprint of Hachette Australia Pty Limited)
Gadigal Country, Level 17, 207 Kent Street, Sydney, NSW 2000
www.hachette.com.au

Hachette Australia acknowledges and pays our respects to the past, present and future Traditional Owners and Custodians of Country throughout Australia and recognises the continuation of cultural, spiritual and educational practices of Aboriginal and Torres Strait Islander peoples. Our head office is located on the lands of the Gadigal people of the Eora Nation.

10 9 8 7 6 5 4 3 2 1

A catalogue record for this book is available from the National Library of Australia

ISBN: 978 0 7336 4086 5 (paperback)

Cover design by Grace West
Author photo courtesy of Jen Dainer, Industrial Arc
Typeset in 12.5/18.3 pt Bembo Pro by Bookhouse, Sydney
Printed and bound in Australia by McPherson's Printing Group

MIX
Paper from
responsible sources
FSC
www.fsc.org
FSC® C001695

The paper this book is printed on is certified against the Forest Stewardship Council® Standards. McPherson's Printing Group holds FSC® chain of custody certification SA-COC-005379. FSC® promotes environmentally responsible, socially beneficial and economically viable management of the world's forests.

For Lily, always

For Robert, I owe you so much
and
For all our trans and queer sibs, you matter.

Turning and turning in the widening gyre
The falcon cannot hear the falconer;
Things fall apart; the centre cannot hold;
Mere anarchy is loosed upon the world

– WILLIAM BUTLER YEATS, 'THE SECOND COMING'

WALLS WITHIN WALLS within walls. Enclaves within enclaves within walls. Lives within lives, living within walls. Everybody is alone within walls, and their enclave is filled with their echoes.

ZOOM – THE GATES

THE SUN IS casting its first light over the town; sneaking up, about to peek over the horizon, like a child stealing a look at grown-ups' party.

Inside the monotonously grey walls: rectangular, chalk-white buses are gathered, waiting. Some are lined up neurotically neat, others more scattered; some appear like gossiping groups, but all are plain, unadorned, identical, nothing on them to identify their owners or speak of their purpose. Outside the gates: black buses are nosed almost perfectly parallel into parking spots. There is nothing to differentiate the buses outside from those inside but the colour and the inside-buses' lack of order. People in black unload themselves from the black vehicles outside, mill about the hardstand before the looming, intimidating gates.

Outside, those people filter into long fence-divided queues, each holding up a card, the size and shape of a credit card; each approach someone in a uniform – from a row of twelve – who holds a machine to those cards. Those whose cards make the machines beep, which appears to be everybody, are waved though a narrower gate. Guards in jumpsuits – bulky in some places that implied armour, in other places that suggested weapons – watch the proceedings, hands on batons on their belts.

Inside, those people pass through the gates, each strolling to a bus, each seeming to know already which one they are heading to; though how they did was anyone's guess. There is no confusion, nobody getting lost; no need for the armoured, armed guards to approach any of them. There seems to be no rush, it is the gate that has bottlenecked them; once through the early-comers feel no urgency.

Outside, the now-empty buses drive away as the last person has their ID card bipped and slips through the gates. The last few through the gates, know they are last and, not wanting to delay their bus, rush to their vehicles. The men with ID machines walk through after them, the armed Security following. The gates close, a hidden beeper beeps, followed by the clunk of an electronic lock engaging.

A lower wall circles the bus park, barely taller than the buses themselves. Wide gates open and let the full buses through. Silence descends; the guards stop long enough to scan the car park once, although through their visors it is impossible to know what they are looking at or looking for, or even if they have faces. Then they turn and walk through smaller doors into another compound.

The sun drags the last piece of itself past the horizon.

A lone figure in black steps out from the shadows of the bus-park wall, following the security guards to the door before disappearing again into shadow.

PART 1

ENCLAVE

FRIDAY

CHRISTINE RARELY REMEMBERED her dreams but of late those she recalled had veered too often into nightmare, waking her in a cold fearful sweat. Jeering faces stared into hers; she saw her friends flayed, gutted, bleeding. Mother's face shattered into floating smuts; Father melted into a puddle the colour of skin; her brother cooked to ash and blown away on silent winds; herself bound, alone with her pain forever.

She woke, barely able to shake off the terror and ponder why she had been so stupid as to sleep another night on the couch. The light of the day had climbed through the window and tiptoed its silent way across the floor, dust motes dancing in its wake. Christine caught it as it stalked the couch where she lay, basking in the colour and movement of the television. The morning sun washed the pixels pale and painted daylight on the yellow-white walls, erasing the blue of television.

The volume on the flat screen was down so low it was almost muted. Hands gesticulated, mouths moved, the twitches of noise that snuck out reminding Christine of moths beating themselves to death against a light fitting or wasps trying to escape a jar. Dut dut, dut dut.

Somebody must have changed the channel to the 24-hour news while she had been sleeping; she fumed at whoever it was and switched channels at random. Anything but the news.

She could not sleep, she could not wake, she could not think. She stared, half-blind, at the cold screen of her smartphone.

Safetynet told her the news: updating her on the crime Safetynet and Security were protecting her from; informing her of the dangers outside, the bad people and dangerous criminals being kept outside the city Wall; of the terrorists threatening her life, buildings falling, people dying. Safetynet told her she had no emails. Safetynet informed her of the latest fads, the latest fashions, the latest pointless things it had calculated she needed.

Safetynet reminded her that there was a new album by the band it thought was her favourite; that there were clothes she might like in the spring collection at what it thought was her favourite boutique; that her hairstyle, snapped by the selfie cam on her phone, was out of fashion. Safetynet asked if she would like to 'click here' to make an emergency appointment with a stylist; whether she would like to one-click-buy the album. Safetynet reminded her that it was her birthday in a month, told her she had no emails. Safetynet said there had been three attempts to enter the city illegally yesterday – contained and neutralised by Security before anyone inside was endangered – and 22,219 attempts to illegally access Safetynet in the past week.

Safetynet told her there were no emails.

She glanced up irritated when the flatulent hiss of bus air brakes sounded in the street outside, considered complaining but couldn't be bothered.

A short, distracted time later Christine heard the expected scratch of a key trying to find its keyhole, the soft clunk as it slid home, the click of the door lock disengaging. She did not hear the door open, someone must have oiled it, did not look up as it clicked near-silently closed.

Someone's shadow drifted past, throwing her face into darkness for a moment while she read something on her phone she did not really care about. She heard 'morning miss' in a false-cheerful tone; lost interest the moment the shadow had gone. She did not care where the servants went or what they did as long as they did their work quietly and, most importantly, didn't bother her.

As she lay on the couch, the staff worked around her, like ghosts; as silent as they could manage, almost as invisible as she desired them to be. They might not have bothered turning up, except that she knew that she would be aware of the mess if they didn't; would be aware if the kitchen was not stocked with snacks or if dinner was not made. If not, her mother would ensure she knew all about it.

Mother would force her to care.

As the sunlight approached the couch on spider-light feet, she dropped her phone and entered another dreamless sleep.

She woke when the sun should have been beating her face sore, cutting her eyes to ribbons, and noticed that someone had closed the curtains to protect her from its rays.

The smell of her house, the smell she had come home to during her years of secondary school, was again in her nostrils: dinner in a bain-marie and some unidentified floral-scented cleaning products that staff were instructed to use. Mother liked the scent; Christine was less keen but it was as much a part of her life as her own smell, or of Mother's perfume, or Father's stale cigar and whiskey sweat.

She checked her phone again. She had waited months, for what felt like years, for a message that had not come, a promise that had not been fulfilled.

Perhaps the promise could not be kept; could never be kept. Perhaps something terrible had happened.

Something more terrible.

The panic penetrated her surface and shook the core of her being.

No longer able to rest she stalked the house, looking for trouble, though what trouble she sought was impossible to identify. Her home was completely empty; she could feel the walls keening with loneliness.

Mother floated through the front door on a cloud of perfume and stale booze. Her outstanding capacity for talk and her even more legendary ability to stay till the end of any event must finally have been expended.

She gave Christine a robotic hug, disappeared upstairs before returning wearing a dove-grey lounging ensemble, then poured a glass of red from the open bottle on the kitchen bench.

'Hello, dear.' There was too much evidence of drink in Mother's usual manicured voice for the wine in her hand to have been her first. 'What did you get up to today?'

Christine shrugged. 'Mostly sleeping, I guess.'

'Perhaps you could have gone and had a haircut. You need to get rid of that ridiculous student hair; maybe have a chance to find a husband. My stylist can possibly fit you in. Would you like me to call him?'

There was a shallow arrogance to Mother's tone that Christine didn't like. She wanted her mother to go out again. 'There's plenty of time to get a haircut later, once I work out what I want to do next year,' Christine diverted.

Mother shrugged, rolled her eyes and said, 'What's there to work out?' Glass empty, she wobbled on her stiletto heels back into the kitchen to pour another drink.

'You could get yourself some decent clothes at least,' Mother said, just loud enough for Christine to hear.

Christine sat and stared without seeing the television, watching the flutter of colour, the movement of nothing. Words appeared and disappeared, scrolled across the bottom of the screen. Christine did not bother reading them, she knew what they would say. She didn't need to watch the news to learn fear.

They were safe there at home, safe in their town. She knew that. They all knew that.

Mother knocked back glass after glass as if it was a race; as if she was worried someone would storm the house and steal the wine before she could drink it all; as if she was worried she would die and there would be full bottles left in the cellar to mourn her. The bottle emptied with a last despairing 'glug';

Mother drunk-stumbled to the wine rack to open another, struggled to strangle the top off the bottle, looked satisfied when the seal cracked.

The roar of an engine echoing from the garage signalled Father's arrival. When he entered there was no glass in Mother's hand, no half-drunk bottle. The only wine not in the rack was the customary bottle open on the table ready for dinner – carefully chosen, by the cook or somebody, to match whatever it was they would be eating.

Later, they collected their dinner from the kitchen buffet, presented the same choices as the day before. Christine watched her parents filling their plates, taking great care to at least change the quantities of each item.

The meal was silent, but not in the 'we're too busy shovelling food in our faces to talk' way. The three of them ate like people who had hours to complete the meal but had nothing left to say to one another. Christine barely ate; Mother and Father had small and pointed forkfuls.

At the end of the meal, Christine made to stand and walk away. Father looked up from his glass. His face turned from pinkish to whitish as it left the well of light reflected from the wine.

'Christine, please. I have something to say.'

'Yes, Father.'

He grimaced. She didn't know what else to call him; no way she was going to call him 'daddy'.

'It's your twenty-first birthday in a month.'

She knew that, obviously; Safetynet Social had probably reminded him only hours before; when it reminded everybody else in town. Well everyone who followed her socials, at least.

'You did remarkably well at university. I'm proud of you,' he continued. She knew that too, not the pride bit though; she had not thought him capable of pride in others. She still didn't. He had never shown her any evidence of genuine pride.

She wondered if there was a point to his words.

'It was quite surprising,' he said.

She waited, not with patience, but rather with a practised ability to shut down her brain and suppress her mouth whenever her parents were talking; particularly Father. Nobody needed to hear what she was thinking.

'Yes, Father,' she said to move things along as her mother raised her glass to her face and hid behind it.

'Tomorrow we are going out together, as a family. I have a surprise for you. A birthday present.'

He stood abruptly and strode from the room. Christine could hear his heavy tread thumping slowly up the stairs before the door closed, so quietly she could not be sure it happened at all. She looked at her mother, saw the confusion she felt mirrored on that familiar face, so like and unlike her own. Father, he of the slow anger and the always heavy tread, was silent upstairs; a silence that seemed impossible when the noise of him overhead had been so much part of Christine's life.

The bottle on the table ran dry. Mother stared at it hungrily like she would wring it out if she could imagine it would work. She glanced at the wine rack in the kitchen, back at Christine, then peered blearily upstairs in the direction of her bedroom. Eventually her eyes landed back on the rack. 'Drink?'

Christine was so shocked to be offered one she could not immediately think how to answer.

'I don't really drink,' Christine replied after the silence had sat on her ears a little too long.

'"Don't really" is not the same as "don't",' said Mother as she almost managed not to wobble into the kitchen for yet another bottle and an empty glass.

SATURDAY

THE SUN OUTSIDE was ugly bright, throwing everything out the window into stark, nauseating contrast. Christine could clearly remember bright sunlit days that did not hurt, did not make her hate the day, did not force her to look for a hole to hide in with a blanket covering her face; this was not one of those days. The light fluttering through the window dug into her brain through her eyes, like drill bits of ice. She had to be sick from some contagion or allergy. Or it might have been the wine.

It was probably the wine.

Christine's hungover, feeble mind wondered if Mother always woke feeling like this. That would explain the expression she wore when she thought nobody was watching; Christine being nobody. It should be impossible to have a hangover like this and stay composed.

It took too long to dress, to slug back a coffee, to make another in a keep cup, to change her shirt for one less bright, to pour more coffee down her throat, to not puke through pure will, to consider changing her clothes again and decide against it, to search for her keep cup to make a coffee for the road and realise it was already full, to grab her stuff and head outside to the car.

Her parents were waiting.

Mother was already in the front passenger seat, showing no evidence of a hangover. She was as upright, uptight, fake bright, sweet-smelling, stiff-necked as always; hair perfect, clothes neat, glasses as dark as deep tannic pools, as the depths of the bottom of the ocean, as Christine's mood. She thought it unfair that she was so bedraggled and Mother showed no after-effects.

The car groaned and roared across town. White, cream, beige, off-white, off-cream, off-beige houses; all neat. The cleaners cleaning, gardeners gardening, repairers repairing; other servants doing who-knows-what. Drones flew overhead and at face-height keeping them safe; security vans keeping eyes on the drones; drones keeping eyes on the security vans.

Everybody keeping watch on everybody else.

Security vans were everywhere, their windows as dark as Mother's glasses.

There were few cars in any driveways. Most people took taxis or called a car. The car and taxi service in town had every sort of car imaginable, from zippy little things through to stretch limos with full bars; Mother must love those. Drivers would turn up almost immediately after they had been requested, so soon that they appeared psychic. Christine felt sure with enough practice that they would learn to arrive even before being requested. She imagined someone not even being aware they needed to go out until their car arrived.

Safetynet just kept getting smarter. She was smart too, she knew how it really did it.

It listened and extrapolated, built profiles, calculated, used algorithms and machine learning, all fuelled by esoteric cognitive mathematics; fed data from Safetynet Social. Numbers were everything. They could explain the world, they could model thought. Christine knew if she could find the right equation she could understand anything.

A black van stormed past in the other direction so fast that Christine barely made out the arrow-shaped 'A' logo of the Agency in matt black on the side, contrasting only against the gloss of the vehicle. Buzzing drones flanked the van, flying overhead on spinning rotors.

Christine poked her tongue out at it too late for the Agency men to see, then back at Father's disapproving glare in the rear-view mirror.

Despite the apocalyptic heat, everything outside the car windows was brightly verdant and aggressively alive. Sprinklers sprayed the air humid, casting sparks on the leaves and throwing small rainbows everywhere. The road was wet with spray, the trees and bushes in front yards glistened. The water did nothing to allay the heat, merely turned it tropical, sweat painting the servants' skin with gloss. It was far too uncomfortable for people to be out in the streets. No doubt the taxi service was having a great day, taking people to the shopping centre, to their favourite cafes and bars, anywhere machines kept the air temperature under control.

Staring out the window, Christine watched a whirlwind dominate the middle of an upcoming intersection, swirling trash and spinning leaves into a gyre, taller than the surrounding buildings. The trash scattered like a flock of birds when their car hit it and Christine turned to watch the loose funnel reforming behind them through the back window.

They passed the church, a tall Gothic edifice of blue-grey stone and wrought iron. It looked older than anything around it in a way that Christine couldn't define. Being a Saturday, there were even fewer people at the church than normal; not that anybody Christine knew ever went inside. Although the entire town was nominally Christian, no one went to church except for weddings and funerals.

She could see no point to church.

They passed a party of people sitting under a tree in a front garden on dining chairs around a cloth-covered table, the location chosen to ensure they could be seen. A portable air conditioner blasted cold air at the gathering, condensation beading on the glasses of champagne like a snowstorm of glitter. Being at home on a Saturday was embarrassing, and the people in town had a morbid fear of shame. The only acceptable way to be home on a warm bright Saturday was to hold a garden party or a barbecue.

Christine knew Safetynet Social would be flooded with garden party photos on Sunday and then next weekend's parties and the social photos would be competitively beautiful. Wordlessly, they passed the colossal white bulk of the shopping centre, then the carefully manicured cafe strip where every shopfront sported ostentatiously different architecture despite all of them being joined at the roof and having obviously all been built at once. The clear glass walls of the leisure centre and swimming pool were so transparent they were almost not there, the people swimming visible.

Silent, Christine checked her emails; what she was looking for not there among the sales emails, the doctor's appointments she did not remember making, the social notifications. She checked Social direct messages, nothing there. Letting nothing show on her face, she quickly checked the dead-drop box they had arranged in a forgotten corner of Safetynet for emergencies. Nothing there either.

They roared past the ladies who lunch, who because it was Saturday were brunching with family; past the fast-fashion outlets selling clothes designed to wear once then be discarded, which because it was Saturday was jammed with people; past the small supermarket with its shelves full of food she could not imagine any citizen would buy except in the direst of emergency.

They arrived at the other side of town, a neighbourhood she could not remember ever having seen. No huge houses on quarter acres, no tall narrow townhouses on one-eighth acres, only ten-storey-high or taller glass and stone and steel buildings with cute shops and cafes on the ground floors.

But it was the people who struck her as most strange on this side of town.

There were men, no flecks of grey in their neatly trimmed beards; some of the beards long enough to dangle arrogantly past the necklines of their black t-shirts. The women wore made-to-look-that-way clothes, where that-way was old and bordering on tatty. Most of the people she could see out the tinted windows of the car were close to Christine's age. The buildings were younger than the people; one was still a building site, thickly staffed with rough-looking workers in dirty ragged clothes; far dirtier and more dishevelled than anyone she would associate with.

At an almost-new building, only a little taller than the edifices surrounding it, the car bumped over a kerb and down a concrete ramp into the thick unctuous darkness of an underground car park, watched all the time by the black eyes of ostentatiously visible cameras.

The car rolled to a stop, the deafening echo of the engine drawing bile into Christine's furry, nauseated mouth. Father opened his door and stepped out into a damp dark space that smelled like lying on the driveway in autumn; concrete, moisture and dust. Mother shrugged, opened her door and eeled out of the seat, wobbling just a little as she forced herself upright.

Christine composed herself, refusing to allow her parents to see the confusion on her face, and climbed gracelessly out of the car to join them.

Mother turned her hunched back on Father, as if to take in her surrounds, and took a furtive slug from a small steel bottle she had surreptitiously taken from her handbag. Christine did not see where it disappeared to, because her mother was a magician. She had more than one trick to make a drink vanish.

The door of an expensive-looking car, the colour of carbon fibre, opened. A strange man launched himself at them from the door. He wore a suit almost the same colour as his car; so plain it probably cost extra. He was striding towards the three of them almost before his shiny shoes hit the ground, his hand already out for a shake with Father. The sound of their hands meeting was as loud as a slap across the face in the cavernous chamber.

Stepping over, he took Mother's hand and shook it vigorously, ignoring the blank face that only Christine knew was Mother's way to show unspeakable displeasure and disdain. Then he grinned at Christine, his expression suggesting they were sharing a secret, and pumped her hand so hard she felt like her arm was going to tear off at the shoulder. She tried not to grimace and failed spectacularly.

He only grinned wider.

With broad, wordless gestures, he ushered them through a door and into an elevator. Christine had last been in an elevator years ago when she had visited Father at work. She still remembered the childish joy of that day, the tall building, the stunningly beautiful but vacuous secretaries, the ride in the lift, the view from Father's office – she felt like she could see forever. She had flinched at the feeling of the elevator going up, like her stomach was falling out of her body, and she did the same again now.

The elevator stopped and the door opened with a whine of electric motors as faint as a breath. The Man In The Suit led them out and into a too-white corridor overlit with bright lights, down the hall to a door so white, so like the walls, it was almost invisible. He opened it.

Behind the door was a short hall leading to what Christine first thought was a small house until she realised it must be an apartment. She had seen them on television but had never been in one before. She had always assumed they were bigger. It was neat, clean, new; Christine was afraid to touch anything lest she damage it, dirty it, smudge it, break it; in case she left dirty childlike handprints that could never be erased.

She stood in the carpeted entrance hall with her white-knuckled fists as deep in her jacket pockets as she could shove them.

Everybody preceded her and then stopped in the middle of the room past the hall to turn and stare at her. Shrugging, she walked into the empty room, white walls and dark matt laminate, the type that seemed designed to show fingerprints.

'Do you like this place?' Father asked.

Christine shrugged again and stared at him, allowing the previously hidden confusion to show on her face. She had never seen anything like it, did not know how it compared to other apartments, could only compare it to her parents' house – it was a lot smaller but she did not know how much room someone would need. She had no idea why her opinion mattered. Suit Man stood with a strange smile on his face and looked to Father, to Christine, to Father, to Christine.

'It's only a month until your birthday,' said Father. 'I have just put this apartment on our family mortgage. It transfers in six weeks. It's yours. I know it's early, but happy birthday.'

Christine opened her mouth and closed it again, looked at Mother, at Suit Man, at Father. Mother appeared perplexed then completely indifferent to the situation. Father looked hopeful, though what he hoped for was a mystery. Suit Man just looked hungry.

'It's fully serviced,' Suit Man enthused. 'Cleaners will come in every three days, or more often if you request it. There's a little kitchenette, a fridge, sink, microwave, just over there. A meal service can stock your fridge with weekly meals. They can be ordered on Safetynet. All you have to do is reheat them. Or a bain-marie can be installed at an extra cost and a meal service can bring your meals already prepared if you'd prefer not to have to prepare meals at all.

'I understand that your father has taken care of a line of credit for the servicing and even for meals until you have your own means of support.'

Father nodded. Christine's head spun.

'No rush,' Father said. 'You have good marks from university. I can find you a job in the Fund or you can try something else, explore, find the right work, even study more if you want, then get married. Until then you can live on the line of credit. We have plenty. It's a trust, really. It will keep you as long as you need it, until you get married at least.'

Christine could hear a slightly predatory tone in his voice, like a farmer talking about a pig he was fattening up. Strolling around the apartment, she attempted to show interest when all she felt was bewilderment. Suit Man's smile followed her around the place, like the eyes of a painter's masterpiece, watching. She wanted to look like she was doing something sensible, like she knew what to do, but she had no idea what sensible activity was in this situation.

What she really wanted to do was run for it.

She walked to the wall that looked more like a window, floor-to-ceiling, corner-to-corner glass; a thick frosted stripe at waist height across the width. Curtains were pushed to the edge. She stared out into the blue distance, out over the village shops, over the two- and three-storey houses, past that. It was a view and an aspect like she had never even dreamed. Past the rolling parkland, she could see the shadowy wall that kept the town safe. Past that was too far to see, even if the Wall had not been in the way. She had never seen over the Wall; she never would.

Christine looked down, suddenly curious as to how high up she actually was. The blurred wings of a drone hovered between the height of the window and the road; she could see the tops of cars, the slightly shiny top of a balding head, the tops of the short bushy trees planted in holes in the footpath.

It was a long way down, at least twice as far as the distance from her parents' roof to the yard she had grown up playing in. She remembered when she was thirteen and had climbed onto the roof – no, not when she had climbed onto the roof, when she had been helped onto the roof.

Her best friend had always been far more athletic, incalculably more fearless, even reckless, than her; she loved that about him. She could do nothing but watch his feet disappear out of her parents' bedroom window. Somehow he gripped the gutter and swung himself over, out and up.

Christine had climbed the rope he had lowered, onto the precipitously sloped tiled roof; had stared in wonder at the blued, blurred, distant Wall, countless, breathless, impossible miles away, as her best friend grinned. 'I want to see what's outside,' he said, and Christine had gasped involuntarily at the audacity of it; at something she had refused to ever contemplate. They had stayed there, in the delirious, shadeless heat that was pinking their skin, talking about the future, as distant and unfathomable as the barely visible Wall.

They had sat staring at the identical tiled roofs of the lower two-storeyed houses around them; she had never noticed before that hers was the biggest house in the neighbourhood. After their first desperate, searching examination in that direction, they stared at anything but the impossibly high barrier hemming the city in. No drones spied them in the hidden corner of the roof.

Their phones warned them it was almost time for Christine's parents to come home. It was then she discovered she lacked the courage to climb down the rope and swing back in through the gaping window. It was then she discovered the rope they had was too short to reach the ground. Her friend stayed with her as long as he could, trying to encourage her down then, when the risk of getting caught became too high, scampered down and escaped through the window.

Christine had not been brave enough to retrieve the rope. She had heard the distant front door slam shut, sat head on knees on the sloping roof too scared to even shake, burned red by the heat, without the slightest clue how to get down.

She had been unconscious with fear and fatigue, with dehydration and exposure – in danger of rolling from the roof – when she was found hours later. Her mother had looked out the window and seen the rope, called Security and emergency services, who discovered Christine on the roof and rescued her. She had spent a couple of days in hospital, then a couple more under observation in a toy-filled room that she had never seen before and never would see again. Some years later she would finally understand it was a psychiatric ward for children.

Even under pressure, she never admitted how she had managed to climb out onto the roof; it was her secret and the keeping of it became a part of who she was.

Christine returned to the present already falling, face-first, towards the window, her eyes fixed on the vertiginously distant ground. A hand gripped her shoulder at the same moment that her forehead contacted the glass, stealing some of her momentum. It hurt, that hand, but not as much as the impact of the glass on the front of her skull. It flexed, as tempered glass does, and ejected her but did not crack. Her face left the window then returned with another thump and slid squeaking down the glass. She landed in a heap, rolled over and looked up.

Father was staring at her with more expression on his face than she had ever thought him capable of. He looked scared, concerned, perplexed, angry; expressions chased each other over his face so fast they collided and blended, fought and formed alliances, which immediately ended in betrayal. She took his quivering outstretched hand and rose to her wobbly feet. By the time she gained her footing, her vision cleared, his face had reset to its customary blankness.

They left the apartment and returned to the car. Suit Man pumped their arms again; Christine felt she needed to reattach hers. They exited the underground car park with a roar. Past the cafes full of people around Christine's age, the shopping mall in the middle of town. They finally stopped in the street near the tall tower of glass and steel where Father worked.

'I think now would be a good time for lunch,' Father said with a cheerfulness that could only be synthetic. Maybe he bought it in a bottle, the same way Mother acquired her tolerance and goodwill.

They climbed out of the car in relative unison, Christine nearly fainting in the heat. Mother stared at the dark reflective glass wall of the nearest cafe with a look of nauseated distaste, the left side of her mouth pinched back in an involuntary expression of contempt. When they entered, Christine could see why Mother didn't like it. It was nothing like the places Christine had collected Mother from in the past; more severe, less homely, more stainless steel and darkness, less red and green velvet and wood. It must have been a businessman's cafe; empty that Saturday, maybe every Saturday when almost nobody was at work.

A waiter greeted them at the door and they were led to a table near the window; the view was clear from the inside despite the reflective smokiness of the glass from the outside. Christine realised there was a treatment on the glass to make it clear in only one direction, giving a view to those looking out while protecting them from prying eyes. There was nobody on the street; the wind blew leaves that a uniformed cleaner chased, packaged in a bag and dumped in a bin on wheels. The shadows in the street were sharp, the sun bright, although Christine did not remember the washed flat light as well as she remembered the heat when they had walked the short distance from the car to the cafe.

It was far too early in the day to start drinking for Christine and, she believed, for most sensible people, yet Father ordered an expensive bubbly. Christine was not keen on the sparkling stuff but didn't know how to refuse. She could see distaste on her Mother's face, which Father ignored. Christine ordered her food without thinking, and Father's eyebrows raised at her obvious lack of care.

Mother ordered ostentatiously, questioning the server carefully, checking every ingredient, asking stupid questions, continuing even after Father glared at her with obvious fury. Christine marked a win for Mother on the scoreboard in her head. Father asked for the 'usual'. The server said she was not there during the week and had no idea what the 'usual' was. Father looked irritated; he said the computer would know. Minus points for Father. Mother slipped further ahead on the scoreboard in Christine's head; she had been winning a lot recently.

The server was patient, calm, took Father's irritation in her stride. She was young, beautiful but not quite breathtaking. If not for the fact that she was a servant, she was someone Christine could imagine being friends with. The server rolled her eyes, tapped her tablet and walked away; Christine was annoyed to have missed the chance to shoot her a sneaky conspiratorial smile.

She wished she had taken longer to order.

'Cameras scan your face when you enter,' Father explained. 'If you are a regular it informs the server what your favourite meal is. The servers can pretend to know your order even if they have forgotten or they are new.' Christine looked around while trying to pretend she was not looking. She saw so many cameras that they were near enough to everywhere. The glass eye of a camera faced her from across the booth, above Father's head. Christine could see her face in the lens. She looked at her reflection with something resembling reproach.

'I've never been here before,' Christine said. 'I don't have a "usual".'

'Well, actually,' Father explained, 'if it's set up right and working, all of the cafes in the city can store your favourite meals and drinks on the "net". It is accessible by every place in town if your privacy settings are on default. So long as they cook your "usual", they can make it for you if you ask.'

Christine shuddered at the knowledge of being watched. There were more than enough camera lenses to identify the diners, to watch over the place. She could not remember being watched everywhere she went before but that didn't mean that she wasn't. It suddenly occurred to her that a 'default' privacy setting on Safetynet implied the existence of other settings.

She decided to ignore the cameras and the unpleasant fact she was being constantly watched slid from her conscious mind.

'The cafes can even predict what you would like from your reviews and posts on the Social,' Mother added excitedly, 'and check on Social what your friends eat to make suggestions.'

Christine was terrified.

Christine and Mother ate and drank in silence once the tradition of a toast – glasses clinking, champagne sloshing – was completed. Father barely ate, seeming to take his sustenance from talking, from waving his arms, from pouring golden bubbles down his fat throat. Christine had never experienced him like that: enthused, gregarious, even cheerful.

Christine didn't want to drink but couldn't think how to say no.

He ordered another bottle of bubbly and this time also a bottle of red, which Christine knew her mother wanted. Mother looked perplexed by the thoughtfulness but poured herself a glass anyway.

One point to Father.

Christine stuck to the bubbly. Once she had consumed a bit she thought it not as bad as she had expected, and forgot she didn't drink at lunch time. Once she drank a bit more she almost thought it quite good. Father ordered more with a smile broad enough to make Christine wonder if he was up to something.

More to drink and Father was slurring his words like he did when he was tired every night when he got home from work. Christine suddenly wondered if he was drunk on all those days he got home from work complaining about an unshakable fatigue. When Father was looking the other way, she saw an expression on Mother's face that might have been her thinking the same thing.

Lunch ended and Father ordered coffees and whiskey. Christine had never tried whiskey before and had to admit, as soon as it hit her tongue, that she was not a fan of the heat and the smoke. It kicked bruises into her already knackered brain. She knocked back the caffeinated beverage, hoping it would blitzkrieg the drink right out of her system. It didn't. She ordered another one and that did nothing useful either.

Father handed her a credit card. She stared at it blearily, trying to work out why her name was on it.

'It's connected to the trust I set up for you,' Father explained in a voice not unlike one used to teach children, only drunker. 'You should have enough to go on with until you are ready to work somewhere. I am sure I can find you a position somewhere in the Fund.' Christine wondered what sort of position she would be given. Perhaps drinking whiskey and eating lunch; for all she knew that was possibly all Father did.

'So, Christine,' Father exclaimed with a grin, 'would you like to pay for our breakfast?'

Did breakfast normally come with that much wine, followed by that much whiskey? was Christine's first thought.

Her second was it doesn't matter, it would be Father who was paying even if it was her card.

Christine shrugged. Father nodded pointedly in the direction of a small box that the waitress had laid on the table. Christine had seen this sort of thing before, when Father or Mother paid for things. She touched her new card to the box. It beeped while a green light flashed.

They stood and walked out of the empty cafe into the blow-torch heat outside.

ZOOM – THE LIGHT

THE CITY DOZES. Watching from high enough the city looks like a polished serpentine, the licorice of the roadways marbling the green of quarter-acre blocks and parkland designed and planted to look natural. It is silent, the reflected light that makes the city visible travels far enough to see it from space (with a strong enough lens), but sound barely travels metres.

Closer in not much is moving. Sundays are almost too quiet, particularly on hot days; the citizens stay home, except for the meagre few who, in their piety, think they need to be in church. The rest of the city sleeps off Saturday. It is not difficult to imagine the city holding its breath, waiting for Monday; when people will go to work, many of them will not quite getting there, stopping on the way for coffee and breakfast and getting no further.

From high enough it's possible to observe the water pipes from the distant bulk of the desal plant, perched on the edge of the windswept denim blue of the ocean, penetrate the city, providing the water that makes the city glisten in the daylight. At that edge the light reflecting off the steel roof of the warehouse is blinding. And the city dozes.

SUNDAY

CHRISTINE WOKE FEELING even more sick-delicate than she had the day before. Her head felt like it was someone else's and not screwed on right or tight; her brain felt backwards, her eyes like they had been taken out, boiled in vinegar and put back in again. She was not remotely certain they had been inserted the right way around. She staggered to the ensuite bathroom, fell to her red-blotched knees on the cold, hard bathroom floor, hugged the toilet and stared into the tiny puddle of water in the bowl.

The last time she had felt this sick was when her best friend had snuck a stolen bottle of vodka from his house. They had drunk furtively under a tree in a park, snatching what privacy they could; Christine had spent days after hugging the toilet, shocked, among other things, at the sounds hacking from her throat. She had told her parents it was food poisoning, not expecting the havoc that would cause; the school cafeteria being closed, school staff being removed. Later, she became certain Mother had not believed her story; she would have known a hangover when she saw one. Maybe it was better to blame the school than admit her daughter had been drinking so young; maybe it was better to pretend to believe that story, to act on the lie, than to reprimand Christine.

Instead of guilt, Christine had hated herself for getting staff fired with her lie. She learned that day that words could be weapons and had vowed to herself to never drink again.

From the vantage point of the bathroom floor, she hated herself again for forgetting that promise.

Foul-smelling, mostly liquid sludge sprayed onto the porcelain from her wrenching stomach until the bile and undigested grog from her gut displaced all the water in the bowl. Then more, pure bilious liquid; then hacking coughs, an empty stomach trying to empty itself, willing to turn itself inside out if necessary. No wonder her mother was always so sour if she felt like this, if her mouth tasted like this, every morning.

Christine left the bathroom – there was nothing in there to make her feel better – and briefly considered searching her parents' medicine cabinet for anti-hangover medication. She could have died there in her room, in her bathroom, and nobody would notice until she started to stink even more than she already did, or perhaps her birthday, whichever came first. She doubted anyone would bother looking for her.

The servants would be the only ones who would notice. They would almost certainly tidy away her corpse, tell Mother she was dead when they could make her listen, although she was not sure they could make Mother care.

She managed to drink the glass of water that had mysteriously appeared on her bedside table then miraculously got back to sleep. When she woke she felt a fraction better, pulled on lounging clothes, managed to stay upright. Staggering, she attempted to walk down the hall to the stairs, held on to the banister like a child as she descended the man-made mountain, closed her eyes when the swimming of the stair treads got too intense. Then more stairs. Never before had she hated the idea of a three-storey house so deeply. Somehow reaching the ground without falling she walked through the living room, the dining room, into the kitchen. There was nobody there. An open full wine bottle teased her from the kitchen counter, an empty, clean glass standing beside it, like a mockery.

Voices tumbled in from outside, voices stripping over each other, words she could not interpret, a burst of laughter then more meaningless words. The moonface of the clock on the wall told her it was just after 10 a.m., even earlier than they started yesterday, too early this time, but her mother had clearly been born with a superpower, or else had spent years developing one.

Through the closed door to the patio, she could hear her mother's distinctly perfect laugh, a tinkling of crystal bells. She had long suspected a speech pathologist had somehow been involved with that laugh; what, besides bending her elbow, did Mother have to do with her time?

The coffee machine on the counter, plumbed into the house – almost fully automatic, the grounds drawer cleaned, the milk fridge and the beans hopper refilled by staff – was silent. There was a clatter when Christine put her cup under the nozzle, a light thud when she almost dropped the saucer, nauseatingly loud grinding and moaning as black nectar exuded in a glacial pace into her cup, a rattle when she put her cup down on its receptacle. She swore involuntarily and covered her mouth.

Outside, it fell silent.

'Good morning, darling,' that perfect, not even slurring, voice sang through the door.

The last time Mother had called her 'darling', she had been a child, and the next words had almost always been 'I am so disappointed in you', followed by some sort of punishment.

Christine tensed, ready to run.

'Could you bring that bottle out here, please? Bring a glass, too. Join us.'

Shit.

She suddenly realised the bottle, the glass, had been prepared for her; a trap, a way to get her outside. She could think of no way to avoid going out there, could see no escape. If she ran away Mother would be 'disappointed', which was worse than angry. If she went out with a glass she would have to join Mother's friends in their drinking. If she went out without a glass Mother would send her back into the kitchen for it, making sure with her tone of voice that her friends would see Christine as a thoughtless, idiotic child.

She could not escape but she could try to prepare.

Christine knocked back the contents of her mug. Too fast, too hot, it seared a path down her throat. She choked for a moment and almost screamed. She wondered if she would have time for another; Mother already knew she was there. Deciding she didn't care if there wasn't time, she made and threw back another coffee. Then she put her mug under the nozzle and left the screen open on her preset, hoping one of the servants would think she was stupid enough to stop halfway through making herself a coffee, finish the job and bring it out to her.

Before she could change her mind she grabbed the open bottle of wine by the neck and the glass by the stem and, lacking a third hand, kicked the door to the patio open. She kicked it a little too hard; it bounced against the wall and swung back. Only a hasty redeployment of her foot stopped the door from hitting her in the face.

Mother's laughter at her discombobulation was somehow sickening, cloying. It embraced her, enveloped her, threatened to consume her, crossing the fuzzy line that existed between a hug and a violent breath-stealing squeeze. She desired to shake the laugh off her skin, but Mother's friends were watching her.

They must have all paid the same cosmetic surgeon, even Mother. Only slight variations in colouring, and millimetre differences, in bone structure enabled her to tell one woman from another. One was a redhead, too red to be natural; another platinum blonde, definitely artificial; golden blonde, might be real; almost-natural blonde, the realest; ostentatious grey, certainly a widow who had inherited everything, proving that she no longer had to prove a thing. Redhead and golden blonde were so similar they could swap identities at the hairdresser. Grey-hair looked no older than the others and probably still had regular top-ups at the plastic surgeon, her hair was already making the point, no need to be weird.

It was her mother's piercing blue eyes that identified her from the others; like sapphires but even colder, all emotion cut and injected out of them by her surgeon. The muscles that created smile lines may as well have been cauterised as there was no evidence of their existence. When Mother smiled only her lips were involved.

Christine had her father's chocolate brown eyes, sensible eyes, earthy, grounded, warm, human. She knew that as much as her mother matched her eyes, her father made a lie of his.

Christine did not recognise any of the women, though that was no surprise if they had been through surgery lately. She wondered how they recognised each other after each operation stripped them of their uniqueness.

She remembered shopping for clothes with Mother when she was a rebellious teen, surly and not wanting anything, Mother insisting. Someone with the body of a middle-aged woman and the face of a teenager approached and started talking to them. Mother was perplexed, a rare expression of utter confusion on her face.

'It's me,' the woman said.

'Who?' Mother replied.

'Me,' the woman insisted and, as if suddenly recognising her voice, Mother smiled and gave the woman a stiff hug and together they dragged Christine to a cafe to talk.

After enough had been drunk, enough small low-carb cakes had been eaten, enough time expended, the other woman left. Before they had even got up from the table Mother was calling her cosmetic surgeon to make an appointment. Christine hated her mother at that moment and that feeling had only grown since.

Christine wondered then if any of the women had ever swapped husbands just for kicks. She desperately stifled a childish giggle. It probably happened all the time.

'Christine, I am sure you have met everyone,' said Mother with a voice like aspartame. She had met them all but said nothing. 'Everyone, I am sure you remember my daughter, Christine.' Mother snatched the bottle from Christine's hand, poured her a drink, tipped some into a glass for herself and then emptied the bottle into whichever glasses had room for more.

Christine stared at a moving bird in the distance, then realised perhaps it was a machine watching them. She could not be sure, she could not hear a buzz, then tried to recall when she had last seen an uncaged bird.

There were more bottles on the table Mother's friends were gathered around in the middle of the patio: reds, whites, bubbles. Some bottles were empty, some were open and breathing, others were half-full and idle; others were untouched just-in-case bottles, proving the bottle in the kitchen was a set-up. Servants were working in the garden; surely at least one was only pretending to be a gardener and was really there to rush to the basement where the wine was kept, in pursuit of more.

Sipping her wine, Christine felt it bounce when it hit her stomach but fortunately it stayed behind her teeth and she forced it down again. She could imagine these women tearing into her like piranhas if she made a wrong move, said anything they did not approve of, looked at one of them the wrong way. The almost-natural blonde one even had the teeth for it. Christine could not stop herself from shuddering.

Piranha Teeth slugged her wine, taking in two-thirds of the glass in one breath, while somehow giving the appearance of daintily sipping. Grey-hair gesticulated with her drink but somehow didn't spill any. Platinum-blonde finished hers and looked disgusted with the emptiness of her glass. Mother stared at the table, like she was wondering how to get more wine without getting up. Golden-blonde stood with a flourish and swooped onto the forest of bottle necks, snatching one seemingly at random. Redhead just sat there; she might have had too much to drink, or it could have been her nature to sit there, do nothing, say nothing, drink alone in a crowd.

Some people could die of loneliness in a crowd.

Christine remembered her best friend once telling her he was dying of loneliness, and she had wondered how he could be lonely when he was her everything.

She suddenly understood.

She was dying without him, alone on this patio crowded with women possessed of the same surgical agelessness as her mother; surrounded by people, yet lonely.

Christine took a big slug of her drink and immediately regretted it, quelled her rebelling stomach by willpower alone, and looked over and saw her mother smiling at her like a tiger at a lamb. Wine appeared over Christine's shoulder – in bottle shape – and tipped, red liquid glugging, then conforming to the shape of her glass. She giggled. It was then she realised she was not quite right.

She could feel it coming, an unnameable thing she did not understand well enough to even fear, a beast from the middle of her self that she kept hidden. She stared at these women: these drinkers and laughers. Were these the women with whom her mother burned all her days? Were these the drinkers and eaters of lunches as long as the day itself?

There was a beauty and terror to who and to what they were, as perfect as sculptures, as hollow as dolls. She could not imagine these women lifting a finger for anything other than to pick up a bottle or a glass. Christine found herself drawn to them, repelled by them, confused and scared and happy. And drunk; very drunk. When her drink was gone she did not question how it got refilled; she had learned to expect it would be.

She began to suspect they were playing with her, getting her drunk to see what would happen and laughing behind her back, but soon she stopped caring. The wine, the laughter, the ugly beauty took hold; if she was not careful it would never let go. Those plastic-perfect faces, those heads of too-perfect dyed hair, became an environment in which to live – drunk became a part of home.

Soon they became beautiful in their own way.

She tried to check her email but her thumbs were suddenly too fat for the icons on her phone. She mashed the screen, kept opening the wrong apps. She did not want the news, or social media, or streamed television. She closed them, opened new apps by accident. Switching her phone off entirely, she dropped it towards the table and missed, knew if she tried to pick it up she would tumble down after it.

She wondered what it would be like to touch those artificially sculpted lips with her own.

Not Mother's. She had not kissed her mother since she was a child. But these women: what would their lips, cut and sutured and filled with collagen, feel like on her own?

Suddenly she was very angry at these empty women, at Mother for being one of them; at herself because she could see her future as one of them.

There was fresh wine in her glass.

As she drank she fell under the spell of these women, their almost identical bell-like laughs; when they laughed together it was like a symphony for carillon. It was utterly mesmerising and inexplicably heartbreaking. It was a bit like love, and a bit like hate.

Christine lost the ability to separate sounds, to break the noise entering her ear into individual utterances. She could hear all of them at once, blending into a roar, like the screams of rioters on television; it throbbed louder then quieter then louder then quieter at the rhythm of her breath. The cacophony, the discord of the room overwhelmed her and washed over her mind as she fell apart.

Christine woke and could not remember where her bathroom door was.

Her head swam and her stomach churned. She staggered, stumbled, almost fell into the ensuite, her stomach emptying itself in a single splattering heave. She crawled back to her bed then back to the toilet, heaved into it again, collapsed there.

She woke again, felt her face pressed into the cold, hard porcelain of the pedestal, felt her stomach lead a rebellion against her rule, attempting to escape the prison of her body. It hurt, so much; she felt this was what dying must be like, what having your guts eaten by worms in the grave would feel like if it was still possible to feel when dead.

Strong, soft hands held her hair back, taking some of the weight of her head. She nearly said 'thanks Mum', remembering when she was a child and her mother had held her hair while she puked, had held her as she was racked with sobs, had whispered comforting things before taking her back to bed.

Someone was whispering words she could not quite understand, but it was not her mother's too-perfect voice, and she was not a child. Someone helped her to stand, and she walked, foot dragging, head hanging bonelessly from her shoulders, a strong-soft arm helping her to bed.

Then she was in bed, too sick to puke, too weak to protest. A thunk and a faint slosh announced a glass of water hitting her bedside table. Hands she did not see tucked her in. She forced her eyes open.

She was looking at a handsome, bright-eyed, brown-skinned woman, wearing a servant's uniform. Her black hair was cropped short, her bronze-amber eyes kind through her stern but concerned expression. She did not seem as disgusted at Christine as Christine was with herself.

'Thanks,' Christine barely managed to say. 'Thanks,' she breathed again, embarrassed she could not think of anything else.

'You should not try to outdrink your mum,' the woman whispered. 'She's been doing it longer than you.' She dropped two soluble aspirin in the glass of water on the table, watched them fizz then turned on her heel and walked away.

'Thanks,' Christine said again weakly, almost certainly too late to be heard, before pouring the fizzing water down her throat.

Christine was adrift in a loveless, lonely void. She went back to sleep hoping to feel better when she woke; and hating her mother, her mother's friends, the wine, the planet that allowed wine to exist.

Hating herself the most.

TUESDAY

NO PHYSICAL EVIDENCE remained of the terrible day before. Her fever-sweat stinking clothes were gone from the floor, and her ensuite was shiny and smelled sweetly of cleaning products. She quenched her lip-cracking thirst with the fresh glass of water on her beside table.

Her phone had also mysteriously appeared. She checked her email and there was still nothing from him, the one she missed, the one, if she could admit it, she loved at least a bit.

Years ago, in high school, the girls would sit around, engaged in giggling conversations about which boy they would marry when they were older. The first time, Christine had said 'ew gross'; she could not imagine marrying one of those smelly, spotty, gangly boys. She could not imagine marrying anybody. But the other girls had mocked and laughed at her so she learned to say she would marry Jack. It was a convincing lie. He was her best and truest friend, the only person she really loved.

And now he was not speaking to her. It tightened her chest, made her eyes water.

Maybe he was dead, the lips that carried his voice stilled forever, hazel eyes sunken and milky. She could not bear to think about it. Yet the town was not that large; she would have run into him by now if he was still alive. He could be dead, and nobody had thought to tell her. That hurt, too.

It was not a nice day outside, the violent blue-white of the sky a warning. Heat from the roadway blasted up to meet the heat raining down from the open sky; these competing heats did not feud, they united, formed a gang, went looking for trouble. She could tell this from the light outside her window, from the haze, from the air beating against the glass. She feared that heat, yet she imagined she would be better off out there in the light and sun than inside in the air conditioning, among the waft of cleaning products, trapped alone with her thoughts, trapped with herself. She would rather be with anyone than alone.

Almost anyone.

She dressed herself in neat, expensively soft jeans and a plain black t-shirt, grabbed her handbag, and walked out the door without looking back. She had a whole day of adventures ahead if she wanted it; an entire day with nobody baying for her attention. The street was green and bright, sprinklers again throwing rainbows at the sky, which consumed them. A scattering of small clouds was flicking the sun's dimmer switch on and off – the land going shadowy then bright unpredictably.

The house next door looked almost exactly like hers but with the top storey lopped off; it looked weirdly cut down like that. The next house along was the same but backwards, as though being looked at through a mirror. The one beyond that had subtle differences in the placement and size of its windows, beyond that a mirror reversal of the one next to it. Another slight variation, another mirror image of that, and then she was standing at the corner. She had never noticed how similar all the houses were before. Her house was identical to the others, but with an extra storey tacked on top like an afterthought.

At the corner, a camera stood on a pole, keeping her safe. She looked behind her towards her house. There were cameras on every streetlight, on every power pole, on every house. When they were teenagers, she and Jack used to sneak up on the cameras, hiding in their blind spots, to try and destroy them. They didn't always succeed but somehow never got caught. She wondered whether they had been seen smashing cameras but got away with it because of their parents; whether they had kept it hidden from her and Jack. Maybe she should test that theory, smash a camera to see if her father would protect her.

Past the corner was a slightly poorer neighbourhood. The houses were still nice, all two storeys tall townhouses, no room for front gardens and butted against each other on the sides. The decorations on the balconies their only sign of individuality. She wondered what it would be like to sit on one of those balconies on a warm evening, watching the road below, not quite able to see the distant Wall. She wondered why her house didn't have a balcony. It must have something to do with keeping the houses secure.

The road was no narrower but it felt like it was, the lack of front gardens helping each house to cut off more of the sky, making the buildings loom. The narrower-feeling road felt dark, somehow cold, and Christine was racked with a whole-body shiver despite the heat.

A drone buzzed overhead. She heard an electric click, resented it photographing her face and poked her tongue out childishly; stared it down until it buzzed away.

After another block she reached her destination. A glass-fronted shop that was covered with colourful and creased advertisements for bright sugary things, chocolate, chips and ice cream. She had drunk milkshakes and dipped chips into pies in there with her friends after school and on countless Saturday mornings, avoiding the passive-aggressive sniping of their respective parents. For Jack and her, it had been their special place.

That unconscious memory must have been why she walked in, why she was at the counter covered with brightly coloured, waxy, sugary crap in boxes of garishly printed cardboard.

It had been a few years since the end of high school when she had last been there, when they had all made promises to be friends forever, vows that not one of them had kept, except her and Jack. She sometimes saw their old friends around town, flapping about with others of their kind; they had not bothered with university and had gone on to live lives like Mother's, trust-fund spending, or like Father's, pushing paper in offices and taking long lunches. She'd try to talk to them but had nothing in common with them anymore.

The shop was the only thing that had not changed in four years or so, not in any way that she could see. Jack had always said the milkshakes there were the best in town, so she wanted one with a quiet desperation.

They had thought it their place, thought they had found it, made it their own. It had not occurred to her as a child, or even as a bratty teen, that the place was as old as the neighbourhood, perhaps as old as the city, that other children had discovered that place, had thought themselves pioneers, had stopped coming when they got older. She pictured a rotating cohort of children and teens; the faces, the hair, the clothes changing, but all the same nevertheless. The place had been built for all of them, for every snotty-nosed kid who pretended to rebel by running away there for milkshakes.

Like she was doing now.

It was early and the place was empty; all the kids were at school. She sat down at a table, then, recalling there was no table service, stood up and stalked to the counter. The server was about her age; she remembered them being older, thinking they looked ancient, fossilised. The server looked at her strangely, like she didn't belong, as if there was something wrong with her being there. Christine bristled. It was her neighbourhood, her milk bar. She ordered a strawberry thickshake, a pie and chips – food she hadn't realised she missed.

She tapped her credit card and the machine beeped, ruining the memory; it was squirrelled-away and sometimes pilfered cash they had spent as children. She smirked at herself in disgust, walked back to the table and sat down with her food, its value embedded in the memories it carried.

Some kids walked in, talking loudly, like they owned the place. They must have been skiving off school. She remembered doing that more than once – always Jack's idea, but she loved it. The kids stared at her with a look that she could remember once wearing; their stances, their body language just like hers had been. Then she realised what it was, they thought she looked old.

The camera over the door stared at her with scorn. She wanted to throw a chair at it.

Christine realised she had unconsciously gone there looking for Jack. She deserved to have 'stupid' tattooed on her face for all to see; of course he would not be there. It had been years since this place had been their hangout, even when they were teens their visits became less frequent; the staring kids would think him old too. She left in a hurry, taking her thickshake with her.

Sipping her drink, she made a decision. If her unconscious was going to force her to look for Jack she would do it properly and with intent.

It was too far to walk to the university, especially in the aggressive heat, and her thickshake had now settled in her stomach like a lump of concrete. She took out her phone and loaded the car company app. A car appeared almost before she was ready. She did not want to know how much the trip had cost when she got to the university.

The university was unchanged – buildings of rough grey stone that looked ancient even if they were not. That had been one of the many pointless topics she and the other students had discussed over endless caffeinated beverages: were the university buildings old or made to look that way? Christine thought the buildings must be as old as they looked, could not imagine why someone would build something to look old, why they would not build the university to be breathtakingly new, a city of glass, towers and spires, a jewel reflecting the surrounding parkland.

Jack had been of the opposite opinion. Then again, he was convinced the entire world was fake.

She went to her and Jack's favourite cafe, which dangled off the side of the food court like a wart. Sitting down, she ordered a long black like she always did, trying to be sophisticated but knowing the university coffee was too terrible to order it short and bitter. It arrived while she was watching the students living their lives, eating and crying and fighting and loving. It had only been a few months but she missed it already: the lifestyle, the classes, her friends.

When her mind rebelled and reminded her that her few uni friends had graduated the same time as she had and weren't at uni anymore, she kicked that thought in the teeth.

As a student she could not imagine graduating; no longer studying, getting a job like Father, or being idle and pointless like Mother. She belonged there, with those fresh-faced first-years, the exhausted final-year students, the lecturers dressed shabbily in clothes that looked as old as the buildings.

She savoured the taste of her terrible coffee and luxuriated in the feeling of the hard chairs she had petitioned the cafe to change on more than one occasion for something more comfortable. It had been one of many madcap plans she and Jack had implemented.

The failure of that petition led to one of Jack's stupider ideas. In the middle of the night, he and a couple of even less responsible friends had broken into the cafe then bolted and epoxied a couch to the ground. He and his two idiot friends from the

Western Civilisation Studies department were hauled before the Vice-Chancellor two days later. She blamed herself. She had been the lookout but didn't think to warn them about the cameras and Jack hadn't thought of them either; in hindsight he was probably aware of them but didn't care. The cameras did not catch her, and her gratitude had been intermixed with guilt.

Jack had returned from the Vice-Chancellor's office sullen and depressed. His friends had been expelled while he escaped punishment. His parents were well connected like hers, his dad paying for the removal of the couch and the repairs to the floor.

Jack had not been the same again. His face remained sullen, the light leaving his eyes.

His behaviour became even more reckless despite her attempts to get him to tone it down, for her, for himself. There was a faint notion her presence could mitigate his behaviour; if she was there, Christine allowed herself to be dragged along with his mad plans. She was terrified of getting caught, he was not.

Maybe he believed nothing bad could happen to him. Maybe he was trying to do something, anything, so unforgivable that he would finally get punished for it. Maybe he had stopped caring. His poetry, submitted for examination, became gratuitously obscene; he struck up friendships with the staff, took up smoking, started getting drunk at breakfast, stopped turning up to classes, shouted abuse at the staff sent to find him. Yet, he somehow qualified for entry to the master's program in poetry.

Then, just after the end of their honours studies while Christine was sleeping off her relief at finishing her thesis, he disappeared. Nobody could find him. The only thing he had left behind was a note, shoved under her dorm-room door. The note, written to her in the code they sometimes used, said he would talk to her soon. If he did not come to see her she should check their secret ways to talk. Then nothing.

Then more nothing.

She had waited for months, languishing on the couch, waiting for a message that would not come.

Christine suddenly decided there was no compelling reason for her to leave the university. She could re-enrol. She had not applied for postgraduate studies, although she must have qualified. Once Jack disappeared, she had not intended to stay.

She was determined to go to the admin building and enquire about undertaking a master's in pure mathematics. She was certain her father or her trust fund would pay for it. He would probably prefer her to study economics or some sort of applied maths, but any maths was good; her father approved of maths.

At the admin building she uncovered two facts. Firstly, Jack was not enrolled at the university. He had graduated with honours like her but had failed to complete his enrolment for a master's in creative writing. They had no other information; at least none they were willing to give her. Secondly, they would be delighted for someone with her university record, the daughter of such a prominent family, great supporters of the university, to enrol in the master's program in pure mathematics.

She filled in her enrolment forms then left before they could see her crying.

Students dashed in all directions within the corridors, all younger than her, some of them looking like children, fresh-faced, surgically dimpled and unprepared for the world. She wondered if her brother was among them, just as excited; away from their parents and free. On further thought she doubted it, he was a business student.

Weak pallid sunlight poked at the windows, splashing through faintly, not doing much for the dreary corridors that seemed designed to absorb the light and stay dingy. In some corners resided shadows that seemed so ancient and primeval that Christine imagined the darkness had been purchased already old and heaped in secret corners.

Christine strolled to the Mathematics department, and past the masses of bright-eyed first-years, bleary-eyed second- and third-years, and dead-eyed honours students, to the postgraduate common room that would soon be hers to mope in. It was beautiful, ostentatiously so.

The furniture was all wood and leather, antique, worn. Yet none of it seemed to quite fit. A dark wooden table floated loosely in a room too big for it, the armrests on the long-legged dining chairs too tall to fit under the table. The couch and armchairs were beautiful but did not match, appearing to be slightly different vintages (or had been made to look that way if Jack was right). The room itself felt younger than the furniture.

She sat down in one of the armchairs. Curved back and curved armrests that joined the back of the chair at the same height. It was not as comfortable as she had expected, the arms were too high, being the height of the back, and the back was too low, being the height of the arms. It might have been her own height that was the true problem, she was often too tall for chairs, but both her back and arms remained unsatisfied.

She liked the feel of the leather though, soft and aged, as smooth as skin, cool like living wood, as firm as her fingertips. She could not keep her hands off it, felt ashamed to be fondling it.

A window opened out into a garden, wetly green manicured lawns and weeping trees, more tendrils than tree; an ornamental lake with ducks and a couple of geese strutting about like they owned the place. They probably did, being geese; she was certainly not brave enough to approach them. Further away, past the lake was a screen of tall trees that almost managed to hide the Wall with its woolly darkness.

There was an oppressiveness enfolded in them. While planted to keep people from investigating the Wall, she could not imagine trees being more intimidating. She resented those trees driving people from the Wall almost as much as she loved them for being a living ancient darkness.

Leaving the common room, she walked to the university food hall. The students were even noisier than she remembered them being, the food far worse. She had loved the food when she was a student and had been involved in long arguments on which was the best place to eat, but surveying the food now, it all looked disgusting. The curries were gelatinous slop, the burgers dry, the pies carbonised.

She chose the least horrible-looking thing: spiral pasta coated with a grey-brown bolognese-like sauce. It was even more foul than it looked; the sauce tasted like raw tinned tomatoes and the pasta was overcooked and slimy with mysterious crunchy bits. She ate it anyway, revelling in the place more than the food; in the energised students, the arguments being held in that tone that said 'I'm an intellectual', which no intellectual used – the more mature students would grow out of it by third year, some would remain prats forever.

The noise, the bad food, the wonky tables and uncomfortable chairs were a reminder of a time that was gone.

Of Jack.

Everybody loved Jack. He was exciting to be around; he made everyone feel like they were better people, because he deigned to be with them. He was powerfully charismatic, always the centre of attention, his self seeming to enter spaces in advance of his body.

He had a special affection for Christine that she could never quite understand; he spent his time on her, not on his many admirers, the women who wanted his love, the men who wanted to be him. He would leave them all behind to be with her, even though there was never anything sexual between them; she was not even sure she wanted that from him.

Sexual feelings never tainted their friendship, never stood between them. They had seen friendships torn apart by dating, by break-ups, by jealousy, by friendship growing into love metamorphosing into hate; they were grateful that their love would never suffer that. They had talked about how such things would never stain the special love they had for each other, their immortal friendship.

Their love that would never die.

Then he was gone. Yet she kept expecting him to return, to walk up to her with the half-smile that he only shared with her; with the pain in his eyes that was there even when he was laughing. Since he'd disappeared, the world had started to deserve the sullen face Jack always showed it.

Tears were burning down her cheeks.

She knew the students around her, the pretty young women and the beige young men, were studiously ignoring her; intentionally not seeing the strange older woman crying at a table all by herself. For most of her twenty-one years she had felt alone but never like this.

FRIDAY

FATHER SAID HE was pleased when she told him she would be returning to university to do a master's in pure mathematics; he probably wasn't lying. 'We always need mathematicians in the Fund,' he said. 'Well done, darling,' he added; then all the other words after that were more nothingness of the same kind. She could not remember him ever having called her darling before; could not even remember having pleased him. He had then gone off to work, Mother went off to have brunch, displaying no particular desire to talk to Christine.

She was alone again.

Safetynet Social had no notifications that mattered, because they weren't from Jack.

Nothing from Jack.

Her email inbox was empty of everything but spam about things she might want to buy soon and information about her future studies. The products on offer were things that might be relevant to a woman studying postgrad maths – computers, calculators, clothes considered appropriate for her new station in life, plain glass lenses in ugly frames to make her look smarter even though she didn't need glasses to see.

Nothing from Jack.

The algorithm seemed to struggle at intervals; the clothes advertised perfect for angsty young men, or vacuous young women, the computers and calculators better suited to undergrads. Other times it found nothing to advertise to her and sent empty offers instead. She considered intentionally bizarre searches and searching for random items to throw the algorithm off further, just for kicks. Then it started learning. It was fascinating. And definitely frightening.

Christine became aware of how the mathematics she loved had become weaponised. And that the only thing she was really searching for was not there.

Nothing from Jack.

There was a forum deep within Safetynet, past the socials and the shopping, the email and the info, dedicated to a long-obsolete phone; a ten-year-old model. Deep within that forum was a poorly visited topic. No one had ever tried to answer the question; perhaps the original poster had not even checked for replies. Nobody had commented, nobody ever would. Unless Jack wanted to leave her a message. This was the agreed-upon place; if all other modes of communication failed, he would go there, post a message in their code.

She slid in there, desperate for some word, certain that if there was no message from Jack, it meant he didn't want to see her again. Or he was dead. She prayed, as she did every time she looked, that he had simply broken his promise and decided he didn't want to see her.

Nothing.

The forum was untouched, the question left unanswered, as were the questions her brain was screaming. She held down the power switch on her phone until it beeped, hit the 'power off' icon and dropped her phone on the polished hardwood floor, not caring if it shattered, ignoring the hollow drumming sound of the wood. She turned to look out the window. The sky was low and dark; it slumped close to the tops of the houses, a sickening, ominous fume.

Desperate for contact, she retrieved her phone, switched it back on, waited too long for it to boot, and left a message.

'Please contact me,' she begged in code.

Fighting the urge to throw her phone through the closed window, she simply dropped it and lay despondent on the tightly sprung couch. The television was turned down low, not worth watching, but what would her life be without its constant boring presence? It was like air itself, like water to a fish, the water in which she swam. She was a creature of information, of television, of Safetynet, of social media. Restless, she poked buttons on the TV remote, trying to make it do something interesting.

Servants quietly bustled around her, doing work she could be doing and attempting to do it without disturbing her. For the first time in her life she noticed them properly. They were healthier than she expected, all young, all fit; all brown-skinned or darker, the colour of servants. All women, they had a robust, powerful beauty she found compelling, far more eye-catching than the identical surgical beauty of her mother's friends and her father's secretaries.

Entering the television's menu, she forced it to scan for channels, watching the progress bar inch across the screen, the number of channels going up.

The random activity did not excise her thoughts. Surgically modified, enhanced, sculpted, exercised, dyed skin and painted faces were had invaded her mind's eye. She became aware of an intense selective pressure. Those who worked hard to look just right were certain to do better in every way and in every endeavour. That was her world.

The world.

Christine had not had surgery yet, though she dyed her hair the same blonde as her mother rather than the dark brown her hair settled on when she did nothing to it. Surgery would be the next step to stop herself from looking old, to get a husband, to be more conventionally beautiful, to ensure a better job, to be like everybody else. Looking at these beautiful women who served her family, it was a step she was not certain she wanted to take.

She flicked channels, resting on a new one she had never watched before. The screen was filled with compression artefacts and pixelated noise, like a channel just out of range, or an eternally buffering videostream. She could make nothing out except occasional bars of blackness that flickered across the screen.

She did not need a husband nor did she need a job; she felt self-contained if a human could be such. She did not want to admit to herself that perhaps her stated and public disdain for surgery was to impress Jack. He hated the homogenisation of faces, as he called it. He wished everybody looked different, which was so alien to the way everybody else thought.

The woman who had held her hair back as she puked was not visible from the couch. Maybe she was elsewhere in the house, or not there that day. She had never wondered before if staff had days off. Christine wanted to thank the woman properly, for caring for her like that, for not embarrassing her by telling anyone.

Suddenly afraid that the woman had blabbed, Christine was consumed by an intense desire to find her and order her not to tell anybody.

She stalked through the house, trying to make it look like it was a general inspection, imagining she could fool the staff into believing she suddenly cared. She was shocked to discover that they varied in looks far more than Mother's friends did; from childhood she had imagined the staff as one homogeneous group.

It was the denizens of the city who were driven to homogenisation.

The woman was not in the house, was not outside hanging out washing on the line, was not in the garden. Christine hated the garden, though she could not say why. Maybe it was because the flowerbeds were too mathematically perfect, the edges where they met lawn cut with razor-sharp precision. Maybe it was the topiary, the bushes carved not into creatures or something interesting but instead into geometric shapes, spheres, cubes, pyramids, balanced on sticks, all that was left of their trunks. The front yards of every second house on her street were almost exactly the same as hers. The ones in between had woolly cascades of weeping trees, puffs and tufts of clumping grasses. There were gardeners in some of the yards, making sure everything was perfect and perfectly identical.

She returned to the house, her house that was almost the same as everybody else's but for the ostentatious extra level, perched on top of the dwelling like a hat. She wanted out, she wanted to break things, she needed a drink.

The television was still tuned to the near-dead channel. It cleared to a black background with the words THEY ARE LYING TO YOU in bold white, for just a moment. The screen went blank and played dead before the television turned back on, showing the news channel. Christine searched. The other channel was gone.

A drone buzzed by on patrol, crossing the roofs of the houses, swerving to pass around Christine's like a bird defying a mountain.

MONDAY

CHRISTINE ROSE EARLY, determined to go down and join her parents for breakfast. She had not ordered anything to be delivered to her, but there was cereal in the pantry and milk in the fridge. She was 'big enough and ugly enough', as Mother would say, to get her own breakfast.

Father was engrossed in his tablet; Christine neither knew nor cared what interested him. Mother had eaten her egg white omelette sandwich and was on what was probably not her first, or even her second, beverage – a king-sized mug of coffee so strong Christine could smell it from the other end of the table. She looked over at the coffee machine and wondered what her mother's setting was; one day she would have to tap that button on the touch screen and see what horrific substance comes out.

Curious about what was happening in the world, she dragged out her phone. Holding a spoon full of cornflakes in her right hand, she loaded the news feed in her left. There was a photo of protesters charging police outside a restaurant called Chilli Peppers, batons swinging over perspex shields, pepper spray clouding the air.

Outside

Gang violence has again erupted as ethnic gangs fight for control of the streets. Police failed to contain the violence as it spread from the central business district into the suburbs. Property damage is expected to reach millions of dollars and law-abiding citizens are afraid to leave their homes.

Outside

Cafe owners are calling on the government to intervene, to make the city safe again so they can reopen.

Depressed, she flicked to the next story with her thumb.

Outside

The government of North America today announced an emergency plan to manage the escalating violence in New York. The city will be abandoned within one month. All residents will be screened before being relocated to other cities. Those with criminal records and those suspected of gang or terrorist affiliations will be sent to a work camp in Mexico.

Somewhere

Mexico has filed a protest with the United Nations demanding that the US government return the land they have annexed for work camps.

Flick

'War in the Middle East should be expected to spread further,' said Professor Mark Jones. 'We must be vigilant and prepared to defend our borders.'

Flick

A march by citizens protesting gang violence in London was attacked by thugs.

Flick

... ethnic violence ...

Flick

... gang war ...

Flick

'We will protect you,' said the head of Security. 'None of the nefarious forces trying to endanger your lives and safety can make it into the city.'

Flick

... government has issued a travel advisory ...

Christine wondered why anyone would want to travel. The unsafe world outside the city jellied her knees, made her stomach weak. She killed the news app, loaded her email. Nothing from Jack, nothing of consequence, nothing from her other friends, from Jack's friends.

Breakfast was silent except for the slurp of mouths on the lips of mugs, the tink and tooth-aching scratch of cutlery on plates, and Christine's spoon hitting the inside of her bowl. Father's tablet bleeped and he abruptly rose from his seat and walked out of the room. Moments later the front door slammed shut.

Christine could see the tension pegging Mother's shoulders to her ears slip away. Silence.

'I am going to the cafe. Would you like to join me?' Mother asked in that artificially bell-like voice of hers.

'I have stuff to revise before starting my master's.' Christine knew Mother could tell she was lying. 'I may as well do it.'

Mother shrugged, made a noise that might have been 'whatever', stood and walked to the door. A car pulled up noisily outside.

The all-news-all-the-time channel was playing loudly on the television in the lounge room. Christine slumped into the emotional comfort of the couch with a long black in her hand, barely able to prevent it from spilling. The remote was missing, possibly under the couch cushions, under the couch, near the television, or in someone's pocket.

On the screen, soldiers and riot police chased protesters through trash-strewn streets and past graffitied walls. The voices of the newsreaders droned over the roar of violence. 'War on the streets,' they told her. 'Stay in your homes.' Christine worried about the protesters, even though she knew her parents would be egging on the police; Father baying for blood. Helicopters chased thieves as they drove fast cars down the freeways, the flashing lights of the police pursuit vehicles painting the roads red as they screamed past an endless array of strange cars. People lay dead on the street; children were starving, skeletal naked. The Chairman of the Agency reassured them that their city was safe; all these things were happening elsewhere, outside.

Outside.

Flags waved, a riot of colour, no two flags the same. Two armies of thugs armed with sticks crunched into a line of back-to-back police trying to keep them apart. Riot police marched into massed bodies, batons swinging. Tear gas drifted in clouds over empty streets. Buildings burned. Open street-battle war. Violence and hate and vitriolic anger.

A camera on a helicopter panned across a destroyed city wasteland, over campfires and people dressed in rags, waving improvised weapons at the lens.

Outside.

It was a war out there and she was glad to be safe, that the Agency was keeping her safe; but a part of her was chafing to get out, to see what was out there.

She was so lonely.

The criminals, the murderers, the attackers, the rioters, the thieves, the people shot by police for carrying guns were all the colour of the staff who had just walked in the door. Christine recoiled involuntarily before remembering that all the servants who entered the town, who passed through the Wall, were vetted by the Agency.

'These are troubling times. The world is a dangerous place,' the voice of the Chairman said. 'I can continue to assure you of this: within the Wall you are perfectly safe.' Christine thought she saw a look of distaste and contempt on a brown face as it passed the television.

She flinched in fear automatically but tried to resist her reaction, understanding dawning that she had been taught to feel that way.

The woman who had held her hair back as she vomited walked past in silence. She stood upright, strong, her face calm. Hers was not the sort of brown face Christine was used to seeing on the news.

There was something about her, a stillness in her stance, a deep kindness in her face, in her golden-brown eyes. Christine could not remember seeing anyone remotely like her before. She tried to stare without looking like she was staring. She breathed deep, sat back on the couch and let the feelings wash over her.

Suddenly she was silently and breathlessly crying and she had no idea why. Her feelings – a malaise of the heart, a crack in her soul – didn't make sense. She wanted to feel and she wanted whatever she was feeling to stop.

The sunlight streaming through the window lay upon her like a lead-sheet shroud. Sounds from the too-loud television, the flicker and light, the shapes and movement, infiltrated her brain. She heard the throaty rumble of a diesel engine, glanced out the window and watched the lumpen black shape of a security van pass, flanked by a flight of buzzing drones.

She did something she had never imagined doing. She turned the television off and closed the curtains herself. Pulling out some particularly difficult exercise, for something to do, she grabbed a coffee.

The sun peeked through the crack in the curtains like a novice peeping Tom, tentative and sly. Christine was engrossed in the work she had started as an excuse. The house could have been on fire and she wouldn't know until her untidy pile of scrawled-on paper caught and burned. The liquid in the cup in front of her was cold. She had not done more with it than touch it to her lips once, not even managed to pour a sip into her mouth before putting it down again.

Still the servants, neat and uniformed, moved around her cleaning, fidgeting, doing busywork, Christine barely noticing when one of them took her forgotten mug away. When a tanned hand placed a new steaming mug in front of her, she felt compelled to look up, to murmur 'thank you', yet she stopped wordlessly.

It was her.

God she was beautiful, silhouetted against the glowing window.

The woman's hair was cut short, like a boy's. Christine could tell from the way it waved that if it was much longer it would spontaneously form ringlets; she had a friend with hair like that. Her friend's hair had been blonde, the servant's was as black as the coffee in Christine's cup, far darker than her own natural colour that she was not brave enough to show.

She had strong but kind features and amber eyes.

Christine was immediately jealous of that eye colour.

'Thank y-you,' Christine stammered. 'You didn't have to do that. I could have made myself a fresh one.'

When she smiled at Christine, it was like someone throwing open the curtains to a sunny day. 'No problem, Ma'am,' she

said. 'You looked pretty engrossed in what you were doing.'
Turning her back, the woman walked away. She had a confident
swagger, like someone who owned the very air they breathed.

'Don't call me Ma'am,' Christine said. 'I'm not my mother.'
The beauty paused for a moment then walked on.

Christine tried to go back to her work but could not concentrate; instead she pretended to work while watching the beautiful
woman out of the corner of her eye. Someone that beautiful should
not have to work; she could have found a husband to look after
her. She could not marry someone in the town but surely even
outside, as dangerous as it was, there would be someone to take
care of her.

The woman finished tidying the mess Mother had left in
the lounge room; scattered fashion magazines, design books,
photos. Mother had stopped working long ago and only seemed
to make a mess to pretend she was working, not just a lady who
lunches, and brunches, and drinks and drinks. She never seemed
to notice that her piles of crap spontaneously neatened every
time she walked away. That was what happened in the ecology
of her mother's world.

The beauty brushed her hair back from her forehead and
went into the kitchen, glancing at Christine as she walked
past. Another member of staff joined her and soon there were
clattering and banging noises.

Christine's stomach rumbled, but she didn't want to go into
the kitchen to make a sandwich while the beauty was in there.
She walked over to the window and twitched the curtains open
to try and see if it was cool enough outside to walk down the
street for a pie.

The sun was a blowtorch creating heat shimmer and mirages all the way up the street. It painted everything metallic, turning the windows into molten bronze. Light bounced from the front window of another passing security van and for a moment she was blinded.

She wondered where Security went when they were not on patrol. They surely wouldn't be paid enough to buy a house in town. She had never met anyone in town who worked for Security or had parents who did. A thought scratched at the edge of her mind. She remembered something from high school, in the class where they had learned about the town's history. Security lived with their families in a village somewhere, walled for safety but outside the town. She hoped they had nice houses. They worked hard to keep the town safe; they deserved nice things for that. She wondered if their kids would grow up to be Security too.

Light reflected from a lens directly across the street. It could only be there to watch the house, to watch her.

Christine abruptly walked out the front door and strolled nonchalantly down the street. She walked back along the edge of the path, almost in the neighbours' yards, across the street from her house. Approaching the camera from its blind spot, she peered at it. It was just out of her reach, the pole too slick to climb.

Jack would be able to think of a way to destroy, or at least disable, the camera. She was not as creative.

She kept walking. A solution would present itself she was sure. She returned to the house and sat back down on her couch, next to her piles of paper, her scrawls.

There was a sandwich on a plate in front of her. She did not know where it had come from, had not noticed it when she sat down. Someone must have read her mind, or heard her stomach – it was loud enough. It was a mystery but a mysterious sandwich was still a sandwich. She bit into it, staring at the equation in front of her, and did not even taste what she was eating; though she knew it was probably her favourite.

SATURDAY

MOTHER ALMOST APPEARED sober when she suggested they all go shopping for furniture for Christine's apartment, which made her suggestion for 'family time' extra weird. Even Brandon, Christine's younger brother, was there, home from university college for the weekend; something Christine had avoided when she was his age. Christine was less than delighted about him being around. Brandon was a little too much a clone of Father, in both looks and attitude; the apple had not fallen far from the tree.

All four of them bundled into Father's monstrous car, which was much bigger than the other cars in the neighbourhood. The purring engine, driven by someone they found easy to ignore, carried them through Saturday crowds, past street parties and markets, to the homemaker centre. The building was huge. A great big windowless box, the outside grey-painted steel, as tall as their house. Christine wanted to see if she could see the Wall from the top but could see no way to get up there.

Their car roared underground. The car park was the size of the building, painted a nauseating colour, something between souring cream and pus-green, lit by fluorescent tubes, blue-white, as bright as day. Something about the colour, the cold light, cut into Christine's brain like a hangover.

She had always hated this place.

Despite it being Saturday the car park was almost empty. The few cars there were huddled as close as they could get to the door to the escalators.

Security's cars could not have been more obvious if they tried. Hatchbacks, sedans and vans, all black. Their windows were tinted; on their bodies, and on their bumpers, were patches of a different texture of black – tinted glass panels hiding cameras.

Around the car park on every pillar, on seemingly arbitrary sections of roof, were conventional video cameras. The cameras were obvious and Christine wondered why she had never noticed that before.

Or had she noticed but forgotten? The thought was slippery; she could not hold on to it.

They exited the car, one of the doors slamming with a dull echoing thump; deafening, startling. Father turned to the sound, the anger on his face uncharacteristic; he normally hid it better. When he saw Brandon, staring into his face defiantly, daring him to react, Father smiled indulgently. Christine fumed in silence.

Glass doors whooshed, the aircon blasted their faces with frigid air, the travelator whirred them up to the shops. The light was so bright Christine felt dizzy sick. She stapled a false smile on her face in a futile attempt to hide how she felt. Mother was giddy, smiling like someone who had overdosed on uppers. Perhaps she was relishing the opportunity to use her university degree in design for something useful for a change.

Or perhaps she had overdosed on uppers.

Father's face was settled in its habitual lack of expression. Christine wondered where he got this blank expression: if it was natural or as trained as Mother's laugh. Brandon was sullen to the point of being surly, walking with his family in silence, barely lifting his feet off the ground.

At the furniture store, a plain clothes security guard shopped with them, pretending to look at the furniture. Surely he and the Agency knew it was completely unconvincing. He made Christine angry, and she was tempted to vandalise or steal something just to see what he would do.

Surely nothing.

Father and Brandon disappeared, leaving her with Mother, which seemed unfair.

Glass eyes continued to watch them. Christine ignored the cameras while subtly demonstrating that she was aware of them, a skill she and the other students had learned back in primary school; each of the girls practising what they had learned from their mothers. She would never be as good at it as her mother though.

Mother's help almost immediately stopped being advice on what would look good in Christine's apartment and began edging closer to shopping for her own tastes in furniture. 'I am an expert,' Mother said when Christine questioned her opinion.

'I studied interior design, you know. I wanted to do art but in the end I did something more practical.'

Christine was not sure whether she cared that Mother was taking over. She knew nothing about furniture, knew she had no taste, would be happy with nothing at all, as long as she had a chair and a desk and maybe a bed.

'Your furniture, how you decorate your house matters so much,' Mother twittered. 'Your living space is your second face.' She stared at Christine and frowned, clearly not liking what she saw.

'It would not hurt to do something with your first face to be honest,' Mother quipped. 'If you continue to refuse surgery – and my surgeon is willing to make time for you even though he is busy – you could at least wear make-up. You are not a little girl anymore.'

Christine's expression probably made her look exactly like a petulant little girl, so she let her face relax into what she thought was a fairly good impersonation of her Father's impassive mask. 'I don't want surgery, Mother. There's plenty of time for that later.'

When hell freezes over, was her rebellious thought.

Mother poked at the tops of tables, opened and closed drawers, sat on chairs and talked animatedly with the shop assistant, a little brown man, shorter than Mother, with strange mannerisms. He was a lot like Mother, Christine realised; maybe it was an interior designer thing. She decided to join them and at least pretend to be interested in buying stuff for what would soon be her new home.

She manoeuvred Mother and the shop assistant to the desks and slid her hand across the top of a wooden table topped with leather. It reminded her of the desk in her favourite lecturer's office, of the furniture in the postgrad common room. Brand-new, it had the look and feel, even the smell, of an antique. It was bigger than the desk Father kept at home but never used, and even bigger than the second dining table at her parents' house that Mother co-opted when she pretended she had a friend's house to design or decorate or whatever.

'That is a beautiful desk,' said the shop assistant. 'I understand you are a budding academic.' Christine wondered how he could know that; perhaps Mother had mentioned it. 'This desk is perfect to create the working environment that an academic, maybe a professor one day' – he winked – 'would find comforting.'

He was right. 'I want that desk,' Christine breathed. She had never wanted anything as much as she wanted that piece of polished wood and green leather. She imagined herself sitting back, her papers on the desk, mug beside them, doing impossible, or at least improbable, calculations.

'It's a beautiful piece,' the assistant said, his voice having a cadence that Christine normally expected from women; from Mother's drinking friends, from Mother when drinking.

'It's lovely,' Mother said, 'but it's not as important as other things if you want to make an impression, meet people, maybe one day meet a man who can look after you. Besides it's too big.'

'I understand,' said the man in a tone that said he knew more than them but somehow managed to not sound condescending, 'that Christine is planning for a career or at least to spend a reasonable stretch of time within academia. The people she will meet in that world, other academics and people who admire academics, appreciate someone who has taken the time to find a good desk, to have an efficient and beautiful workspace in their home. This desk' – he touched it with a loving caress – 'says all the right things to the sort of people that Christine would likely be meeting at university or later in her line of work. Especially the men.'

Christine smiled even though she did not need to impress any men. She didn't care what else Mother bought for her apartment, did not care how her place was decorated, as long as she got that desk. She would smile at anything to get that desk.

'Adding a couple of beautiful bookcases – and we have them to match the desk – would create a workspace that would not only be inspiring but also give the right impression.'

Four security officers jogged past the glass partition that separated the furniture store from the rest of the centre. Christine watched them until they disappeared. She hoped something was actually happening; an emergency evacuation, or even a terrorist attack, would be better than shopping for more furniture with Mother.

'You should try some chair designs, see what you like, what feels good when you sit on it,' said the sales assistant. 'When you find something you like we can customise it to whatever covering you prefer, like leather for example.'

Christine stared at him, trying not to appear suspicious but wondering how he knew so much about her tastes. Had someone, or something, at university watched her caressing the postgrad common room chairs and stored it on Safetynet? Had someone seen her, snapped a photo, and posted it on Safetynet Social?

She watched him as they walked to the area with desk chairs, saw him glance at a device in his hand. She wanted to snatch it off him, see what was on it. Was it her Safetynet Social account and data? Something else? Was someone keeping a database on her, predicting her likes and dislikes? Safetynet was good at sending targeted advertising. Safetynet knew everything. Christine suppressed a shudder.

She wondered whether it was possible to completely confound the machines.

As Christine bounced on a chair the shop assistant's device made a sound like a phone ringing. He put it to his ear, listened to something. As he took it away, Christine noticed a tiny hole like a piercing on his earlobe. He must wear an earring there, perhaps when not at work. Christine could not remember ever seeing a man with an earring. She liked the idea.

'I have to take this,' the assistant said. 'Continue testing the chairs and let me know which one you like when I return.' Christine watched him walk off to the other side of the store.

'I wonder how he knows so much about me,' Christine mused, as she sat in another chair. 'He knows my aspirations, what I do, even seems to know what I like. He knows me better than I know myself.'

'Great, isn't it?' Mother giggled. 'Makes it *so* much easier to decide what you want when people only show you things you might like.' She stretched out the 'so' like a schoolkid, long and tunefully. Christine could not tell if the tone was sarcastic; with Mother she never could, never had, probably never would.

'I don't like people knowing so much about me.'

'Don't put things on the Social then,' Mother replied.

Christine bounced in another chair like a child, grimacing at the security camera in the centre of her vision and ignoring the others she could not see. She wondered if the cameras were analysing how she sat in the chair; if they would use AI and biometrics to work out more about her. Sitting bolt upright, she tried to appear adult and capable, realised she looked quite silly and burst out laughing. She resisted the urge to poke her tongue out at the camera, tried to relax into her habitual posture, failed, too self-conscious, and slumped back down like Father did on his desk chair in his office when he thought nobody was looking.

'This one,' she said. The chair was like a narrow armchair without arms, upholstered in horrible black fabric that made it look more like a suitcase than a chair. Although she was not certain about it, it felt important to say something.

The shop assistant chose that moment to return. 'Perfect.' He beamed. 'We can have it upholstered in any fabric you choose. For example' – he led her to a couch covered in weathered reddish-brown leather – 'this is the exact antique leather we used on some of the leather armchairs we had made for the mathematics postgraduate common room at the university. I am sure you are aware of those particular chairs. They are popular with some of the academics.'

Christine nodded, desperately trying not to show the fear and bewilderment in her eyes. 'Yes,' she said with a patently false calm that Mother and the assistant seemed to find genuine, 'that would be perfect.'

They wandered the store, looking at other furniture, the assistant and Mother debating what would look good in Christine's apartment. The shop already had the dimensions, and a 3D render of every room, knew the colours, knew what would fit and what wouldn't, could tell how daylight and the artificial light in the night would affect the space. Mother was having the time of her life.

Christine followed, making noises when she thought they expected her to have something to say. They did not seem interested in her opinion, only her assent. She was quite aware that the assistant kept letting Mother think she had won, complimenting her constantly but subtly on her taste.

It took less time than Christine had expected it would to furnish her whole apartment. Mother told her it didn't matter if they got it wrong, they could always replace things later. For some reason, Christine was disgusted by that.

They went for lunch. Christine did not see Mother call or message anyone, yet Brandon and Father were waiting at the restaurant when they got there. Brandon had a bag from the computer games shop, which looked big enough for a new console.

Christine ordered the seafood special, whatever that was; she liked seafood. Mother ordered the same and a drink for her and Christine, who suddenly wished she had been more creative with her order. Father ordered steak and Brandon followed his lead. Beer for Brandon and for Father. Drinks arrived; Mother drank her first glass of red too fast, ordered a bottle as soon as a server walked past. Christine sipped hers. She did not see Brandon or Father drink from their glasses at all. Food arrived; small serves for Christine and Mother, huge chunks of meat for Brandon and Father. They ate in silence, except for Mother flirting with the server whenever he walked past. 'He's cute,' Mother said. 'He would be perfect for you if he was not a server.'

'You are not flirting for me,' Christine said, then silenced herself by shoving a fork full of food into her blushing face. She did not know if Mother was being sarcastic or obtuse. Brandon laughed, Father ignored them both.

The server came and picked up their plates. Christine's was empty, Brandon's looked like it wouldn't even need washing. Father had eaten most of his steak and none of his salad. Mother's plate looked like it had hardly been touched. There was a forest of empty glasses and spent bottles on the table, although Christine could not remember them being ordered. She counted three bottles labelled 'red'. Her glass was full, but she couldn't remember anyone filling it, nor could she remember her glass ever achieving emptiness.

Mother was talking too fast, describing the furniture they had ordered in tight detail and with a passion Christine had not heard from her before. She wondered why Mother no longer worked as a designer, if she ever had.

Brandon was staring at her with a look on his face like he had trodden on dog shit and couldn't quite scrape it all off his shoe. Christine stared back, wearing a facsimile of her father's blank face. Brandon had always been a bit of a dick but seemed worse now he was at university.

Father and Mother were involved in some new permutation of their cold war; the silence escalating. They each stared at the other, wearing their habitual faces – Father blank, Mother cold – as they pointedly ate desserts they had surely not given any thought to ordering. If there was a way to utilise silence as a weapon, one of them would have found it; perhaps they already had.

Servers came and went, lunch went on and on, and eventually became nothing other than drinks.

The tension was so thick Christine thought she could dance on it. She wondered what her parents got from each other; there was nothing obvious unless both of them thrived on passive abuse.

Christine and Father both looked over at Mother. She was staring down at the table, a faint self-satisfied smile on her lips; it did not reach even a millimetre past the perfectly drawn edge of her lipstick.

SUNDAY

SITTING IN HER room was so boring Christine briefly considered looking for Brandon, looking for Mother, looking for trouble. She even considered seeking out Father, although she knew that would be pointless; he would be off playing golf, or doing whatever other mysterious thing he did most Sundays. He was probably off bonking one of his secretaries and, if he was, Mother probably knew about it and didn't care.

Christine opened her window. She could barely remember when she had last done so. The whirring of the air conditioning increased in pitch as it attempted and failed to cool the incoming heat. Not bothering to close the hole she had created in the security of the house, she dropped her pyjamas on the floor and threw on some jeans and a plain black t-shirt. She stood with shoes in one hand, socks in the other for a moment, wondering if the street would be too hot for bare feet; wondering what people would think of a barefoot adult. Sitting down again, she put on her shoes.

Stuffing her tablet in her handbag and phone in her pocket, she walked down the stairs and out the front door before anybody could notice she was leaving. As she stepped out a drone buzzed past overhead, hovered just outside her open window and whirred away.

When Christine was a kid she had thrown the window wide to catch a breeze that she was certain smelled of the ocean. She had never been to the ocean but it was described in the books she read; that briny smell on the damp breeze, sand and seaweed. She had lain in that breeze, dreaming of places she had never seen, might never see, because the ocean in those books, in her dreams, was not there anymore. That's what she'd been told.

That early morning she'd tumbled back into sleep, to dream, she hoped, of the ocean. She had been woken by Mother, breathless and wide-eyed, throwing open her bedroom door, two men from security behind her. Christine had not needed to be reprimanded, the look on her Mother's face was enough.

She was an adult and didn't think her window was anybody's business. She had something she needed to do.

She was not ready to give up on Jack.

After Jack went missing, leaving her broken, Christine had gone to his parents' house. Jack's father had hissed, spat incomprehensible words at her and slammed the heavy wooden door that protected their house in the face of her shocked silence. She did not want to brave him again but she had no choice. Jack's house was not far away.

Moving stiffly and mechanically like a puppet without volition, like a voodoo zombie from an old movie, she walked until she reached Jack's house. The garden was perfectly maintained and the facade of the building manicured. She knocked on the door, waited, knocked again. Still no answer.

The windows were blinded by curtains, but there was a crack of light between one set when she looked closer, in the window of what she remembered as the family room. She peered through it intently. Nothing. An empty room, the lights even starker with no furniture to shine on. There was nobody, not even a cleaner or servant. It was the saddest room she had ever seen.

Nobody was there to see the tears rushing down her face.

At first she did not register the sound penetrating her ears, but then insight came to her in a rush, a small drone buzzed towards her at top speed. They were watching. They would see she was peering through the windows of an abandoned house and she did not want to have to explain why. She kept the back of her head between her face and the invader of her personal space, knowing that a drone that size would not have a very good lens, would not have chemical sensors or be able to steal her hair for DNA. It had been fun as a teenager with Jack, trying to figure out what each type of drone could do, seeing how far they could go without getting caught.

She also knew that more drones would be on their way. Some of those machines would be able to count the hairs on her head and steal some of those hairs to identify her. Some would have chemical sensors and would be able to track her across town like sniffer dogs. Her parents would know what she was up to. She suddenly feared being caught.

Christine walked away briskly, racking her brain for a public building nearby to lose herself in. She did not know how long the batteries of the machine would last, if she could keep ahead of it and run its batteries low; she might get away before a bigger machine joined the chase, before Security became interested and attended.

Maybe she should give herself up. She had only been looking in through the window. She could explain, surely it would not take long; she could lie, that would be even easier; she could tell them she was looking to buy the house. And yet. She did not want anyone knowing she was so desperate to find Jack that she would invade his family's privacy.

Once she looked like she was running away, once she looked guilty, she had made it harder for herself.

From childhood, she had been told she had nothing to fear if she had done nothing wrong. Christine no longer knew what 'nothing wrong' meant.

The sound of the micro-drone was becoming quieter. She did not risk looking back, did not risk showing her face, but she hoped it was falling behind, nearly out of battery. Normally drones did not risk running down or not returning to base, otherwise a security officer would have to come collect it and take it to a recharge station. It must be very interested in her or have orders to keep its camera on her for as long as possible.

She could hear no others. Not yet.

The buzzing stopped. There was a faint clatter; it had landed on the road, camera trained on her. She dared not hope its lenses were broken. Not that it mattered, it streamed its data to base anyway.

She began to run, trying to get away before more machines came, then stopped, knowing that Security's AI would identify her terrified pace and become interested. A sudden turn, another, down a cul-de-sac and then down a narrow alley between houses. She could not hear any distant machine noises. She was in a small park, hidden between the back fences of houses; she could see no roads.

Scattered raggedly across the field of trimmed grass were gum trees, some of the biggest she had seen outside of the large parkland that ringed the town, before the Wall. Somehow the trees seemed older than the nearby houses, than the town. She could rest a while in the dark green shadows, the colour of licorice. It would be cool there, safe from the eyes of the high drones that constantly quartered the sky.

Christine sat in the shade of the tree, leaned against the great bole and closed her eyes. The area smelled of mown grass and eucalyptus, of damp and small wriggling things. When she opened her eyes again, dark was falling; she must have fallen asleep. She scrambled to her feet, brushed dirt and who-knew-what off the fabric over her arse and started walking. Home was not out of reasonable walking range.

In the darkness she was tempted to call a car but suspected they tracked car call-outs and might connect the woman fleeing from an empty house with the woman calling a car from somewhere nearby. She did not want to have to think of a lie. Lies bred lies until the truth drowns under them.

Security had become increasingly intense throughout her life. She was not sure whether it was because the surveillance became more noticeable as you grew older. When she was young, she didn't pay attention. She was used to being watched, accustomed to the anti-crime cameras and the security vans, the agents and the drones. They were there to keep citizens safe. But she noticed more now and she was no longer sure how long she could tolerate it.

Christine walked past houses made ominous by the dark. She felt the flakes of light coming through the gaps in window coverings were watching her, the red eyes of camera on-lights were stalking her and following the little dot on the map app on her phone, like she was. The Agency could track her through her app use, perhaps even track her phone in general.

She turned the corner to her street to a flashing, crowded commotion.

There were Security everywhere in the street outside her house, their lights strobing blindingly off the neighbouring houses that appeared to be crowding around her like flies around a corpse. The neighbours had their blinds open, rooms in darkness, making it impossible to see if there was anyone standing behind the glass, watching.

She knew there was.

From those dark windows, the neighbours watched as she walked towards her front door. A brace of Security stepped out from the flashing lights and approached her, grabbing her arms. Their hands were slick, like cling wrap, like a condom. They must have been wearing gloves of some kind.

Mother appeared, looking confused, relieved, curious, cold, then angry – all within less than a minute. 'Where have you been? Your window was open and you weren't there. You could have been kidnapped, attacked, dead. There could have been an intruder in the house. I saw the window and I was frightened. I didn't go in.' Mother's voice was stuck in that tone she usually used for the lower classes, for staff, servers and Security, like a volcano under an ice sheet.

Christine shook off Security's hands disdainfully, just as she imagined Mother would do if she ever stumbled into that situation.

'If you never went in, how did you know I wasn't there?'

'Security told me they had been chasing a suspicious person through the streets,' Mother continued. 'I was so worried.'

The security operatives, in black one-piece uniforms, gloved with glistening white, dropped their hands to their sides and took a step back, as one.

'I went for a walk,' Christine said with a false haughtiness. 'I lost track of time. I don't remember doing so but I must have left the window open.'

Mother stepped forward and embraced Christine. It did not feel like an authentic embrace, it felt like Mother was acting, like Christine knew she herself was. Mother was stiff and robotic, none of the ice in her bones had melted. Christine knew the hug was for the benefit of the neighbours, not for her and certainly not for her mother.

MONDAY

MOTHER MADE A show of going to work. At least that was what she said she was doing. She had always claimed to be an interior designer, or something like that. Christine had never really cared and suspected nobody else did either. But her mother hadn't been into an office for years, if ever.

Is she a designer if she never designed? Christine felt underqualified to answer that question.

'My daughter is moving out, my son is at university,' Mother had exclaimed. 'I need to do something with myself.'

She almost sounded excited.

Christine couldn't understand why Mother hadn't worked before knowing she had no hand in raising her children. When they were kids there had been nannies, then school and after-school activities, with a driver and staff to get them to where they needed to go. Mother had all the time in the world and nothing to do with it.

With a bang of the front door, Christine was alone, except for the servants. The curtain that normally obscured the front yard was open. A tall dark man was mowing the lawn, sweat blasting from him and gluing his shirt to his back. A woman in a servant's uniform, her hair short, black and wavy, her skin glowing gold in the sun, sauntered over to him and they dived into what they must have thought was a secret embrace. A moment later they separated and the woman went to hang out the washing while he went back to the mowing.

Christine smiled to the empty room.

Though she had never quite seen the point of that, throwing yourself into the arms of a strong man, damp with sweat, smelling like Father, whiskey, man smell and aftershave. That man outside would be hard-skinned, carved of granite and wrapped with leather; unlike Father whose muscles had the texture of pudding. She could see muscle dancing under the wet fabric over his back. She could not imagine such hardness. But she could understand the need for a cuddle, a smooch, and perhaps more than that.

She was glad her mother was not there and hoped the eyes of the Agency, those glistening glass lenses, had not seen them. They were taking a risk; they could be fired or separated.

The sky looked like it was planning to unleash a storm, the clouds obscuring the sun, so dark grey they had passed through it back to blue, much darker than the clear sky. The low sky touched the top of the Wall like a ceiling.

She felt trapped.

Although it was just after breakfast, Christine slipped back into the kitchen, hungry. The beauty was working, cleaning pink stains off the white benches. Christine opened the fridge and poked around, not sure what to eat, glancing from time to time at the woman scrubbing the bench with a lithe efficiency.

Christine filled her arms with a salami, half a ham and a jar of pickles, stepped backwards and felt her back colliding with a moving object. The things in her arms began to slide away and she tipped forward, trying to catch everything. Strong arms caught her as the food dropped, but she could not stop herself from falling nor could the woman who slowed her collapse and lowered her gently to her knees.

The ham was on the floor, the salami rolled away, the pickle jar exploded. Christine slipped back into those arms despite herself, could hear and feel somebody's breath, could feel another's heartbeat against her own.

Christine scrambled on her hands and knees to the island bench, and pulled herself up to her feet. She could not catch her breath; her chest hurt in a way she could not identify. It was quite difficult to stand.

'Sorry, are you okay, Ma'am?'

Christine turned to the servant, embarrassed. 'It's fine. I'm fine,' she stuttered, backing away. 'Don't call me Ma'am.'

The woman watched her, staring into her eyes wearing an expression Christine had never seen before. There was a fire in it.

She felt an overwhelming shame, and something else she had never felt before, in the pit of her stomach.

'Clean up this mess,' Christine said as she blindly groped for a bottle of wine from the full rack. She walked towards the door and, feeling unexpectedly guilty, added, 'Please.'

Her lungs felt too big for her chest as she walked to the stairway and laboured up the stairs. Her bed was cold and lonely. She missed Jack. She was angry and confused and did not like it.

She lay there, shaking, did not want to stand up again, wasn't sure she could. Finally, she twisted the cap off the wine bottle and it cracked like a finger breaking. Holding the bottle in a trembling hand, she raised it to her mouth and glugged. The tannic dryness made her even more thirsty. She drank more, then more and more.

She dropped the empty bottle to the floor, not concerned about the last drops dripping into the carpet. Somebody would clean it up. She was not sure how long she had been lying there but she needed to see a friendly face, a familiar face, or even an unfriendly one.

Father was at work. Mother was at work but might not be. Brandon was at university.

She felt woozy and boozy but unaccountably energised. It was a strange feeling, a different drunk this time, like the world was hers if she would just take it. Standing, she swayed slightly in a non-existent wind.

Checking her room was secure – she did not want to face Security and Mother again – she left the room, a little unsteady. At least now there was a reason for her slight shaking. She carried nothing but her phone and credit card. A car arrived with prophetic rapidity after she summoned it, and she demanded to be taken to the university.

The familiar campus buildings were rendered sinister by the sunlight, the alcohol in her gut and her inexplicable mania. The grounds were wet, but she could not remember when it had rained. Sprinklers sprayed and painted the walls brown, the hard water from the bore almost the colour of tea.

Brandon would be somewhere in the Business department, in class or with his friends, the others who were clones of their fathers, wearing business suits even as students, even in high school.

That place was where the first-born sons congealed; where the second-born tried to prove themselves and hoped the privilege would rub off, hoping their fathers would be able to find them a decent job or, failing that, their older brothers would die young. That place where the boys with older sisters grew bitter and desperate. They were scared, those boys, and the few girls who had no brothers; scared they would be infected with the uselessness, the idleness of the students in other parts of the university who were unlikely to ever be CEO or company president or run a trust.

Her postgraduate ID card seemed to be enough to get her in through the fortress doors that kept the business students safe. The halls beyond the security station were stark white, painfully impersonal, having nothing in common with the new-old look of the rest of the campus.

Walls within walls.

A young, too-confident undergrad delighted in providing her with directions to the cafe; down one hall, follow the cream carpet, left turn, right turn, right turn. The cafe looked nothing like the halls that led to it. If anything, it looked like a replica of the cafe where Father lunched every day, all chrome and black, smoked mirrors and dark wood; but instead of businessmen it was packed with students of all ages in suits.

It was silent. Everybody was eating with quiet efficiency, as if they had no time or energy for anything other than shoving food in the holes in their faces; or at least wanted it to appear that way. Every table was a two-seater, and every table had only one person sitting at it holding a tablet or with a laptop open. Perhaps they were all keen to demonstrate that work was more important than anything else.

Brandon was alone at a two-seater table, eating and staring into the screen of a tablet, the backlight of the screen lighting up his face, starker and uglier than usual.

Christine strolled across the room with fake arrogance, ignoring the stares from the other students, and pulled out the chair from in front of Brandon. The chair was as uncomfortable as Father's silences. She squirmed, trying to soften it with her buttocks. Brandon looked insulted at having someone join him even before he looked up, and then when he did, he looked perplexed. He raised one eyebrow in a perfect facsimile of Father.

'I needed to see a friendly face,' she said. 'Not knowing where to find one, I settled for a familiar face. Couldn't think of anyone familiar, so family had to do.'

Brandon grunted at her attempted levity. 'And how did you get in here?' he asked arrogantly. 'This is the Business department. We have secrets here, things others are not allowed to know. You can't be here.'

Christine laughed, then shrugged.

'We like our quiet in here,' he said. 'We need to concentrate because we will be running the place soon, running this town, the businesses that own the town, the Agency, the trusts, the banks.' Christine suspected the work Brandon was doing was nowhere near as hard as her work. The business course had a low-entry requirement but astronomically high fees compared with other subjects, so families saved up to buy their way in. Most families – even the super wealthy ones – could only send one child. Christine was sure she was smarter than Brandon, yet he would still be the one running the place. This revelation made her furious, but she couldn't let him know that.

She shrugged a 'whatever'.

'You can't be in here,' Brandon snapped again.

Christine heard voices, whispers. A faint smile slipped across Brandon's lips, and she saw a spark in his eyes she had never seen before; there was a cruelty there, colder than Mother's. He was looking over her shoulder.

'Ma'am,' a firm voice said from the direction where Brandon was looking. Christine could imagine his stare had summoned the voice. 'Can I see your student card.'

Christine looked behind her, saw the familiar uniform of campus security, a pretty woman, not much older than her, inside it. Christine unclipped her ID from where it had been hanging on the hem of her t-shirt and handed it over. The woman frowned as she read it.

The woman had a tablet in her hand, tapped it, handed Christine back her ID.

'Sorry, Ma'am,' she said, unnecessarily conciliatory, 'you can't be in here. The business faculty is a restricted area.'

Christine gestured loosely to Brandon. 'He's my brother.'

Brandon looked horrified, but nodded.

'Sorry, Ma'am. You can meet your brother all you like,' the woman said, 'but not in here. Come with me, please.'

'Bye, bro.' Christine laughed. 'See you next time you deign to come home – if I'm still there.'

Not caring enough to resist, Christine let the woman lead her out of the Business department. It was always good to learn something new every day and today she had learned two things: the Business department was completely out of bounds and Brandon was even more of a total dick than she had always thought he was.

WEDNESDAY

THERE WAS A copter outside, cutting the air into slices, destroying the entire neighbourhood's ability to hear anything other than the rhythmic thumping; churning Christine's stomach. Both her parents were silent in the house, or missing; she hoped for the latter. The house was too well lit; the cleaners preferred it that way but she wanted darkness.

There was a coffee before Christine's face by the time her vision stopped swimming. She could feel it doing her good before it even touched her lips. This time she had done nothing to deserve how bad she felt; it had to be a migraine.

The copter departed leaving a heavy silence in its wake. Christine swore at it silently.

She poured her morning sacrament, as black as her mood, down her throat. Unable to resist the urge to sleep, she placed her head on the kitchen bench. The smell of coffee roused her and there was a full cup before her again. She sat upright long enough to drink that too, stood to make another, fell rubber-kneed.

Before she hit the ground, she felt strong arms holding her up again, felt her hip against something soft and bent around it, placed her face in what felt like the curve of a neck, smelled skin. She rolled her head to the side and saw a face; the beautiful one.

'We must stop meeting like this,' Christine quipped, then felt her legs go weak again.

The beauty laughed, not mocking or fake like Mother, nor pained like Jack.

Christine let herself be led to the couch, let the beauty lay her down on it. She looked at this woman, who was fussing around, making sure the pillows were in the right place before walking away and returning with coffee and water.

On impulse, she half sat, draped an arm around the woman and kissed her hard, like she had done only once before with a boy. That time, it had been sticky and slimy, his tongue attacking her mouth. She had felt sick. She had told everybody she was never going to marry, because the words 'you may kiss the bride' made her feel ill. Mother had laughed and Father had despaired. Perhaps her father feared he would have to look after her, pay her way forever.

This kiss was different. She felt like she was dying; and if she was, she was ready to go. The woman leaned hungrily into the kiss. There was a warmth that melted all her joints away, that made her heart hammer, that stole the air from her lungs. The hair on her arms stood up on goosepimples, her stomach shook, her chest contracted, her brain was elsewhere. She felt a tingle that went to the tips of her toes. She knew, finally, what a kiss was and knew she would do anything for it to continue.

She feared she would die if it stopped.

But it ended. The beauty pulled away and ran back into the kitchen.

Christine pined for what she had just lost, for that moment that had felt like forever and had taken all her years away from her.

The back door opened then slammed closed again. The house was silent. Christine was alone. She could hear the bus outside picking up the staff and she wanted to chase it down, desperate not to be alone.

Yet she believed that alone was all she would ever be; all she would ever deserve.

FRIDAY

THE AIR CONDITIONING blasted, burning electricity all day to keep Christine cool as she lay in bed reading a book. There was nothing she wanted to do so she could see no reason not to stay in bed all day. She assumed Mother had gone to a cafe to meet the ladies who drink.

She sat back on the too-soft mattress and watched the clouds chasing each other across a blue-screen sky out the window. The sun threw light at the windows across the street and the windows retaliated. The world had a shimmer to it, like compression artefacts, like the first signs of a migraine, like the wobble the world got for someone so tired they were about to collapse.

Not that long ago, in the final year of her undergraduate degree, she had an exam to study for, but instead of cramming she had spent the whole night on the phone to Jack who was freaking out about something. He said he trusted her but wouldn't say what was wrong, only that whatever it was, it was enough to make her hate him. Christine had not believed it.

She could never hate him.

The next day she'd sat the exam, nearly fainted at her desk, finished what she could, raised her hand to leave and stumbled from the hall. She had found a park bench under a tree. The world had swum nauseatingly like this. The path before her had flowed like a river across her vision, the grass beyond that had flowed in the opposite direction. This time there was no reason she could think of for what her brain was doing; she was not tired enough.

She could not stop thinking of the woman. Kissing her was so wrong and so painfully right at the same time. She should not have done it but knew she would do it again. She was desperate to do it again.

The door opened, startling her nearly into screaming.

The woman walked in as if she had been summoned by Christine's thoughts. Her beauty was breathtaking. The women in town must be jealous of her bronze skin – no time in a tanning salon could match it – yet Christine knew most looked down on women like her.

How did that make sense?

She was suddenly overwhelmed by competing desires: the desire to hold the woman in her arms and the desire to be that beautiful.

'Ma'am,' the woman said.

'Please don't call me that,' Christine snapped, surprising herself. 'I am not my fucking mother.'

'Christine,' the woman said this time. 'We are both in danger. I don't know what to do, but I have to warn you. I could lose my job. I need this job. If your parents knew, I don't know what they will do, what they *could* do.' She paused. 'They could make life hard for you too.'

Christine didn't want to think about it. 'I don't want you to lose your job, but I don't give a fuck about what they do to me. What's the worst they can do? Ground me?'

'They can do far worse than that.'

'Shhh.'

All she was interested in was more of yesterday; the hunger was something she had given up hope of controlling. She rose from her bed and stepped towards the woman.

'You know my name, but I don't know yours,' Christine said, then realised she did not know the names of any of the staff who worked to make her comfortable. 'It seems unfair.'

The nameless woman stared for a moment at Christine's face, looking for something. They faced each other, the air from their lungs meeting in the charged space between them.

'Sienna.'

'Hi, Sienna,' Christine said, her voice near breathless.

Sienna oozed forward, the word 'hi' squeezing out with her breath the moment before their lips met.

The air conditioning kept the room cool but Christine nearly swooned with the warmth that flushed her head empty. Sweat stuck to her back, ice ran up her spine; the sweat and ice somehow filling her lips with heat. She was prepared to burn alive if that was the consequence of this moment.

Sienna kissed her, their hips grinding together. They were the same height, but Sienna was stronger and more lithe. Wherever Christine wriggled, Sienna's hips were there to meet hers. A strong hand held the nape of her neck, held her in that embrace, in that kiss; even if she wanted to there was no way to escape. Chill and heat chased each other up and down her skin, fought for the territory of her face.

The hand fell away from her neck. The mouth she would die for pulled away from hers and she chased it, almost caught it before it spoke.

'Christine,' Sienna warned. 'We can't get caught. We need to stop this. I don't want to, but we should.'

'No,' Christine moaned. She had never felt like this before. Her mouth chased Sienna's mouth again, to stop those words.

'This is dangerous. What about your parents?'

'Fuck 'em,' Christine hissed. She went over to lock the bedroom door and close the curtains before returning to where she knew she belonged.

Sienna pulled her closer, their mouths sharing air, swapping spit. Christine slipped her hand down and found a buttock more taut than she had expected. She felt a hand on her crotch and was surprised by her sticky reaction. Licking sweat off Sienna's neck, she grabbed that hand instinctively and pushed it down the front of her pants, fumbled for the zip on the front of Sienna's coverall, lost the fight, moaned with frustration, then found it open. She slipped her hand in, first over a bra, then down lower.

Putting her hand down there felt like touching herself, but not; having a hand down there felt like touching herself, but not. They fell into the bed in a tangle of clumsy limbs, Sienna used her free hand to stop Christine from screaming, shook her head and said, 'Shush, quietly.' In silence they painted Christine's bed with their sweat, their breath keeping time, until, with a shuddering rush Christine had not expected, Sienna's hand stoppering her scream, it was over.

She did not know if what she was feeling was love or just afterglow. Frankly, she didn't care. She just wanted it again.

MONDAY

THE HOUSE WAS empty. Christine was packing her few meagre belongings that had survived the purge while she was living at the university. Even then, she was not taking much; more would be going to the trash than to her apartment. Her memories were held in her head, not in things.

There was a bell-like sound, one she vaguely remembered but rarely heard. She recalled it being the front doorbell; she could not remember the last time someone had been at the door unexpected. She waited for the sound of the door opening. Mother would take care of whoever was there.

There was a faint tap on her bedroom door as she packed her advanced maths texts; she had already packed her favourite novels and trashed the rest. She thought of Sienna and the last time someone had come in through that door. With what felt like her last breath, she said, 'Enter.'

It was not Sienna. Christine could breathe again.

An older woman she did not recognise stood at the door. Her face was lined in a way that nobody who lived in town would allow, her thick grey hair in a ponytail. She was almost skeletal in her overalls.

'Yes?' Christine said.

'There's someone at the door, Ma'am.'

The words 'Don't call me, Ma'am' staggered to her tongue then died unuttered. She shrugged and followed the older woman down the hall, down the stairs, and across the lounge room where Mother's magazines and empty wine-stained, lipstick-smeared glasses were still scattered.

There was someone just inside the closed door. A sickly pale man, not much older than Christine. He was dressed in the black suit, white shirt and charcoal tie of an Agency man. As a kid, she had been taught that the Agency men kept them all safe. They controlled Security and kept watch while Security enforced the rules. They were staff but not, the same class as servants but not; both her equal and above her, they spoke for the Agency but had no positions, or identities, of their own.

They were nobody. She did not even know if they had names.

They could enforce the law no matter who broke it.

The Agency man was handsome in a certain kind of way, although not to her taste. Mother would have been all over him if she had answered the door.

He held out his hand and Christine took it without thinking. 'You must be Christine?'

His grip was warm and firm and she could feel the muscles twitching under the skin of his palm; his face muscles were crawling like a bag full of snakes.

'I am here to see your father, but I have been informed he is not in.' His voice was bizarrely flat.

'He is probably at work,' Christine said, wondering why the man hadn't left when he discovered Father was not present, why he was there when nobody had visited looking for Father before. She hoped her father had done nothing to warrant an Agency investigation. She wished the door was open; it would be easier to steer the man out if it was. Even more, she wished he was not there at all. 'I don't know why someone didn't already tell you that.'

'It was nice to meet you, Christine.' Something about his voice made her skin crawl.

'Nice to meet you, too.'

The Agency man turned abruptly, opened the door and stepped out. On the road, there were five or six security vans gathered like a conspiracy. Before the door clicked closed, she could see armed Security getting back into their vehicles.

The front curtains were open, leaving the couch in view of the street. She did not want to sit there where passing drones could see; where Security men in their black vans could see; where the camera across the road could see, where anybody who cared to look could see. She fled back to her room and resumed packing with increased urgency.

TUESDAY

'I SAW YOU on video,' Father spat. 'They showed me.'

Father's expression was frightening. Christine had never seen him this furious. His eyes were dark and sunken, the warm brown of his irises had transmogrified into molten lead, his cheeks were flushed with the fire of rage.

'I saw you kissing that black . . . that animal. I saw you. My own daughter, a filthy dyke, a monster, an Abo lover.'

She had never heard those words before.

'I look after you. I give you everything you need, everything you want. I would do anything for you and this is how you treat me, how you treat this house, this family. Kissing a woman is disgusting enough, but she is not even *our people*, not even our colour, not even our class. I thought . . .' – his voice dripped with disdain – 'you were better than that.'

She backed away, not caring in which direction, only knowing she wanted to escape the roiling caldera that had replaced her cold father, who, she had always assumed, had loved her, who had only recently expressed pride in her. Mother stepped between them and held up a hand to Father, who stopped, surprised. She turned to Christine.

'I understand the desire to kiss a girl,' Mother said, glancing back guiltily at Father. 'I flirted with the idea for a while when I was your age, but you should have stayed with your own type, with our class, with our race. Why couldn't you have done this with some girl from your school, with someone like us, like everyone else?'

Mother continued. 'If you had just been more discreet and closed the damn curtains, there were things we could have done. Now we are being investigated for letting this go on in our house.' There was something unsaid in Mother's tone, but Christine's battered mind could not get a handle on it. She did not want to imagine what would happen if they knew what had gone on in her bedroom behind closed doors and curtains.

Shaking with fear, she wanted to tell them it was only a kiss. But that would be lying. That it was only that once, only once, and she was over it, long over it. But that would be lying. She wanted to tell them that Sienna meant nothing to her. Maybe they would forgive her if she promised to never touch that woman, any woman, again. But that would be a lie too. She knew she would do it again.

Sienna meant everything to her. Sienna was her breath. And even if she could never see Sienna again, her feelings, for a woman, perhaps for all women, had been let out of the bag – and the bag was too small to squeeze those feelings back in.

She had no voice and no use for it; nothing to say and no way to put it in words if she did.

Father forced his way past Mother, throwing her off balance. She rebounded hard off the hallway wall with a surprised grunt. 'We can't have you in the house,' he growled, grabbing Christine by the arm with enough force that she could feel bruises immediately forming under his fingers. 'Something like you doesn't belong here, little dyke, race traitor, bitch.'

She looked to her mother for help. Mother's eyes were glass, the skin around them cut and shaped by surgeons until they were expressionless. She did not resist as Father, whose strong arms and big hands had held and comforted her when she was a little girl, forced her out the door.

The last words she heard as the door closed were 'Good thing I still have a son.'

@

Christine arrived at her apartment building as the sun collapsed drunkenly behind the city, the falling darkness making it even harder to see through her tears. She waited as she adjusted to the twilight. Her tears turned the city lights into stars.

She strolled to the glass and steel front door with a nonchalance she did not feel, then stared at the closed door, not wanting to move. Finally, she slipped the key card from her pocket and tried the lock.

A mournful bleep, a flatulent buzz, then nothing. Sobbing, she put her key card away and tapped the touchpad with a quivering finger. A grid of numbers appeared, lightning blue on grey, too bright in the darkness. She had set the code just yesterday, before the world had ended. She tapped in the code, another mournful bleep and nothing, the sliding door simply didn't.

She wanted to scream but couldn't spare the breath. She wanted to kick in the door, but didn't. She tried her card again and again. Nothing.

'Having trouble with the door? It happens to me all the time,' a voice boomed behind her.

Christine jumped, containing a squeak behind her teeth. Turning around, she was confronted with a black beard sparkling in the faint light of the screen, eyes glistening above it. The man was huge, lumpen and even taller than Christine. She refused to be intimidated. 'Sorry' – not sorry, her tone said – 'you startled me.'

He shrugged, reached past her with a card and bipped the scanner. The door opened. Turning his back on Christine he lumbered into the building. She slipped through just before the door slid shut.

The LED strip lights in the hall were an uncomfortable blue-white, the colour of the sun in the middle of the day but not as bright. The halls were a white that might have been chosen to reflect painfully, to make the light ugly, everywhere she turned her tears turned to diamonds in the stark light.

The man who had let her in was not in sight by the time she reached the elevator. Good, she did not want to talk to him, to have to explain anything. The elevator chimed when the door opened and again when it had completed the climb to her floor. She walked to her apartment, breathed, stopped, breathed again.

The lock stared back at her, daring her to try it. She had no choice but to take the dare, call the bluff. She touched her key card to the sensor and again nothing happened. She tried the handle, hammered her code into the door plate. Nothing. Tried the card again. Still nothing.

All her things, what things she cared about anyway, were in there.

She kicked the door, knowing it would do no good; screamed, knowing it would do no good. Losing her temper at the door would probably make things worse but she was unable to stop. She hammered, kicked, screamed, smashed the touchpad, kicked harder at the door. Down the hallway a door cracked open, a face peering through the gap. Christine screamed again and charged the doorway and the person staring at her; the staring face disappeared and that door slammed right in her face.

Christine wailed.

Somewhere sirens were trying to out-scream her. They grew louder until her voice was drowned out under their weight.

Christine sprinted for the elevator and kicked the down button so hard it cracked. It lit up nevertheless. After an eternity, the door pinged then moaned open. She dived in, hit the button for the basement, the damp car park.

If Security were coming, she could hope they would come in through the front door; hopefully there was somewhere to hide and time to get there.

The elevator door opened and she skittered across the brightly lit car park and behind the only parked car in the building. Christine tried to make herself as small as she could but the car didn't provide much cover. Terrifying blue lights on the roofs of Security cars fought the LEDs overhead for the right to paint the roof blue, white, blue, white. Frantic to find somewhere better to hide, blue, white, Christine ran across the car park, dived into a giant skip bin, pulled the lid shut over her head and buried herself in the refuse. The flashing blue somehow made it in. She could see it even with her eyes closed.

She crouched, entombed in unnameable filth, could feel the stench working its way through her clothes, into her skin, into her pores, and into her blood; threatening to make her one with it forever. She had no idea how long she had been hiding in there before the flashing lights went away. She peeked out of the skip towards the entrance. There were no security vans, but she was still afraid to leave the car park. They might be out there, might have killed their lights and moved their cars; they might be waiting. Somehow she fell asleep.

She woke and gasped with pain, the involuntary intake of breath sucking more stink into her nostrils. Her cramped muscles screamed. She climbed out of the bin, wincing when the lid slammed shut. Disgusted at the smell, she snuck quietly to the car-park entrance, on the lookout for Security.

It was a frigid night. Her phone told her it was three in the morning. Thumbing the taxi app, she stared in disbelief as it told her she had no credit in her car company account, no credit on her card, no money in her bank account. It would not be sending a car for her. She could not stand in the street, looking like she was up to something, so she started walking, brushing herself as clean as she could.

She had a bit of cash in her pocket. That, her dirty clothes, her phone and stench were her only possessions. The truth was, she was more worried for Sienna than for herself. What would they do to her? What could they already be doing?

It became starkly apparent she had nowhere to go. Somewhere, surely, there would be a cafe or bar open, somewhere she could get a hot beverage and sit at a table in a warm room until she finished it, somewhere that might take cash. She walked through the neighbourhood that was supposed to have been hers, looking for somewhere safe. The warm yellowish lights of an all-night cafe bar enticed her. Young men with beards and young women without make-up sat around tables in groups, in couples, none of them alone.

A couple ostentatiously wore pyjamas and dressing gowns; another woman wore pre-distressed lounge wear; the servers were in collared shirts, bow ties and old-fashioned waistcoats. Surely ironically.

The server looked at her strangely when she ordered a black coffee and even more strangely when she paid with cash. Christine raised her eyebrows and tilted her head like she had seen her mother do when people irritated her, and the woman blanched slightly, shrugged and put the money in the till. The only table available was by the window, with a view of the street; somewhere to see out and be seen. Christine wanted somewhere more private but sat there anyway.

At least she was warm. The server arrived with her coffee and looked like she was about to say something, but didn't. People strolled past the window and Christine used the pretence of people-watching to keep an eye out for people looking for her. Security passed in a black van but did not slow. Someone in staff overalls seemed to be on an errand, but she could not guess what it could be at that time of night. Another security van and drone passed noisily.

If they were searching for her, they didn't yet know where to look.

The people inside the cafe bar were eyeing her. She watched the window, she watched the bartender hoping she would not call Security, she looked at her phone, not really seeing it but hopeful it would give her the illusion of a purpose. She worried she smelled like shit and garbage but had lost the ability to smell it herself.

A small black car with flashing lights, so blue they were sickeningly ultraviolet, crawled past, flanked by buzzing drones. It kept moving, either heading to the wrong place or on another errand. Christine could barely contain her panic. It was only a matter of time. She checked the time on her phone. Half-past four, nearly dawn. Any idiot could guess it would be easier to find her once the sun rose, despite the increasing crowds.

She checked her email.

Safetynet gave her a NOT CONNECTED message.

She stared at her phone.

Safetynet stayed disconnected.

She switched it off and on again. It flashed back on with nothing but a frowning face and the words 'no account detected'.

She could hear a distant copter carving the air into ribbons.

Gulping the last liquid from her mug, she put her phone back in her pocket. Christine stood and went to the counter, asked where the restrooms were. The server, with an expression that said 'you idiot', gestured to a sign saying 'Toilets' at the back of the cafe bar. She walked down the corridor and into the disabled toilet, locking the door carefully.

She stripped naked in front of the sink and washed her face, her neck, her hands, any part of her that had been outside her clothes when she was in the skip bin; the water was freezing cold but it was all she had. Indigo marks bloomed on her arms where Father had manhandled her and on her knees from the hard floor of the skip. She ached in places she didn't know were places.

Shaking the worst of the crap out of the creases of her clothes, she checked her face in the mirror; big-eyed, blotchy, hair forming wet waves on her shoulders. She looked pale and there were red rims around her eyes from crying and lack of sleep. She had nothing clean to change into so she put her dirty clothes back on.

Christine left the bathroom, fighting to demonstrate calm she did not possess, her muscles vibrating with fear. The server was at the entrance to the corridor, not even pretending to clear a table, watching for her. She ignored the server, who looked like they were about to say something, and walked out of the cafe bar, the cold air poking through her thin clothes like someone had thrown a handful of pins hard against her body.

Swerving breathlessly through the streets, she could feel the desperation in her walk, in her pace, and hoped nobody could see it. From the road, she spied clothes hanging on a line; someone's servant had been negligent. Sneaking down the side of the house, she found a long businessman's overcoat, grabbed it and pulled, sending pegs flying in all directions. She put on the coat. It was too big for her but it was warm and at least a partial disguise.

Lights flared on in the house and she ran.

WEDNESDAY

IN FEAR, SHE had run to a place with good memories, with illusory safety; a clearing in the woods, between the university and the Wall, with an ancient-looking gazebo, the wood cracking and faded grey. The gazebo seemed older than the forest, a strange sort of magic. The glossy green of middle-aged pines surrounded her, the bones of the trees coarse and rough-barked, crowding in so close she could barely see the cloud-grey sky. It was colder in the resinous darkness, the dead fallen pine needles a dark bronze in the shade between the bone-grey of fallen limbs.

She and Jack had found this place one day when skiving off from class. They had sat for hours on the benches, grey and splintery, attached to the real-wood table. Very few people ventured there, to this artificial woodland, perhaps planted for recreation, perhaps decoration, perhaps intimidation. It was too similar to the world outside the Wall they all feared.

The light of morning, poking through gaps in the clouds, was painting the tops of the trees with glitter. For a moment she could breathe, she had space to think, but she was not sure she wanted to. Sitting in her memories of Jack, she felt even more utterly alone. Yet, for some reason, she believed she would be safe here. Bundling her coat into something that resembled a too-hard pillow, she stuck it under her head as she lay on the bench. The sunlight dappled and danced its way through the trees in a way that was almost pleasant, almost comforting, lulling her to sleep.

When she woke, the sun was peering into the clearing from above, no longer hidden behind the trees, peeking around the edge of the gazebo roof. The light drilled into her eyes, destroying any chance of sleep. In the light of day, she felt stupid, running to a place she had remembered as safe, which was outside and not hidden at all. The university was nearby; she could go there, disappear in the familiar halls, disappear among the students, classrooms, couches in the postgrad lounge.

She rolled to her feet, pulled on her coat, brushed the pine needles and dirt off her clothes, and walked over to the campus.

The university was bustling as always, but this time it felt alien, irritating and claustrophobic. The students all seemed to be photocopies of one another. The young men were ugly chunky things; the young women were hollow-faced and shallow, early prototypes of Mother and Mother's friends.

She and Jack had thought the students were rebels and rabble-rousers, that they were nothing like their parents, but Christine realised they were wrong. Her parents had been to university too; there were diplomas on the wall of the house. She did not doubt that her parents had thought of themselves as rebels too. Maybe at university they were.

She wondered if one day some force would turn her into her mother.

Then it was almost like everything changed, or she did, and she could see. Here, a boy who could not quite cover up a girlishness in his manner, there a girl wearing an oversized man's shirt, here a woman with her hair cut a little too short to be acceptable, there a boy with hair past his collar and eyeliner darkening his eyes.

In a corner, a boy looked at another boy like Christine knew she looked at Sienna.

Those motes of resistance were like a flash of sunlight on a rainy day. It was Jack who had explained to her that on a sunny, rainy day you had to turn away from the sun, keep the sun to your back, in order to see the rainbow.

In the postgraduate lounge, she snoozed on a couch, then went to the cafeteria to find food, bought nothing but chips – her cash was not bottomless – and ate them in the common room where the coffee, at least, was free. At the end of the day when a cleaner found her there and stared at her meaningfully, she left.

With nowhere else to go, she returned to the clearing in the forest, wrapped herself in her coat and sat, staring at the stars, distracting herself by attempting to do calculus in her head. Every so often there was the buzz of a passing drone, but she saw none flying overhead. Unable to fight sleep, she wrapped herself tighter in her coat, stuck her arm under her head and felt herself slipping away.

The next day she woke from a sleep deeper than she had thought possible and returned to the university, where she bought chips again for breakfast. If she was careful, she might last a couple of days before she would start to feel hungry. She ate the chips on a bench out in the sun. A student wrinkled their nose at her, no doubt smelling the nights she had spent outside.

Christine went to the gym, a part of the campus she had always lacked interest in, and headed to the showers. She turned the water on hotter than she could bear and stepped under the showerhead. Somebody had left behind a flake of soap and she scrubbed herself with it, then dried herself off with one of the gym's towels. Feeling clean, Christine nearly vomited when she had to put her dirty clothes back on.

When she returned to the postgrad lounge there was someone at the door, an old man wearing a badge that read 'Campus security'. He asked for Christine's student ID and looked at it as if he knew what he was going to see. He bipped it with a scanner in his hand, then put it in his pocket.

'This ID is invalid,' he snorted disdainfully.

'How?' Christine asked, desperate but unsurprised.

'Your fees have not been paid and I understand they are not going to be paid. Please cooperate as I escort you from campus. If you don't cooperate, I will have to call Security.'

Knowing he would hand her to Security anyway, she turned without a word and ran out the door, dodging the students, the clones, the hollow men and cut-out women, security guards and the rising cacophony of pursuit. Breaking free of the buildings, she dashed into the dark green of the woodlands before realising too late that cameras would have watched her as she fled. They would know exactly where she was and she had led them to her sanctuary.

THE GYRE

CHRISTINE CLIMBED UP and stood atop the Wall, considered throwing herself off. Better that than being trapped there, caught by rough hands and taken. Wherever they planned to take her, it wouldn't be somewhere she desired to be. Drones circled her. They would be transmitting images of her scared expression to Security, where they would undoubtedly be forwarded to Father, to Mother, to identify her.

'Is this the daughter you disowned and kicked out into the streets?' the Agency would ask. Her parents would see how filthy she was; they would be disgusted by her expression of melded despair and fury. She must look like the distorted angry monsters, violent freaks, rioters and criminals outside the Wall.

The sun above seemed to share the sentiment. It screamed at her, at the city, at the Wall. The sky felt bright enough to see right through her like a fluoroscope, to see who she was more than she knew herself. She wanted to scream defiance at that arrogant sky.

If she died on the Wall they would not need security footage. Her parents would stand impassively in the morgue and stare at whatever remained of her. Perhaps there might be tears, or perhaps they might say, with characteristic lack of emotion, 'That's her.' She could throw herself off the Wall and spare them that, could die outside, when her living bones, and her mortal flesh, impacted on the world outside the Wall.

She could rot out in the wilderness with the other monsters.

She did not know what she missed most keenly: the university, her home and family, her companionship with Jack, or the unfathomable feelings she had for Sienna. Her life was already over. All that was missing was the formality of a coroner's report and a funeral if they deigned to commemorate the end of her life. She was almost certainly destined for a quiet cremation, her ash thrown over the Wall to scatter in the breeze. At least then she would be free.

But if she died, she would never see Sienna again. That would be as bad as dying twice.

Security paced towards her along the walkway on the Wall, between the railings and the sparking diamonds of razor wire. Black-dressed figures without features, masks hiding their faces. No Agency men on the Wall, with their slick suits and blank faces. A flock of angry machines gyred lazily, like vultures in an old movie waiting for someone to take their last breath.

The men moving towards her were in overalls, bulky with padding and armour, armed with something that looked like a cattle prod, two electrodes on a long pole. Christine did not want to be zapped. It was better to surrender, better to rob them of the satisfaction of zapping the disgraced daughter of someone so powerful as Father.

She remembered she had the dead-drop forum open on her phone, where she had waited too long for a message from Jack. A ridiculous conceit when she had no connection to Safetynet, to email, to Socials. She was suddenly consumed by the perverse desire to turn to the razor wire, to the world outside the Wall, and throw her phone as far as she could. If she could not use her phone, nobody could. She could see the frustration in the shoulders of Security as they watched the phone leaving her hand. Some of the drones turned to trace its path, but she was less interested in where it landed outside, and more interested in the knowledge that her messages to Jack were safe.

Just like that, the last vestige of her life, her last chance of finding Jack, was gone.

Security continued pacing towards her from both sides, their faces covered with the mirrored visors of riot helmets. They might as well have been robots, automata, machines made to look human. Christine was desperate to see something recognisable in their faces, desperate to see their eyes, lips, a curve of a cheek. All she saw when she looked at where their faces should have been was a dark stretched reflection of herself – filthy and terrified.

She wanted to reach out and tear their visors open but knew they would not let her get close enough before they hurt her.

She did not even know if they were male or female. She did not know if they were the same colour as her and her parents or as Sienna and the other servants. She hated knowing nothing.

'I know I should not be up here,' Christine said. 'I'm sorry. I was desperate to see what was outside the Wall. That's all.' She was not stupid enough to imagine they would believe her. They had chased her up there and their mannerisms indicated that they were not delighted by the exercise. 'I'll go home now.'

They did not react.

'I surrender, okay?' Christine said as the front guards raised their stun rods. 'No need for the zapping. I will come quietly.' She laughed, but even she felt it was fake. There was no evidence they had heard her or that they would care if they had. 'Look, my father is a powerful man. He's actually probably your boss. We have been going through some rough stuff lately, but I am sure he would not be happy to find out you zapped his baby girl when she had surrendered.'

The first jolt felt like her body was on fire. It radiated out from where the prod touched the skin of her arm, sparking through her muscles and shaking her like a ringing phone. Her skin crawled and would not stop. She danced an involuntary tarantella, vomited into her mouth and collapsed to her knees, screaming then choking. The second stab of a prod, straight through the clothes on her chest, threw her spasming onto her back. She rolled into a ball on her side and hugged her knees, a sound between a scream and a sob escaping her lips. Again and again the probes sparked into her skin, again and again she felt her heart jump, felt like it was trying to break though her ribs.

Again and again.

Again and again.

When mercifully they stopped, she had not enough strength left even to uncurl her hands.

Her heart was jumping, then faltering, then kicking. She was going to die.

ZOOM – SECURITY

THE SECURITY ENCLAVE hangs off the side of the town like a tumour, grey and black, concrete and steel, contrasting strongly with the green of the greater city. There's life there, some trees and shrubs, but they are choked off, like the stone-grey pavement is trying to strangle them. It's dry, and in the middle of the day the sunlight throws up heat haze so strong it blurs the view and hurts the eye; even from orbit it would be possible to tell the heat was a killer.

People in this place scurry like worker ants, dressed all in black; even the children move like soldiers. Where the wall between the Security enclave and the bus park meets the outer Wall of the city near the gates, the Security edifice stands, ready to intimidate both the inside and the outside.

THE CENTRE CANNOT HOLD

THE CELL WAS windowless as were the corridors Christine had been dragged through to get there. The whirr of fans was hypnotic, moving the air she needed to breathe out through vents. She had spoken to nobody, did not think it would make any difference, had been moved firmly but non-aggressively down hallways. Only when she had resisted had the force been increased, but only enough to ensure compliance. They took her to her meals, to the exercise area, wherever they thought she should be, whenever they thought she should be there.

All without saying a word.

They were all dressed the same, black one-piece boilersuits, balaclavas with the eyes covered with bulging ovals of fine plastic mesh. If they were not dressed like that to scare her, it had the effect regardless. She could not see them, could not see any emotion except the occasional bulging of face muscles under the cloth. After a few days she had been desperate to see a face, any face.

When not somewhere else, she lay on her bed, staring at the blank cream ceiling, at the cold-white LED strip light. She could see the faintest of marks in the paint, shallow linear marks, almost like writing, like someone had scratched messages into the walls and maintenance had simply painted over them.

Christine cried in her bed, cried in her sleep, cried for Jack and for Sienna, wondered if either of them had been here in this prison, wondered if anyone even cared where she was. Out of desperation, she had asked to call her father. None of the guards showed any signs they had heard her.

Then the beatings began, light, almost polite, at first, like a warning, then escalating. She feared they believed her father's protection had evaporated, that she was fair game. They punched her in the face when she stood her ground, then forced her to wherever they wanted her: the cold showers, to the medic – who studiously ignored the bruises – the empty cafeteria for taste-less meals. If she fought back, swung a punch or a kick, they stun-gunned her until she collapsed, then dragged her quivering body back to the cell.

After a while she began to believe they must be enjoying it. She fell asleep every night in almost intolerable pain.

Over and again, she dreamed of someone coming for her. One night this someone came with paperwork, letters or documents to set her free; another night she dreamed of a lithe body sliding through the vent in rescue. In every dream it was the same face, the same amber eyes, the same black hair.

Sienna.

Every day she thought of Sienna, worried about where she was; and of Jack, worried he was dying in a cell in this place. She even wished for Mother, for her cold expression and the disdain she would have for the complete lack of decoration in the cell.

Nobody came to save her.

Then one day she was dragged weak and bruised down the halls to the room. An agency man, bland, so much the everyman, a nobody, as faceless as the masked guards even with his naked face sat behind a desk. He was the Agency embodied, dressed in a plain black suit, white shirt and tie. When Christine tried to get a handle on his humanity, tried to see the human behind his eyes, her mind slipped off his identity like he was greased glass.

'You have been charged with being in the city without accommodation or means of support,' he said, 'and of being of bad character. You have been found guilty by the Agency Security Committee.'

'How? Charged, how? Guilty, how?' Christine interjected with shock. 'There was no trial. I haven't had a chance to speak to anyone about my case. How can I have been found guilty?'

She had nothing but the air in her lungs, and she willed it to the vent, to take a message to anybody, to Jack, to her parents, but mostly to Sienna.

'This enclave, Safetown,' the nobody man said, 'is a private facility, private property. We don't need to hold trials on cases of lack of accommodation or support. These things are defined clearly and indisputably as trespass. We could have held a trial for the bad character applications but considered that a waste of time. You are already a trespasser. We have kept you here as nothing but a courtesy. You have no money in the Fund, or in any bank account; no job, no home. Nobody is allowed inside our Wall unless they own property or shares in the Fund. This is private property and your presence here is illegal.'

Black smudges danced in Christine's vision, met and multiplied; the whirr of the fan transmogrified into a roar. She was a trapped pigeon, her breathing laboured as a vice crushed the thin bones of her chest; she was dying. She opened her mouth to speak, to mention her trust fund, her father, an important man in the Fund, who own the Agency. Her mouth opened and closed, but barely any words came out.

Nobody man stared at his notes.

Something about her father must have tumbled out of her mouth because the Agency man responded.

'Yes,' he said, without malice, without anything in his voice at all, 'your father.' He flicked through some papers on the table, then stopped. It didn't seem like he had even looked at them. 'Trying to talk to him delayed the carrying out of your sentence somewhat. He was away, in Kingstown I believe, had been for the entire time since you left his house. There was some difficulty contacting him. He did, however, inform us when we eventually made contact that you were not welcome in his home and all your credit had been cut off.

'We allowed him some time to change his mind, hoping, as you are his child, that he would talk to you and sort this out. We might have considered dropping the bad character charges if your father had asked us to, given you a chance to change your behaviour, but he is less forgiving than us. We explained that once you are exiled, once you leave the gates, you can never return, that it's important to maintain the integrity of the Enclave, to keep undesirables and undesirable habits outside our gates. He informed us that he is okay with that.'

Christine could taste something metallic in her mouth, blood or vomit, maybe both. She had nothing left to resist when they came to take her away.

PART 2
THE WORLD

ZOOM – SEATOWN ONE

SEATOWN ONE, FROM an approaching helicopter, looked like a semicircular string of green and blue pearls floating on the surface of the Pacific. When the Island it sat over had been submerged by rising sea levels, when the tiny oceanic nation ceased to have land to live on, when the local populace became climate refugees in Australia and New Zealand, Seatown Inc. had purchased the shallow reef that remained. It had built the floating islands, gardens and swimming pools with a mansion in the middle of each, manufactured and towed into place, and then attached the gantries, walkways and supply cabling.

The islands and mansions became smaller as they approached the Anchor, a floating hexagon covered with solar panels and water desalinators, wind generators and hydroponic farms, harbours, warehouses and security offices.

The last barge before the Anchor was the biggest, other than the Anchor, of course. Half of it was a floating apartment block, its roof shining with solar panels, the walls fuzzy with hanging gardens. It was there that the workers who did not live on the island of their employer resided. The other half of the barge was shops and cafes, restaurants and open spaces, where the workers on that side could see and long for the privileges of their betters.

The first shots fired did not surprise any of the residents. Tensions had been brewing for months between the security forces of the Ashley and Novak-Smith families. The two families who co-owned the town made up only a small minority of the population. They had argued recently about nearly everything involved in the management of the community. Ashley were the biggest shareholders in Seatown Inc. and therefore had more votes on the town board. Novak-Smith, always paranoid, had the largest security force.

A passing unmanned freighter had its long-range cameras aimed at the floating atoll – a major shipping hazard – when the lights went out, leaving the reef and lagoon in darkness. The AI on board reported the sound of automatic gunfire bouncing across the water, running away from the muzzle flashes.

The freighter's AI informed the media and sent a report to the Australian Defence Forces, who had policing and defence responsibility for that section of ocean, then launched a swarm of semi-autonomous camera drones it kept on board – such news footage would be worth a lot of money for the conglomerate who owned the freighter. Small arms fire erupted as residents and non-security staff of the two families armed themselves and fought each other and even unrelated folk who had bought homes there, attempting to take control of their floating city, to protect their homes, taking the opportunity of the chaos to end petty feuds permanently.

The lights of small boats started drifting away from the city, then all twelve helicopters registered at Seatown One took off in quick succession, their lights escaping into the distance.

The fighting and the exodus continued all night as the freighter slowly floated past on its electric motors, sending out autonomous lifeboats to search for anyone floating in the water. By the time the naval helicopters and army paratroopers arrived the next day, the security forces of Novak-Smith had occupied the Anchor and the security forces who used to work for Ashley had occupied the Apartments and they had each declared the city to be their free state. The fight was protracted but in the end the navy won; the security on both sides were offered amnesty if they lay down their guns.

Seatown One, the first seastead built by Seatown Inc., the last to survive, had died.

DAY 1

THE GATES SOMEHOW made no noise closing. Christine's life was over without even a whimper.

From the outside, the Wall was hideously ugly, grey concrete and a full four storeys high, looming over her like an abusive parent; the Wall tut-tutting, raising its hand ready to strike. It appeared to lean but that was surely only an illusion. In places the rebar showed itself, bleeding rust, which streaked down the grey like bloodstains. In other places the Wall was warty, where repairs and additions had been slapped on without care, any protrusion someone could use as a hand or foothold wrapped in razor wire.

The guards standing just outside the gates stared dead ahead, straight out from the gates. The visors on their helmets showed nothing but misshapen reflections of the wasteland and the sea of concrete before them. Christine walked away and looked back; they had not moved. Perhaps they would only respond if she walked towards them, towards the gates. She was not brave enough to find out.

Past the car park was a ruin. Burned and broken concrete buildings, gaping eyeless sockets where windows used to be, plywood nailed over window frames like eye patches. Piles of rubble, stone and bricks, and twisted rusted steel. A pile of what might have once been cars sat on the edge of the hardstand, pushed against a broken building, rusty and blackened. Maybe they had been on fire in the past, throwing flames far into the sky. Once the paint had burned off, the rust would have taken hold.

The ruins, a walk of mere minutes, was too far to go. Christine lacked all volition. The sun dipped behind the Wall as she stood, too terrified to move, yet she knew staying where she was would be a mistake. As night fell, floodlights blasted on, lighting the Wall blue-white as bright as noon, shining on the bitumen so that the embedded stones sparkled like the night sky.

Red-orange light flickered, coating the ruins in patches. Christine realised they were small fires scattered throughout the labyrinth. She could not bring herself to approach the ruins, to go towards whatever people might be sitting in those patches of light, more afraid of the unknown than of the guards.

She started to walk back towards the gates. A guard's hand twitched towards a gun she had not noticed before on his belt; his helmet shook slowly from side to side.

Christine stopped, backed away a few steps and collapsed boneless to the ground. With the last of her will, she forced herself to a seated position, crossing her legs.

A light, the colour of fire, moved towards her, bobbing and weaving. It lost momentum and backed away before again moving closer. She realised it was a flaming stick held at head height, by someone she could barely see. As it came closer she saw a woman, maybe Mother's age, shorter than her, skeletal scrawny and dressed in rags.

'You, you can't stay here,' a nervous voice said. 'If you are still here when the buses come in the morning, those fucking bastard guards will shoot you. They will just shoot you and drag your bloody corpse into a gutter.'

Christine said nothing, had no idea what to do. The woman leaned down and grabbed her by the arm, tried to pull her to her feet. Christine fought back, trying to unseat her grip but the hands that looked like twigs were as hard as steel.

'You can't stay here,' the woman said adamantly. 'You have to come with me. Please, girl. I know you are scared, you don't want to move, but you have to come with me.'

Christine stopped resisting and allowed the insistent hand of wire to pull her to her feet, allowed herself to be dragged to the ruins. They passed a beaten car, a conical pile of rubble, a charred mass of something unidentifiable; everything dark red in the warm flickering light of the flame. She smelled something that made her think of death. On what must have been a road, she almost tripped over an obstruction, but those steely hands held her upright.

Finally, the woman pulled her through a door into a building that appeared even less livable than the street. There was rubble and trash everywhere, knee-high piles in places, waist-high drifts in others. The light of the burning stick flickered in the enclosed space, enough to make her nauseously dizzy.

The only place clear enough to walk was a dangerously narrow path leading to some stairs, the treads bowed with age and neglect, and covered in places with patches of carpet-like scabs. Christine stood at the bottom of the stairs, staring at the dark gaps where entire treads were vacant, shaking her head. The pressure on her arm was relentless; she knew if she refused to climb she would be dragged up, thumping against every step.

She climbed.

At the top of the stairs was a hallway with ancient wallpaper festooning the walls and dead plants in pots. Under a carpet so stained its colour would be unidentifiable even in daylight, the floor creaked and bowed down underfoot as they moved down the hall. There was a mysterious smell that Christine hoped was the carpet and not something worse.

The doors to the rooms they passed were open. Christine peered inside. The rooms all looked ransacked, with scattered and broken furniture, and charring and scorch marks on random spots of carpet and bare floor. The next to last door was closed, a bolt and a chunky padlock securing it. The woman stopped dragging Christine and let go of her arm. Christine stood there like a switched-off toy. The woman took out a key, opened the padlock with a sound resembling the tick of an ancient mechanical clock, the sliding of the bolt like a knife against a whetstone.

The strange woman bustled Christine through the door, closed it and slid a bolt on the inside. The room smelled of stale smoke and was neat compared to the outside. The furniture was mismatched, most of it damaged or scorched in places, but relatively intact. Christine imagined every piece had been collected from a different place.

There was a makeshift fireplace of mortarless cracked bricks, the coals of a dying fire glowing within; a pot and a kettle sat on the edge of the fire. What light there was came from candles in cups and solar garden lights wedged into wherever they would fit. She wondered where they had come from.

The woman spread a dirty blanket onto a filthy couch, poured clear liquid into a muck-smeared mug with a cracked rim and closed the curtains over the room's single window. Christine had a moment of panic when the view outside of the car park and the Wall disappeared.

'Toilet in the bathroom through there,' the woman said, pointing though one of only two doors. 'There's no running water, so flush the toilet if you have to with a bit of the water in the bucket. Not too much or you will have to go out and find more. I'm not gonna get water if you waste it. You can't have a bath or a shower, there's not enough water.'

'Who are you? What's going on?' The fear came out in Christine's shaky voice.

'I'm Becka,' said the woman in a way that implied she thought Christine should have already known that. 'I used to live over there' – she gestured to the Wall – 'like you, I lived there. Like you, they threw me out, chucked me out here and now I am here.'

'I'm Christine.'

'Sit,' Becka barked, pointing at the couch.

Christine collapsed onto the seat.

'I am going to sleep now, so you lie down there. Go to sleep too,' Becka said. 'I have been watching the gate quite late for days because it had been a while, a long while, weeks, since they had kicked anyone out. They are not going to chuck anyone else out tonight. If they chuck out two in a night, they do it at the same time. So the gate is not going to open tonight again, not again, so I am going to sleep'.

Becka disappeared through the other door that didn't lead to the bathroom.

Christine sat on the couch, her tear-filled eyes locked on the edge where the filthy wall met the smoke-stained ceiling. It was over. She was outside the Wall. She was dead, or as good as. All her life she had been told how dangerous it was outside. Now, the rest of her life, which will be short, would be outside.

Inevitable death would be a relief.

Realising there would be no chance of sleep, she twitched the frayed, half-rotten curtains open just enough to look out, but not for anyone to see in. Floodlights from the Wall lit the pockmarked, potholed concrete field before the gates. The guards were no longer standing at the gates, but Christine knew the cold black glass eyes of Security would be watching. As children they had been told about the guns on the Wall that killed everything that came too close. It was part of the system designed to keep them safe. She knew the moment someone approached the Wall they would die, one way or another.

Security were there to keep others out, and she was now one of those others.

She stood there, desperate to return to the safety within, but knew assaulting the Wall would be suicide. When she was ready to die she would do it. She would charge the Wall in the certainty she would fail, and she would die.

But not yet.

Not while there was a chance of finding Sienna.

DAY 2

SHE STOOD THERE, watching the Wall and the lights all night, tears blurring the lights in her eyes until the sky above began to glow. Until the light of the sun made the building she stood in cast a shadow on the wasteland before the Wall. Until the light of the sun washed out the lights on the Wall. Until the lights on the Wall, only just visible in the burgeoning daylight, went dark.

A gate opened and figures stepped out, faceless, black-clothed, so de-individualised that it was impossible to tell if they were the same guards who had removed her unresisting body from the city less than a day ago.

Christine was startled by the sound of engines, of tyres crackling on gravel. Not unlike the sound of the bus that brought Sienna to her parents' home and into her life. A bus exited the ruins to Christine's right, groaned its way over near the gates and stopped with the hiss of air brakes. Another came, and another. A buzzing flock of camera drones exited hidey-holes in the Wall and swarmed over the car park.

Becka surged out of her room and threw the curtains open.

'Good—' Christine started to say, but Becka knocked her down before she could say 'morning'. Christine jumped to her feet ready for a fight, but the other woman ignored her, focused on the car park, on the buses, on who was exiting them.

Soon, Christine was also fixated on the scene.

She had not known there were so many servants. It looked like there were thousands – tens of thousands – of them climbing out of bus after bus, walking to the gates, lining up, being scanned, and walking in. They had two things in common that Christine could see: they were all dressed in the uniform of Agency service employees; and not one of them had the same pasty skin colour as Christine and Becka.

She could not understand. She felt like there was something she was missing.

Christine looked at her own hands, filthy after her time in detention and only a day outside the Wall. She knew that underneath the dirt her skin was blotched with pink and between the blotches was the cold pasty colour of the belly of a fish, of uncooked dough.

Same as Mother, same as Father.

Realising she would never see them again, tears filled her eyes. She had expected to cry at being taken from her home, but she had not expected to be crying over missing her parents. Not after their betrayal. Not after they had exiled her. She should hate them, but couldn't.

Her head hurt. She did not know if it was due to the light streaming in through the window – even that looked different to the light 'inside' – or withdrawal from caffeine. Even in detention she had still drunk coffee. She had screamed and wailed until they brought her what she demanded, her headaches and heartache soothed because of that familiar black sacrament. With a coffee in hand, she could pretend she was still living.

Now, outside, she silently thanked them for that tiniest of mercies. It mitigated some of the hate she felt. Even that prison, with its dull mundanity, the pain and threat of injury, the fear of torture that eventually eventuated, was incalculably better than out here.

She wondered what Becka ate. There was no fridge, or bain-marie. 'Becka,' Christine said, 'is there anything to eat or drink other than water?' She had last eaten in the prison but could not remember how long ago. 'Becka,' she said more loudly. 'Becka,' she said again, almost shouting.

The other woman continued to ignore her, back quivering like a bird in hand; one scared, panting breath after another. Christine realised Becka was talking to herself, but not in words that could be understood easily, maybe not in words at all. She moved closer.

'I have to get back, I have to get back, I have to get back, I have to get in, I have to get back, I have to get back, I have to get in,' over and over again like a Catholic chanting the rosary.

'Becka, please,' she said, laying a hand lightly on the woman's shoulder.

Becka turned, her eyes shining with rage, and swung a tight fist. Christine felt it hit far before she could even imagine Becka hitting her. There was not enough weight behind the swing to knock her from her feet, but she still dropped to her knees, shocked.

Becka's eyes were fire, her face ice.

'Please.' Christine did not know what else to say.

Becka looked at her like she was something to be scraped off the sole of a shoe, with the same contempt with which Mother used to look at the servants. If Christine was honest, that was how she used to look at the servants, too.

Becka turned back to the window.

Christine crawled to the couch on her knees, put her head in the bowl of her cupped hands and filled them with tears.

©

The servants were now all unloaded. Christine hated herself for not looking for Sienna. She might never see her again, might never touch those lips, smell that skin, touch that hair. Their time had been too short.

She was shocked by the strength of her desire.

Becka turned away from the window a different person, the intense look of desperation, the flame of frenzy in her eyes, the fever, gone once the gates had closed and the bus park had cleared.

In the light, Christine could see that Becka was perhaps younger than Mother, but her plastic surgery had been too long ago. Her face was sagging, the wrinkles around her eyes pronounced. But now the madness had gone, her eyes were kind.

'How are you, dear?' she asked with a saccharine cheerfulness that reminded Christine of Mother. 'I know it's difficult being out here but we make do. Keep your wits about you and you will be fine.'

She walked over to a battered tin on the bench, pulled the lid off with a pop, took out a handful of biscuits and handed one to Christine. 'Well, not fine,' she continued, 'but we survive out here. We get on with it.'

There was a shrink-wrapped case of bottled water on the bench beside the tin. She tore two bottles off and handed one to Christine.

They ate and drank in the desperate silence of the truly hungry.

'So,' said Becka with a questioning tone, 'what brings you here, what did you do, who did you piss off to be thrown out here with the rest of us reprobates and discards? I was an academic, and before you ask, I wrote an article that was critical of the Agency.'

Christine stared like Mother would.

'Well, not an article, barely a Safetynet Social post. I guess I was just a bit too radical for them. I thought they had too much control, owned too much, thought letting us come and go would be better. So, what about you?'

Christine filled her suddenly dry mouth with water, swallowed. 'I kissed a servant,' she said finally. 'I was caught on camera. My parents threw me out and I had no money of my own to buy a house in the town.'

'Was he worth it?' Becka asked, a laugh behind her teeth ready to escape.

'She,' Christine said, the words like sweat on her tongue.

Becka stoppered her mouth with a biscuit but her bemused grin was impossible to hide.

'Sometimes in prison I wasn't sure, particularly when they beat me, but yes, she was worth it,' said Christine, sounding to herself like someone underwater. 'She is worth it.'

'Well,' said Becka cheerfully, 'you can help me watch the gates, maybe you will see her.' She laughed. 'It doesn't matter if you have a house by the way. You kissed a black girl and got caught, but your parents must have intervened. You're still alive.'

DAY 3

THE MIDDAY SUN was harsher in the ruins. It ate her skin, boiled her eyes, reflected and radiated from the asphalt and concrete. The water bottles they carried, one each, might not have been enough. Becka chastised her like a chattering bird, hurried her whenever she slowed, when she was too tired to move, when she hesitated because she did not know where they were going.

Somewhere in the ruins someone, or some beast with a voice like a human's, screamed. Becka stopped, stared for a long time in the direction of the sound, quivered like someone ready to flee. Christine could feel her pulse in her ears, hear her blood rushing.

The line snaking through the ruins was as orderly as the people in line were not. They were dressed in rags and tatters, sunburnt brown and wrinkled, scarred, leathery and knot-haired.

It was her clothes, Christine realised – her tracksuit pants plain but unholed, her t-shirt neat, her hoody filthy but untorn – that made her stand out in the crowd and marked her as newly exiled.

Some wore items that did not match the rest of their clothes – filthy rags with brand-new jumpers, shredded jeans with near-new shoes, old trackpants with new shirts. Christine assumed they had robbed someone just out of the city, like her, or had traded new clothes for something people just out were desperate for.

There were faces snarling, faces brain-burned and expressionless, faces with streaks of tears in the dirt they all wore like foundation; faces so blank they were barely faces. There were dreadlocks and heads with scars and nicks where people had shaved their scalps with blunt razors; one or two heads wore matted baskets of hair. She knew the faces, under the grime, were all as white as hers and she knew it was only a matter of time until she would look as brown as they did. But even under the dirt, many did not look like they got any sun, like they hid in caves, in holes in ruined buildings, like movie vampires, only emerging to feed.

Christine caught herself staring at a better dressed woman, who had sharp cheekbones to admire, soft curved lips to kiss. She would be stunning if she ate some decent food and cut her hair. 'Don't look at everybody so much,' Becka hissed. 'Some people, being on the outside, they can't take it, become a little bit irrational, a bit mad. Or madder.'

Christine couldn't quite keep in a snort of laughter at the irony.

'Some of them are dangerous,' the woman of bone and wire continued. 'They might think you are looking at them funny, might object and make you regret not looking away. They could make you regret breathing.'

'Thank you,' Christine said. 'Thank you for telling me. Thank you for helping me too, for getting me out of the car-park grounds, letting me sleep on your couch, bringing me here.'

'I didn't do it for you,' Becka said. 'I did it to spite them, to spite everybody in there, every one of them. They want us to come out here and die quietly. If they thought they could get away with it they would just chuck us off the Wall, I reckon. Watch us splat onto the pavement. They would laugh at that, take bets on how many times we would bounce. It's against policy, I think, and they are big on policy, on rules, on order in there. I don't know if the people running the place in there would sanction murder. Much better to push us out of sight, out the gates, out here.'

'Thank you, anyway.'

'Also, you have a face, it almost looks okay, almost like I can trust you. You can help me watch the Wall, watch my stuff.'

Christine only nodded. She thought everybody had a face and didn't imagine Becka had stuff worth watching.

A gap appeared before them and they stepped into it, and again when the line moved forward, and again. Becka walked backwards, talking to Christine, her patter increasingly disordered as the heat hammered down on them. Christine took a sip of water, edged forward some more. At the front of the line was a line of women in white. Most of them looked older than anyone in Safetown. One of them handed an opaque plastic bag to Becka.

'No soup today?' she quipped in a voice that was half-laughing, half-admonishing.

Christine stepped forward and someone handed her a bag. It was heavy. She stepped away, following Becka's whip-thin frame. The rough ground held dangers to trip up the unwary and Christine was that intent on what was in the bag – a packet of biscuits, two of what she thought must be protein bars and six half-litre bottles of water – that she stepped on a wobbly half-brick and tumbled forwards, barely getting her hands out to break her fall and protect her face.

Her bag fell open, its contents scattering out into the dirt.

Becka wandered on obliviously as Christine sat up and examined her palms. The skin was damaged, pinpricks of blood rising. A small stone was embedded in her left hand. She stood slowly, gingerly put weight on her legs. Her ankle hurt, but she could stand on it so it wasn't broken. Becka was still walking away. Only her head was visible above the broken bricks, rusted metal and burned trash. Christine picked up her scattered food, stuck it in the bag and hobbled after her as fast as she could. She did not know how to find Becka's apartment, had no way to be sure which one of the ruins it was in.

Christine moved as fast as she could, a limping, stumbling lope, almost catching up with Becka as she walked into a building. She hoped she would not lose her only guide in that labyrinth, hoped she would remember which apartment to go into if she did. Through a door, hanging from one hinge, the lock long ago destroyed, over pile after pile of debris, then, up the stairs to the second floor.

Someone huge, like a movie ogre, burst through a door, bumping into Christine and knocking her into a wall. She was reminded of the day her life had ended, the day her father had bounced her mother off the wall and forced Christine from her home. It was that, not the pain of her shoulder striking the wall, that pulled tears from her eyes, that made everything hurt.

She wept all the way to the next staircase and her questing foot hooked through some stringy threadbare carpet that tore free a moment after it tripped her up. She fell forwards again, caught the banister with her better hand, but did not have enough strength to arrest her fall. When she landed, she slid down a couple of steps on her stomach, then crawled the rest of the way to the landing on hands and skinned knees.

She kept climbing despite the pain in her legs, knowing that Becka was on the top floor, imagining she would kill to ensure she had the best view possible. She could not remember having climbed two flights of stairs before.

Then there was no more height to gain. Still no sign of Becka, who had either not noticed Christine was not behind her or did not care. Christine was desperate to find the right apartment before something bad happened. She didn't know what hostility she would find behind any wrong door she opened.

At the top of the stairs, the hallway was clogged with trash in both directions. Plasterboard fell off the walls like sunburnt skin, and a ceiling thick with spider webs hung down like Becka's uncorrected face.

She tried to remember the view from Becka's window and turned right, stepping gingerly over more debris, placing her feet in holes in the knee-high shit. Surely there must be vermin in there, filthy cockroaches, dangerous spiders or rats; surely there were things in those piles that could jab her in the leg if the stacks subsided, spill her blood and inject filth and infection under her skin. The cuts would fill with pus and bacteria, and with no doctors outside she would die in excruciating pain.

She stopped at an open door and peered through. A man stood before the window, frozen, joints calcified, empty water bottles and crumpled biscuit packets surrounding him. Rats ate around his feet. He was thin, like someone who lacked even the drive to eat. Christine carefully backed out of the doorway.

Next door, locked. The one after that had so much trash in front of it that it surely could not open. The next door opened, but she was afraid to step through, afraid of what could happen. She looked around the frame, terrified.

Becka was pottering about, putting biscuits in the tin, storing another unopened packet in a cupboard, humming tunelessly to herself.

'Shut the fucking door. Get the fuck in or get the fuck out and shut the fucking door,' Becka screamed.

Christine shut the door behind her and stood inside the entrance of the apartment. She did not know what to do.

'There's a lock, you know,' a mercurial Becka said sweetly.

It occurred to Christine suddenly that Jack might have done something to earn the ire of the Agency, like her, and been turfed out here, although she was certain he was too smart to get caught doing something as stupid as kissing a servant.

The thought of him out there, filthy, knot-haired and dressed in rags, poured ice down her spine.

She could look for Jack while she waited for Sienna to show herself. And yet she was scared to search too hard for him. What if he was brain burned? What if finding him damaged was worse than not finding him at all? What if someone took objection to her search, the sort of objection that would inspire them to leave her hurt and bleeding or dead on the road?

If only she could try to contact him, but she had thrown her phone off the Wall. She slid the bolt with a snick.

When the thought sank all the way into her brain, cutting through the cobwebs and overgrown vines, she dropped her bag of food and fell to her knees.

Her phone. She had thrown it off the Wall to the outside.

She was outside.

DAY 12

A FENCE, COILED barbed wire and razor wire, rusted to poison, tangled with brambles, imprisoned a space near the Wall that was filled with nothing she could see but gravel, broken glass and yellow-grey scraggly weeds. A section of the fence was brown and bulky, not much like a fence but a raggedy wall of fur, feathers or leaves. Christine closed the distance and saw dried flesh, mummified hide and small bones; smelled something sickening sweetly nauseating.

She could not stop herself from approaching, saw a tiny rodent face, and another, the drying of their flesh carving their faces into rictuses. Then another, rotten down to strings of flesh holding tea-brown bone together. Then another, maggots writhing in tiny rotting eye sockets. A small bird, scraps of feathers hanging off its flesh. A rabbit, its yellow teeth screaming.

The first security drone she had seen in a long time buzzed towards her. She covered her face with her arm, threw a broken-off length of rusty wire at it, but missed. It started jinking, trying to get a good look at her face. She picked up a stick to fend it off, knocking a rat skull off its dehydrated corpse. Dropping to her knees, she hacked up bile.

The angry machine buzzed so close to her head, so close to the hands that were covering her face, that she could feel the breath of its blades. She heard it fly away, looked again at the fence. There must have been hundreds of rats hanging on hooks, their bodies and mouths contorted, their blood blackening the ground, dried and still sticky. Christine felt certain many, if not all, of the rats were alive when they were hung on the wire, pierced by the barbs of the fence, bleeding out in the sun.

She did not want to meet someone whose mind would compel them to slaughter animals and build that display.

Almost as if her thoughts had summoned it, she heard a noise from a small building nearby. It was the sort of voice she would expect to hear coming out of a ruined face; it made her hair stand on end, made her heart jump. She could not make out any words and was not sure she wanted to.

The noise was approaching. She wanted to run, but the cameras, the drones, the guards atop the Wall with binoculars and rifle scopes, would see her face if she uncovered it. The brain-ruined voice grew louder.

The drone returned with more friends. She could feel the downdraught of their propellers. There were so many they looked like willie wagtails mobbing a crow, like flies surrounding a corpse.

She heard the voice retreating; perhaps they were even more afraid of the drones than Christine was. Some of the flying machines peeled away, in the direction of the voice. She hoped the drones would find that more interesting to chase. She hoped the others would bore of her.

She did not know how long she stay curled there, tense and afraid, her heart beating against her chest like a rat trying to escape. The plastic bodies carried on, buzzing wings batted against her like moths against a light. Fear had eaten her ability to move, her ability to think. Then silence. She could hear nothing but the wind in the grass and the sticks.

Fearfully, she opened her eyes. The sky was dark.

Christine surged to her feet and ran into the darkness, far from the Wall and Security, far from the mad voice who would surely soon be on the chase. Security had night-vision cameras on spinning wings. If they found her, if she did not get to cover before they arrived, she might not get away at all. She ran into the darkness, tumbled over a brick and tangled herself in some wire. Dancing to untangle it from her ankles, she bounced from a knee-length wall and somehow kept her feet.

In the darkness she ran on, terrified of what was behind, terrified of what she might collide with, hoping she would be able to feel any obstacle before she ran headlong into it. She ran on, hands outstretched like a rotting dead-thing in the zombie movies all the kids in the town had loved. They had imagined the world outside the Wall might be like that. Suddenly, her hands touched something, but she did not stop fast enough. Her arms collapsed at the elbow painfully, firmly enough to sprain, her face hitting a wall, much of the force stolen by outstretched hands.

In the darkness she didn't want to scream, something might hear her.

On hands and knees she felt her way along the base of the wall, found an opening, a doorway perhaps, crawled through. Feeling her way along the inside wall, she came to a box, a space, some sort of hidey-hole, crawled into it and curled up.

She managed, somehow, not to scream.

DAY 13

SOMEWHERE IN THE long grass and the weeds was her phone, probably ruined by the rain if it had survived being thrown from the Wall. Still, there was a chance of finding it. It held her memories, her hopes, the only chance of finding Jack. Without it she despaired of ever being able to look in the dead drop.

She walked across the broken, gravelly ground, more black than green on it: the scene was the colour of licorice. There had been a fire recently; she hoped it had been before she threw her phone. The scraggly weeds, all the golden dead-burned away, held on to the ash as they would the elixir of life.

There was no clue to hint at what had started the fire; perhaps a cooking fire from the ruins had escaped its confines; perhaps a lightning storm had struck the ground, sparking a conflagration; perhaps someone frustrated at being stuck outside the Wall had started a fire for no other reason than to see something burn. More likely, this close to the Wall, Security had torched the area, firebombed it, to keep the view clear for their cameras, for their guns.

There were no ruins past the wastelands; instead a wall of forest, dark, wild and oppressive, loomed. She could see no way to press through that wall of green, not from a distance. She feared approaching. There might be wild beasts in there, feral people, worse than those in the ruins, as wild, dark and animalistic as the landscape itself.

A flash caught Christine's eye from among the ash and weeds, from about fifty metres away. She ran to it, roughly parallel with the Wall, kicked through gravel and broken glass, over rough ground, barbed wire and scattered foot-eating nails. Dust and ash puffed up from her feet, making grey ghost-shapes before falling to Earth, the last airy fragments stolen by the wind.

There was nothing there.

She looked around some more, pushing the tall spikiness of a thistle aside with her foot, stamping the glassy green of a nettle into the ground. There she found it, the glint. Nothing but an ancient amber glass bottle. Disappointment surged through her body. She sat down, defeated, gravel-dust-ash throwing itself into the air in the process. She breathed some of it in, heavy in her lungs, itchy in her nose and throat.

Tears poured out, washing her cheeks. She tried to stop her sobs and could not. She did not know where the tears came from. She cried for Jack, for Mother, even for Father, but not for Brandon, not for her house, not for the city, nor for herself.

Then she was crying for Sienna, for the memory of her smell, her touch, her lips. The feel of Sienna's arms. Christine had never experienced this quivery feeling in her gut before and wondered if this was love.

She felt sick. The realisation she might be in love kicked the last thoughts out of her head, left her empty. Soon no more tears came. She pulled a battered aluminium flask – worth every biscuit and bottle of water she had bartered for it – out of her pocket.

Christine had been surprised by the economy outside the Wall. Biscuits and water traded for favours; rat meat and skins traded for moonshine; weapons, acquired and improvised, traded for pretty much anything their owner wanted when not used to kill, maim or steal. Stolen goods traded for stolen goods. Even bodies were commodities, which sickened her when she first heard of it.

The hooch in the flask was so harsh she gagged, but she forced it down, burning her nerves to ash, her pain dulling in a moment of fire. She ate a precious biscuit. It tasted strange, too sweet while simultaneously too mealy after burning her mouth clean with moonshine.

She watched the looming bulk of the Wall. It was not far. She knew precisely how close she could get before the cameras and drones showed interest. She was safe where she was. Long before she was close enough to risk being shot, they would warn her to back away. If she ran at the first warning, she would get away, she would survive.

As the sun cut out from behind a cloud, there was another flash of light in the weeds, like a murderer drawing a knife, between her and the Wall. She stood up too quickly. The combination of sunlight, food and wasteland-distilled ethanol made her wobble. It was difficult to stay upright and keep her eye on the knife blade of light. She knew she was getting too close as the sound of buzzing machines erupted from the Wall.

At the same moment she almost stepped on her phone. She moved her foot to the side before it was too late, but not early enough to do it elegantly. She staggered and skipped a couple of steps before finding her feet, grabbing her phone before she lost sight of it again.

The drones sounded furious. She laughed at herself and how weak her throw from the Wall had been. The machines laughed back as they flew angrily at her.

Holding her treasure tight to her heart she ran from the machines, sending rocks bounding. They sped up to catch her and she covered her face with her arm as they flew over, then she kept running as fast as she could. Tripping on a length of wire that spanged away she managed somehow not to fall. She stepped on a stick, and the other end jumped up in the path of her other foot, and she squealed with the pain lancing into her ankle, managed again somehow not to fall. The machines fell behind. She kept running as they turned away. Then she was sprinting free across the wasteland towards the scraggly edge of the forest, far from the ruins around the gates.

Out of breath, she stopped as she reached the tangled edge of the trees, afraid to go in any deeper. She looked at the phone in her hand. The screen was cracked, the battery flat, the casing damp; the phone likely irreparably dead. But she had found it. That had to mean something.

DAY 17

CHRISTINE SAT ON a tall, narrow stool in the most cluttered room she had ever seen. There were screens that looked like big tablets on stands, others that looked like crates with one glass side. There were computers, most of them useless; tablets, most of them dismantled; tangles and drapes of wire and cable. Among it all were coffee cups and biscuit packets, water bottles and dirty bowls; everything studded with bits of this and that and festooned with wires.

'I think I can charge it, but I don't have a screen and digitiser to fix the broken screen,' a nasally voice emitted from somewhere in the mess. 'Even if I charge it, it might not work. It might be water damaged.'

'How much to charge it then?'

'What you got?'

'Biscuits and water,' she replied. The voice in the pile snorted.

It was all she had. She had found other things to eat, things she found intensely distasteful but worth far less in trade than biscuits. But she had not foraged enough to make up for the loss of the biscuits she saved to trade. She was getting thin. Soon she would be nothing but skin, bones and wire. Like Becka.

Christine had gone back to the apartment, to watch the gates at night while Becka slept; careful to hide her phone, even from Becka. She could've probably just slept and made sure she got up before Becka did, but she was too honest for that. Watching the gates ate her sleep, but she didn't really mind. She still had held hope that she might catch sight of Sienna.

Not much happened at night. There were occasional buses, probably carrying the night shift for the restaurants and cafes, shops and car services. When a night-shift bus arrived or left, the parking space lit up like day. Once, when the lights had flashed on, she saw a man creeping towards the buses. The sound of a gunshot tore through the silence and the man stopped moving.

Becka had paid her in food. That was where Christine had got some of her stash. Becka had never divulged where she got the extra biscuits and water from, what she had to do to get them, and Christine did not care, did not want to know what someone was willing to go hungry to pay for.

Then abruptly, like a switch had flipped in her brain, Becka lost what sanity she had left and Christine fled the apartment. She wasn't sure how long ago that was, but she was on her own again.

'What else do you have?'

'More biscuits and water. It's all I have.'

'Come back for your phone tomorrow,' the voice said. 'Don't worry, it's not worth my reputation to steal your fucking phone. I won't even ask how you got hold of it.'

'It's my phone,' Christine snapped.

'I won't ask how you got it past Security and brought it out here then,' the voice said. 'It's charging. Leave the food, come back tomorrow. Bring more when you come back. When you have enough food to make it worth my while, you can have your phone back.'

DAY 20

THE LINE FOR soup was longer than normal. There was a wall of people, most of them older than her, many of them dirtier, scabbier, more ragged. A long line of knotted hair, of torn and stinking clothes, of grey beards and bare feet, of wounded faces and cracked minds. She knew it would only be a matter of time before she too looked like that, before her mind also fled.

Everybody carried a vessel for the soup: dirty plastic bowls, cracked coffee mugs, dented saucepans, miraculously unbroken jars, plastic water bottles cut in half. Christine had none of those things. She had an old tin, the paper label rotted away long ago, the inside scrubbed as clean as gravel and water could get it. The scratch of the sand had removed the seal on the inside and she was losing the war against rust. Every time she scraped the rust off, the tin got thinner and weaker.

Becka was there and looked at Christine like she didn't recognise her. Perhaps she didn't.

She tried not to catch the attention of anyone in the line. People stood talking, old friends or maybe those thrust together. Other people were glumly silent, turned inwards, seeing only the worlds in their heads; still, others faced their minds outwards, rage and hate all they had left to offer the world.

There was one man who roved wildly between those two states. One moment he was silent, eyes closed, a faint smile on his lips, humming a thin tune that was not quite possible to follow. Maybe in his head he was at a concert. Maybe music had been his hobby inside and he was reliving the memory of playing, a memory that should have made him happy. The next moment his eyes would burst open and he would scream out of a red-rimmed toothless mouth, swinging at anyone nearby with whatever was in his hands, or his fists, until everybody moved away, until a stronger man eventually knocked him down.

It had happened yesterday. He had gone from absent and harmless to dangerous in a breath. That time, his friend, a bearded monster of a man who seemed to hang his identity on the madman – she thought maybe they were lovers – knocked him down and sat on him until he stopped flailing and started humming again.

Christine felt a madness tickling her consciousness, but she pushed it away.

Suddenly, a man broke away from the line and ran wildly at the Wall, screaming. Christine could not quite make out the words but thought 'let me in' was probably the sentiment. Drones swarmed from the top of the Wall before he was halfway across the wasteland. Christine wanted him to stop. Sit down, stop screaming, her mind silently yelled. Be as still and silent as the grave you will never have. If he was quiet and peaceful, they might leave him where he was.

The man ran on, swiped wildly at a drone that buzzed close to his face, stumbled and almost fell. Christine hoped he would not find his feet. If he fell and lay there, he might survive. But he regained his feet and ran, lumbering like he had pulled a muscle in his near fall. Someone in the line howled like a wolf then began whimpering like a wounded dog. Drones circled the running man like bees around a hive, almost landing on his head. If his hair was not so matted, the wind from the machines would have made it dance.

There was a bang. The man kept running. Another crack echoed and the man stumbled and screamed, half-loping, half-limping. Then rapid-fire sounded, like hail on a tin roof. His screaming was audible, even over the stuttering of automatic gunfire. The man crumpled to the ground.

The guns kept firing, misting the air above his corpse red.

Everybody turned back to face the back of the person before them in the line, stepped forward when the line did, stood in silence when the line stopped. Nobody wanted to look at the spot where the blood was soaking into the ground.

More steps forward, then a couple more.

One of the soup-bringers held up a ladle of soup, looking at her with an unspoken question in her eyes. Christine held out her tin and the soup glugged in. Another soup-bringer handed her a plastic bag. It weighed like there were a few bottles of water and maybe some muesli bars in it. Perhaps some biscuits to trade.

She walked over to a smashed bit of wall that was smooth enough to sit on, where she had sat alone for the past few days, and raised her tin to her mouth, not tasting the food. Those with places to go had gone back to their squats. The soup-bringers, those angels in clean white, fanned out from their table and spoke to the stragglers, to those with nowhere to go. Nobody had told her where the soup truck came from or where these volunteers who came every day to feed the hungry went when their truck was empty.

One of the soup-bringers approached her. She turned her head away, stared at the most damaged part of the ruins, the fallen walls and bent twisted metal. Cars, with noses up, noses down, with tyreless wheel rims, pointed jauntily at the sky. She didn't think anyone lived there, how could they unless they were a rat, or had someone found a car right way up, tunnelled down to it and was living there in a metal and fabric cave.

Maybe those stronger, or madder, or those less concerned with getting back into the city, did indeed live out there in the wastelands, preying on rats, on cockroaches, on other people who strayed too close. Perhaps that is what she should do, become a hermit of the barrens, live on rats and pigeons caught with her bare hands, eat them raw because there was probably nowhere to make a fire. She could sneak back from time to time and watch the Wall for Sienna.

Someone was talking. The woman, the soup-bringer, was talking to her. She felt like she was underwater, could only hear snippets of sound. None of it made sense. She closed her eyes and concentrated. What was this angel saying to her?

'Christine?'

Her name. It had been a while since she had heard it.

'You are Christine, aren't you?'

'Who are you?' she snapped, terrified at what someone knowing her name might mean.

'My friend Sienna asked me to look out for you. She gave me an old security photo. You are thinner and the time outside has not been kind to you, but you look enough like the photo. You are Christine, aren't you?'

Christine stared, processing, freaked out. Then nodded.

'She heard you had been evicted, exiled, but didn't know where to look for you. It's not safe for her here or else she would have looked for you herself. A lot of the people kicked out of the city keep their prejudices. They think brown people, black people are nothing but dirt. They try to hurt people, try to enslave them. Even removed from that place they think having black servants is the natural order of things.'

Christine remembered a desperate man, not too many days before, running at the servants as they exited the buses. He had grabbed one, almost dragged her away, before Security beat him. Later someone told her he had died, been beaten to death.

'Yes,' she barely breathed. 'I'm Christine.'

'She asked me to give you this.' The stranger handed over an envelope. 'It has a train ticket to the mainland, to the city where Sienna lives, and her phone number. It's not a short walk to the train station, but it looks like you are still pretty fit. You have survived here a while, you might make it.'

Christine nodded.

'This is from me,' the woman said, handing her a small package. 'Hide it, quick, you might need it. You need to be prepared if you are going to make it to the train.'

Christine hid the envelope and the package in her layers of rags. Her heart was beating too fast and her mind was blank. She could not see through the film of tears. Realising she had not thought to say thank you, she turned back to the woman. But the soup-bringer was gone.

After eating her cold soup, she scrabbled into the barrens and found a cave where a fallen wall had hit. She crawled in. Only when she was certain nobody could see her did she lean into the light and look at what she had been given. In the envelope was a train ticket and a piece of paper with a phone number on it. The other package contained chocolate.

DAY 30

THE WORDS NOT CONNECTED stared back at her, mockingly. She should not have been surprised and regretted bartering so much food to charge it. Of course it wouldn't connect, it had not connected to Safetynet even before she had thrown it off the Wall.

She sat in her cave, a burnt car body half-buried in tumbled buildings and debris, lined with scraps of cloth and rat hide she was sure were doing little but attracting vermin. With no Safetynet she would never find Jack. It was stupid to hold on to such a fool's hope outside. Yet she still couldn't bring herself to dispose of the phone.

What if she never left, what if she lost her mind, what if Sienna forgot her? It was time to go.

She had all she needed. A backpack patched with rat fur and scraps of fabric stitched together with string and copper wire, a working phone with no connection, two packets of biscuits, six bottles of water, one block of chocolate and the clothes on her back. Sienna's number was in her pocket along with the ticket for the train.

A small boy, no more than ten, had taught her how to catch rats, pigeons, and rabbits with snares made of wire. She thought he must have been born out there in the wilds, and she was just as sure his parents were dead. She remembered the soup-bringers chasing him, trying to offer help, but he always evaded them, running across the rubble as fast and agile as a cat. Rat meat, as distasteful as it was, had supplemented her meals and enabled her to conserve the biscuits.

It was time to leave. It was time to find Sienna.

Digging into the debris through a smashed side window, she opened the top of a buried cardboard box, stuffed her bag in the cavity, and reburied it. Not all that secure but it was all she could do. She climbed out of her hole and slunk off to check her trapline. The first two snares had nothing in them and she cursed the waste of time. In the third, she found a rat. It was scurrying back and forth, squealing with every movement that pulled the line tighter. Christine smashed its head with a rock, undid the snare, picked the rat up by its tail and reset the snare. There was a mark on its neck where the snare had cut in through the fur, drawing blood.

Returning to her cave, she stopped suddenly. Something was wrong, something she should have noticed. There was someone there, she could smell them.

She was silent, a rat in her pocket, a foot-long piece of rebar she had sharpened on a fallen piece of concrete– the handle wrapped with plastic bags and melted in her campfire – in her hand. She snuck towards her hole in the rubble, holding the shiv against her leg. If they had found her stash she would hurt them, if not she would let them run.

'Girl,' a rough voice echoed from the entrance of her safe haven. 'I know you have a shank, I have an axe. I will kill you. I just want to talk.'

She snuck closer.

'I can hear you,' the man said. 'Don't think I can't hear you. I don't want to hurt you, a pretty girl like you. I like you.'

The man climbing out of her car was huge, carved muscle, like the ancient statues she had seen in the museum in town, but for his pot gut. He had one great dreadlock down his back and an explosion of beard poking out from his face. She had seen him skulking around the food line in the past, a man everybody feared.

He held an axe in his right hand, beckoned with his left, and looked at her with a raised eyebrow.

'You want to die?' he asked in a voice that held nothing but curiosity. 'Some women out here just want to die. Are you one of them, or do you have a reason to live?'

Christine handed her shiv to him. He took it and dropped it to the ground behind him. It clattered across the concrete and jammed itself between two pieces of rubble. Christine's adrenaline-heightened senses recorded where it landed.

Reaching out, he grabbed her by the t-shirt, pulled until it started to tear. Christine tried to pull away. He let go and punched her, fireworks going off in her head. She screamed.

'Don't be stupid, girl,' he said, dropping his axe to the ground, where it thudded against rotten concrete. He grabbed her throat and threw her down, held her breathless, pulled at the waistband of her pants and yanked with enough force until they tore loose and slid down.

He reached towards her filthy underwear. She wriggled on her back like a snake, willing her back muscles to carry her away. He slapped her and she writhed harder. He slapped her again. This time she stopped moving. He reached again for her underwear, pulled it down, pulled down his own pants, exposing himself.

Christine was ready to die.

She thought of Father, his big hands and his strength. She thought of Sienna, who she would never see again if she died now. She thought of this man taking the last thing she had left of herself.

There was nothing of her left.

Christine closed her mind, ready to die, opened it and lived for Sienna.

She found a rock and swung wildly, blindly, relying on luck and fate, felt it hit him on the side of the head with a sickening crunch. The man fell on top of her, his dick out and flopping against her naked skin.

Crawling out from under him, she tore the skin off her back. She stood and kicked her pants off then started backing away. As she did, she felt something hard against her ankle. It was her shiv: sharp but barely, dangerous, but only a little, She bent down and picked it up. Half-naked, she stood poised, hiding the shiv behind her back.

The man's eyes opened, first filled with confusion then rage. He stood up unsteadily and stepped towards her.

Christine did not hesitate. Using his momentum and bulk, she stabbed him in the gut, so deep she felt her hand thud against his skin. He screamed, backed away, showing a fear that did not rest easily on his face. His backward momentum pulled the shiv out of his flesh. She followed with a single step forward and stabbed him again. He turned to run and she stabbed him in the back. He fell down; she stabbed him again. She straddled him, digging the spike of steel into him again and again and again.

She remembered her father, the men who had beat her in prison, the faceless figures who had zapped her on the Wall, forgot for a moment who she was, stabbed the man until blood splattered her face. She remembered being kicked out of the town, the betrayal, the hate, the faceless men and cut-and-paste women. She screamed as she stabbed.

She remembered Jack, his smile, his eyes, her love for his bountiful soul.

She remembered Sienna, the smell of her neck, the feel of her breath on her own.

She stopped.

The man was dead.

DAY 33

THE FIRST LIGHT was only just appearing when Christine climbed out of her cave and shrugged her bag onto her aching back. She had the shiv in her belt and an axe in her hand, a corpse at her feet, and nothing left to lose.

There were no rats in her traps. She dismantled them and put the wire in her bag, too.

It was time to go. She could not risk another man coming to take from her the only thing she had worth stealing.

Walking away from her cave, she manoeuvred over concrete blocks that wobbled dangerously under her feet. She was dressed in tatters and the dead man's coat and his sturdy boots; too big and stuffed with rags. She had messily cut her hair a centimetre short, stealing scissors from Becka while she was away. She walked where she could see the road, through the rubble and the death. It was the only clear space, carved and bulldozed through the ruins, metre-thick concrete laid over the existing chaos, patched repeatedly whenever it cracked. She dared not take the road: cameras and lights on poles lined it, making it visible in a way that could only be intentional.

There were bones in the ruins, of the people who were there before the city was built, of the people ejected from the city, of the outsiders from elsewhere who had tried to enter the city and been killed. Even the car park where the buses parked was built on the corpse of an old city. Under a slab of concrete, a cave where she might have camped, she found a corpse lying on a brown stain, an opened belly full of maggots, limbs torn, clawed and bitten, what might have been an axe wound in the face.

She didn't recoil, didn't vomit; faced the death and decay with impassivity. She knew then that Christine, the girl from the city, was dead.

Night fell and she slept in the nearly intact room of a ruined building. Fear gripped her when she heard dogs howling, yet she dared not light a fire and tell other humans she was there.

It was a restless cold night. She was hungry and tired. For breakfast, she ate biscuits, but would have preferred anything else. The road taunted her but she ignored it, stuck to the rubble and the sticks and the prickles, the glass, wire and tripping hazards. This slowed her pace, but she could not trust the road. Surely they would be watching it.

There was less and less evidence of humans as she travelled, and more and more of nature beating its way through the concrete, taking back what never really belonged to the people.

Here, a tree ladened with apples, small and tart, had shouldered its way through broken concrete. Christine hungrily filled her belly, her pockets, her bag. There, a shallow cavern, too low-ceilinged for Christine to enter on anything other than hands and knees, empty but for the smell of dogs. There, wheeling crows revealed a corpse, mummified skin and rotting guts, the glossy black birds feeding on the flesh and the maggots; the skin peeling back from the skull in the heat.

Here, a human skull. There, a broken plastic toy, the colours faded, hiding among ferns. Here, the blackened remains of a campfire older than the last rains. There, a plum tree, the fallen fruit squishy and stinking of stale wine under foot.

At regular intervals during the day, she could hear buses roaring down the road. Not long after, she would hear them go the other way. Sometimes she could hear the sound of a distant drone, but she never saw one. Still, she kept her eyes peeled.

An eagle drifted overhead. She had seen them flying over the town from time to time, when she was a child, but outside in the wastelands, where there was nothing to live for, the great bird carried a new meaning. She was awed by it, a little scared by its silent drifting, drifting, looking down on her like an angel, like a god. She thought it would see her as insignificant, just a human; pathetic and pointless to an eagle's eye. If there was a god, surely the eagle was his messenger.

She needed light and heat and life; she lit a campfire that night at the entrance of a cave she had found where a building had not quite fallen. Ivy scraggled across the ruins, morning glory fought it for space; blackberries formed an alliance with barbed wire creating impassable thickets. She lay among those vines, scant shelter in the thin warmth of her fire. She could have set snares, caught a rabbit, a rat, a cat or some other small furry or feathered thing, but she was too tired.

She wished she had not dreamed, because she dreamed of women, her mother's friends, their faces doll-like, constructed of glistening wax. They laughed at her when she came close, threw full wineglasses at her, called her a 'dyke', the red of the wine mixing with blood where broken glass penetrated her skin. When she screamed hate at them, their faces melted down their chests, over their breasts.

When sleep finally left her it was still dark, the stars fading in the first light of sun. She thought she could smell a phantom trace of Sienna's hair.

The day dawned red and she left the safety of her hole to watch small clouds scudding across the sky. She feared it would rain, that she would not find shelter fast enough; exposure could kill her. Yet she needed to move on, her food would not last forever. She had nothing but tart apples for breakfast.

She walked as the sky grew lighter, then got darker again, stopping only to eat biscuits and cold rat. When it was too dark to see, she wrapped herself in her coat to sleep. She walked on when she saw the ruins getting lower, the hills of debris almost low enough to see over. She walked on until a wall of green became visible, resolving into the densest thicket of trees she could imagine.

She stopped when the ruins ended and only the road continued into the forest. Then the rain started.

In desperation she ran and found cover under one corner of a fallen house at the edge of the tree line, a fragment of its roof intact. She grabbed what dry wood she could, broken furniture and fallen sticks, piled it under a concrete slab where it would stay dry. The rain was so heavy she thought it would drown the world.

©

The stars were out but there was no other light. Christine pushed the leaves and branches she had covered herself with aside. She shivered, soaking wet, as she felt her way to the firewood she had stashed, prayed it was more dry than her, piled it up by feel and sparked the lighter she had looted from the corpse of her would-be rapist to life.

She had become skilled at lighting fires in her time outside. Those who could not control fire did not survive.

The flames caught, but her wet clothes insulated her from the fire, sucking the warmth from her skin. Stripping off her clothes, she hung them up as close as she could to the fire to dry, sat naked on her coat, hugged her knees to her chest and prayed for the sun.

Dawn was a long time coming, a twilight glow crawling into the sky, the sun peeking over the top of the trees, its first light bringing welcome warmth. She stood in that light, her back to the fire, arms outstretched to catch what light and warmth would come.

The early morning sun bleached the sky, rendering the forest before her even darker. The wall of green was overgrown, the road cutting into the darkness and soon disappearing from view. She feared that thicket, despaired of getting through it without walking on the road in full view of cameras or coming buses.

She stood indecisive for a while, catching the sun on her naked skin, like something solar powered or cold blooded. Moving seemed impossible, the impetus lost, so why not stand there, getting warm? Suddenly, in the hot early morning light, a bus exited the forest onto the roadway, then another, and another. She had to move or risk being seen.

Diving under her pathetic postage stamp of a cover, she threw sand on the coals of her fire from her hidey-hole, and pulled ivy, morning glory, sticks, leaves, branches, whatever she could find, over herself. From her trash pile she could see out through a gap where the leaves did not quite cover her eyes.

Over the bus, a Security quadcopter flew, barely visible in her confined field of vision. It slowed and hovered about halfway between the end of the ruins and the start of the forest, where scraggly weeds and the tendrils of vines embraced and tangled with wires, deadwood and the rusted corpses of cars.

She had little doubt there were bones in the wasteland too, people who failed to cross that space of sharp edges and glass, animals that hurt themselves there and crawled into holes to die. She was scared she would soon join them. Distant buzzing presaged the arrival of a flock of drones, big and small, dozens of them, zipping back and forth, spiralling, circling, zigzagging; every machine taking a different path, dancing in the sky like flying leaves.

Were they looking for her?

She silently begged the darkness and the debris to keep her hidden.

The buses kept coming. She could hear them before they revealed themselves, bus after bus, rolling down the road at over a hundred kilometres an hour, their big diesels roaring. Every bus was full; there must have been hundreds, maybe thousands, of people passing.

The buzzing, the roar of the copter, the ragged beat of her terrified breathing, continued until she felt that white noise was all there was to her life. The thunder of the copter faded first, then the sound of machines died, until there was silence. Proper silence. It was so silent she worried that the machines had rendered her deaf.

A small animal ran for the bushes, making the fallen leaves rustle. A crow somewhere squawked out its disdain at the noisy human machines. Somewhere in the distance an eagle called and another answered, and as if the world had been waiting for that, the forest started breathing again.

Christine crawled out of the hidey-hole, brushed sticks and leaves off her skin. She wondered what had brought the copter there, was almost convinced they must have been looking for her, had tracked her down somehow. Perhaps it was there every morning when the dawn buses came; though she couldn't remember having heard it.

She brushed herself off some more, put on her dry clothes and went looking for more firewood.

Christine was afraid of the darkness in the forest and had to admit to herself that she was stalling. But she was also cold and hungry. Rummaging for her snares in her bag, she climbed into the ruins to set them and to collect more firewood. She built a windbreak from sticks that would also shelter her from prying eyes from the road.

The buses roared past in the other direction. She hid behind her rough wall of crap but did not hear a copter this time.

When the last bus had passed, she waited for life to return to the world again before inspecting the five hundred metres of wasteland between her and the forest. Exploring it proved dangerous. There were pools of fetid water, biting creatures, broken glass and barbed wire. She stood on a slab of concrete that wobbled, threatening to throw her off. Stepping off from it, she fell into what turned out to be a grass-covered hole, filled with broken glass. Her stolen boots, too big and stuffed with cloth, saved her life.

As the daylight slid away, she returned to the comforting ruins, lit a small fire and watched the road.

DAY 44

CHRISTINE RAN HER fingers through her hair. Even as short as it was she could feel the potential for it to knot. If she did not want dreadlocks she would have to cut her hair off before it grew too long and trimming her hair with the piece of broken glass she skinned rats with would not be fun.

She picked at scabs and brushed off dirt as she absently watched the morning buses pass. They had dropped off their cargo of people and were now going back to wherever they had come from. Every day she had watched and knew that the longest break between traffic was after the morning buses returned.

It would give her enough time to get to the forest.

She carefully crossed the wasteland, almost tripping on a length of wire that jutted from the ground. She made her way over a wobbly slab of concrete the size of a house, dodged a snake that saw her and spat its disdain before slinking away. Rubble scattered underfoot like a shoal of tiny fish. A gunshot crack warned her she had stepped on plate glass, and she took her weight quickly onto the other foot.

She was not prepared for the heat. The sun beat on her like fists, sizzled her skin like a stun baton. She wanted to sit down in the cool shade; she wanted a sprinkler, like those at home, to follow her and mist her skin. She was going to die, she didn't want to die.

A few more steps, her ankles scratched by blackberry vines that had long ago dropped their fruit, barbed wire tangled among them like a dog among wolves. Loose gravel stole her balance and she nearly slipped into a hole, the bottom invisible in deep darkness. She tripped on a coil of wire, mercifully not barbed, turned her shoulder to the ground and rolled to protect her already sore and bloody hands.

She felt she had hardly covered any distance at all, the obstacle course making her progress slow. Sitting on a pile of rubble, she picked a painfully sharp flake of glass out of her arm, wiped the blood away with a dirty thumb.

Finally, she reached the darkness at the edge of the forest and the temperature dropped from a blowtorch against her skin to frog-skin cool. She staggered, dropped her bag and sat in a puddle. Such a short distance and she felt like it had nearly killed her. Even the hardening she had received in the fallen stone and broken concrete of the dead city near the Wall had not prepared her for this.

Soon she almost wished she was back in that familiar labyrinth rather than in the twisted alien shadows of the forest. Branches grabbed at the rags of her clothing, at the straps of her bag, tripped her up, tried to strip her naked. After only a few steps pushing though the sharp-leafed, thorny scrub, she was bleeding on her arms and face in several places. She would have turned back but for the fact the direction she was moving towards might lead her to Sienna.

That faint thread of a chance was all she had, all she cared about. The bush seemed to despise her, seemed to want to keep her from passing. She kept going.

She stumbled over a rock and slipped into a narrow stream with a tumbling splash, threw herself forward so that the top half of her body scratched between the branches obscuring the other side, rolled over and sat up with her feet in the stream. She sat there on the creek bank and caught her breath. Up above, she could see the sky for the first time since entering the forest.

There she ate some meat she had snared the day before, a long-eared rabbit that looked so much like a storybook character that she had almost felt guilty killing it. She risked a small fire in the mud by the creek; the animal was not bad cooked, unctuous but not fatty. She had skinned it with a shard of a broken bottle, blood from small nicks in her fingers joining that from the animal.

The noise of a copter assaulted her and she nearly screamed. She froze and watched it drifting overhead. It did not slow and she started to breathe normally again as the noise disappeared. When the sound was gone, she drank from the stream and filled her water bottles. Her bag was heavier, satisfyingly but almost uncomfortably so, when she moved on.

That night she slept in a scratchy cavern, axe-carved, pushed and scraped out of the thicket. Leaves and bush were below her, all around her, above her. She could not light a fire, there was no clear ground; she could imagine what would happen if a fire took in that place, in those resinous smelling trees. It scared her.

Years ago she had watched a brushfire unfolding on all the news channels and on Safetynet. Solar flares, change in orbit, whatever, it didn't matter, the world had got hotter. Everywhere was afire. Great forest fires consumed entire cities in their path, ate lives too. But not in her city. The Wall, Security, fire services, sprinklers; they all protected them. The people in Safetown sat and watched as most of the world burned, talking about it obsessively and incessantly on Social.

Lying there, where she could smell oils and resins, things that smelled flammable, where her bed was dry leaves, her walls dry sticks, her roof resinous leaves, she felt fear again. If a wildfire started, she was dead. As she walked she had seen evidence of old fires, charcoal on the ground, scorched bark on the shrubs, blackened topsoil. The thought was terrifying.

But she was freezing, still damp from slipping into the creek, from brushing all day against damp foliage. All she had to keep herself warm was her memories and the hope of love that was driving her forward. She woke in darkness, knowing somehow it was morning, the sun needing hours to build up the strength to fight its way into the scrub.

Christine decided to move on even in the dark. Half-crawling, desperate to remember which way she had been travelling, she felt the scrub, pushed then half fell through it, felt for another gap, managed to step through sideways, pushed through another gap even though it was too narrow. She moved forward slowly, hoping she was going in the direction she wanted, that the holes she was falling through were not letting her go around in circles.

As the sun rose higher it lit the scrub but, as she expected, it was not much help. It was still dark under the trees, a dank green, buggy and spider-filled darkness. She moved myopically though the claustrophobic thicket, falling into an almost trance-like movement, pushing on but barely registering the creatures, the scratches, the relentless trudge.

Something hard like concrete hit her knee and she fell out of the forest onto the road and into broad daylight. She lay there for a moment in the sun before imagining the cold eyes of the cameras on her, thanked the trees themselves that she had landed face down, kept her forehead on the concrete as she scrabbled backwards into the scrub.

Catching her breath, she decided she would move with more certainty and be less likely to get lost if she stayed close to the road.

It was both easier and harder at the same time. The trees were looser, further apart, and she could dodge between them with less effort, saving her arms and face, not getting snagged as much. It was warmer too, the sun pushing further into the edge of the forest, heating the air. However, the ground was more overgrown, wet grass dragging at her feet and vines tripping her up; and it was also wetter, her shoes getting stuck in pools, puddles and patches of mud. Her boots were so big that every sticky patch, every grabbing vine, tried to pull them off. Hearing the buses pass, she would step away from the roadway and crouch deep into the scrub, waiting before moving on.

When darkness embraced her, she turned her back on the streetlights of the roadway and felt her way deep into the darkness. She could not find anywhere to sleep so she wrapped herself in her blanket and lay down, hoped there would be no animals to burrow into her flesh, no humans to grab her in the dark, no rain to soak into her bones.

Dinner was the last crumbs of biscuit from her first packet. She wanted rat or rabbit but hadn't caught any.

When the light of morning painted the tops of the trees with gloss, she walked back to the edge of the road. A noise alerted her to the morning buses. She dived into the trees and crawled away. Over the monster roar of the diesels, a copter and its airborne escort could be heard, flying backwards and forwards over the convoy.

The buses disappeared and she ran as fast as she could along the edge of the road. In her haste she sometimes she had to jump onto it to duck around a shrub, around a thicket too thick to push through. It would not be long before the convoy returned, maybe with an escort; there was no way to guess what was coming.

They came and she was again in the bushes, terrified. The copter stopped, hovering closely like it had seen her, before moving on.

The buses finished passing and the road was empty. She took a chance and ran for it; jogged for a while on the white concrete roadway, dived into the trees when the road crossed a small creek, sat on the bank, drank water and ate some of the horrible biscuits. Back to the side of the road again, moving as fast as she could through the trees until the next convoy came. Then the next and the next.

She measured her day by the movement and sound of buses and convoys. She realised she had not seen the soup van for days, worried for the people starving in the wasteland around the city, worried it was her fault. There was nothing she could do about it but feel guilty.

A strange noise, like wheels on concrete but unaccompanied by the sound of engines, stopped her. She cast herself into the angry bush, crawled as deep as she could, the trees punishing her. She could not turn around, the scrub was too thick. It grabbed onto her clothes and skin like hands full of pins. The song of wheels had been joined by a faint motor sound. She knew the sound. An electric car was moving slowly down the road.

She crawled out of her cover once it passed, turned to face the road and dug herself as deep into the wiry scratchy bush as she could. The wait was not long. She barely had enough time to catch her breath before the electric car moaned back the other way down the road, Agency men at every window staring out intently as it travelled by.

Shaken, she crawled deeper into the trees and didn't move for hours. Here, she spent another restless night.

The next day, between the first bus of the morning and the last bus of the afternoon, she made it to where the forest ended. Ahead was a field, no cover to be had. She would have to cross this expanse in full view of drones, of copters, of anyone who looked. She was tired and hadn't eaten today; soon she would collapse no matter what she did.

She sat down on a stump at the edge of the forest, ate her chocolate and cried.

THE CENTRE CANNOT HOLD

SHE HAD NO alternative. Christine crossed the open ground at night under the cover of darkness, crawling through grass, getting caught on blackberry vines, picking thorns and small stones out of her hands and knees. There were still buses, but not so many; there were still cameras, but she hoped they would not be able to see her in the dark.

Across the field, surrounded by razor wire lit with painfully bright floodlights, were buildings five storeys high and boxy. If they were apartments, there was room for hundreds of people. There might even have been more buildings behind them. Room for thousands. She couldn't see that far. It looked like a prison camp from an old movie.

Nobody and nothing moved around outside.

She crawled slowly through the night, closer to the fence and the lights and the cameras. In the morning she hid, prone on her belly, in the best cover she could find, a yellowing thicket of barely waist-high ferns. She could see the fence from there and hoped nobody, human or otherwise, could see her. People started to mill around before there was light. She was not close enough to identify any of them, but from a distance, they looked to be wearing the black of servants as they passed through the splash of spotlights. Eventually, the bus convoy roared out a gate in the fence.

She could see no way in through the fence but the gate, which was flanked by guard towers and auto-guns. When the buses returned, they entered the compound through the same gate and disappeared.

Christine did not want to go into that place, where the servants must be imprisoned, where she herself could be caught. Security would find her. She smelled so bad she was surprised they could not smell her from inside the fence.

Even in the ferns, the air was hotter than her blood, sucking life from her; the sunlight poked through gaps in the foliage threatening to burn. She tried sleeping on the soft damp ground, with the warmth of the sun on her face.

She could not sleep, she could not wake, she could not leave purgatory. She could not even die.

From time to time she was shaken awake by the noise of the buses leaving, a copter flying overhead, smaller machines pursuing it, the buses returning. Her sleep was fitful. Every noise was Security coming to get her. Every sound – mouse feet on sticks, the hoot of an owl, the rustle of leaves in the wind – shook her to full wakefulness. Every time, falling asleep got harder.

Every dream she remembered when waking was of Sienna.

These were not happy dreams; she saw Sienna chained, Sienna in the prison she herself had been a resident of, Sienna beaten by Security, zapped screaming to unconsciousness by stun prods.

More buses, big and small, came and went. More drones too, circling widely but somehow, miraculously, not passing over her. The copter passed overhead. Christine prayed the ferns and the ragged filth of her clothing would shield her from prying eyes.

When darkness fell she rose from her hiding place, edged to the fence, and stayed on the penumbra between the lights and the night, not knowing how close would be too risky. All night she walked. Another road on almost the opposite side from where she had started led to a scattering of lights, like stars thrown carelessly on the ground, like Mother's jewellery box struck by a beam of light.

It was too far away to make it to this new landmark before dawn. Finding a thicket, she scraped her way in. The only noises were the scritching and scratching of small things in the undergrowth, the breath of the wind and the keening of her soul. Despite her fear, she slept.

That night she rose with the mist, walked through the grass-land and the low scrub to the distant lights.

It looked liked a town but without a wall or a fence, an exposed place anyone could enter. The houses would have no protection from people like her; damaged people from the wilderness. She walked towards it slowly, the lights resolving into the windows of single-storey houses scattered across a low hillside.

She walked.

Low houses, what looked like a row of shops, no security she could see, no wall or fence around the town, no lenses sparkling in the lights, no blinking red LEDs. Streetlights lit the streets just enough to see. She snuck to the edge of the field of lights and looked for somewhere to hide.

There was a road that came out into the field, ending abruptly like something unfinished. She followed it and passed the front yards of houses, the light from the windows and occasional streetlights revealing little about them. A crossroads appeared, houses down every street. She kept walking and came to a public square, a stand of trees in the middle of it. Finding a clearing in the trees, she sat down.

In the distance, the sky grew light in the east.

Christine feared what would happen if she was caught in that town, in those trees, with no permission to be there, nowhere to go; but she saw no option but to stay and hide. She prepared herself, ready to run, as people emerged from their houses. Across the road a person walked into a shop, turned the CLOSED sign to OPEN; someone walked in moments later. A car exited silently from a driveway, turned and drove away to Christine's left. She watched it until it was out of sight.

A sudden noise to her right made her turn her head. A woman stood near the trees. She was not as white as Christine but not as bronze as Sienna, and dressed in clean but old clothes. She was smiling at Christine. It made her nervous, but the smile was open and trusting; there was nothing sinister about it.

Not a familiar expression for someone from Safetown.

Regardless, Christine turned to run, suddenly deeply afraid.

'Don't run,' the woman said quickly, reaching out a hand. 'I won't hurt you, I promise. Nobody here will hurt you. You are safe here.'

Christine took a step, stumbled to a stop, her mind stuck between fear and resignation. She turned around again and faced the woman, might not have done so if she was not so tired, so thirsty, so unbearably hungry.

Christine sagged, ready to die; already imprisoned, she felt the next breath would be her last.

She could do nothing but try and catch her breath.

The air moved like the sky was breathing, making leaves dance, brushing through her hair like a soft hand. It stole her breath, stole the tears from her eyes, took her hope and carried it away; she hoped Sienna was waiting for it somewhere. The other woman, the outsider, was talking but she could not hear the words through the roaring of blood in her ears.

Christine waited to die. She waited for this woman from outside the Wall, this carrier of disease, this criminal, this terrorist, and the monster of all her nightmares, to kill her. But this woman did not look dangerous. She was probably less dangerous than Christine, who was aware of all she had done to survive outside the Wall.

She had a shiv in her pocket and an axe in her hand. What could happen that was worse than what had already occurred?

She could not die here, she would not run; her breath belonged to Sienna. If this was a trap, she would fight. She hoped she wouldn't have to hurt anybody.

'Where, what is this place?' Christine asked. 'Where I come from, they said . . .' She petered out, not sure she wanted to say any more.

'I know where you came from,' the other woman said kindly. 'We see people like you sometimes, people from that place, that walled city. You are scared of us out here, think we will hurt you, but we won't.'

'I'm so tired,' Christine said. 'I have nothing left. I don't think you alone can do much to me and I'm not sure I'd care if you hurt me right now.'

The other woman laughed, then covered her mouth, looking mortified. 'That will have to do, I guess,' she said. 'Why don't you come with me? I can buy you breakfast.' She took a few steps. 'Come on, there will be coffee, I promise.'

Christine followed reluctantly, clutching her near-empty raggy bag, keenly aware of her smell as the woman led her away from the park. The cafe they went to was all whitewashed furniture, raw wood and brass; tables mismatched, each chair different.

'Coffee?' The woman laughed. 'I saw the hungry look on your face. I know that look well. How do you have it?'

Christine nodded so vigorously it made her head spin. 'If there's coffee first I don't care what happens after,' she said. 'Strong and black.' After all she had gone through, her body hadn't forgotten coffee. The desire for it crawled across her skin.

She didn't even notice the woman walking off. She hoped the woman was not calling Security.

'Where did you find her?' Christine heard from the direction of the counter.

'In the park,' the woman said. 'I don't know how long she's been out for, but she doesn't seem as damaged as some of the others. Either fairly fresh or stronger than average. Long black for each of us and a big breakfast for her.'

She thought about her family. She should not have been surprised that the smells of the place would bring them back.

'No,' said the other voice. 'No need to pay. I have this one.'

'I can't let you do that. This one's mine. I found her.'

'It's my place.'

'I found her.'

Christine could not tell what was going on, tuned the words out.

She had nearly dashed away when a hand touched her elbow. It was the woman. She gestured to a seat. It was then that Christine realised she was standing in the middle of the busy cafe. People flowed around her like water around a rock. She hastened to sit down.

'You can put the axe down.'

Christine startled, saw she was holding her axe and dropped it with a clatter. 'I'm sorry,' was all she could think of to say.

Coffee came first, a strong long black. It ran a live wire to her face and her heart, cut into her gut and shook her awake.

The taste brought it all back. Christine felt tears pour down her face. If the people in that town were not evil or criminal, as the Agency had told them, what else had they been lied to about?

What were her family involved in? Why was Sienna working for them?

She was not sure who the tears were for. Looking at the kind, warm amber eyes of the woman across from her, she could think of nothing to say, nothing to express her feelings except 'thanks'.

Saying that word, she lost control.

MONDAY

CHRISTINE'S CLOTHES WERE SO new they were making her uncomfortable. She was so clean she was surprised she didn't squeak when scritching the scabs off her arms.

The shelter – that's what they called it – was empty except for Christine. There were six empty bedrooms, all identically furnished in blonde wood and cream, plain comfortable furniture. She had the choice. She chose the first floor, a storey above ground, not as high as her childhood bedroom had been, but higher than the dirt she had been sleeping in. They told her that people from where she came from turned up sometimes, even whole families, or groups travelling together. The shelter was there, they said, so people like her could get back on their feet.

'What happens later?' she had asked the volunteer. 'What happens when people get back on their feet?'

'Some people go back to the ruins, to watch the Wall, they want to get back to that place, but at least we can feed and clean them up, give them medical help first.' She said that last bit like it was a slogan. 'Some stay here in town and work, some settle down, get married, raise families. Some get on the train, go to the mainland.'

There was nothing to go back to. The choice was to stay here or go elsewhere. Then the thought that had skimmed her brain came back and slapped her.

'The train is here?'

@

Once she had been told the train was close she could not stand being in that sweet little town anymore. The train could take her to Sienna.

The whole town knew she was leaving, that she was chasing a lover she didn't know how to find; they even knew it was a woman and taught her a new word.

Lesbian.

Women who love women.

They told her it was not a bad thing, just a thing; even a thing to be proud of.

She wept. She had never imagined her love being anything other than a crime or a problem.

They gave her a backpack and packed her lunch. A volunteer drove her to the train station.

There was a smell to the air, a metallic scent, rot and sulphur and the stink of a road after rain. The volunteer who had driven her to the train station told her it was the taste of the sea, carried on the wind from kilometres away, the breath of life. Christine considered asking to be taken there, to see the ocean, the waves something she had always imagined, but she said nothing. She had relied on their help too much already.

She had somewhere to be.

What she had imagined on the air in her parents' home was only a ghost of what the sea really smelled like, and what it smelled like was like nothing else.

The train was leaving soon and she was determined to be on it.

The ticket collector did not check her ID, which was lucky because she had none. She had nothing from her old life except her useless phone. They waved her through the gate in the chain-link fence, rusty in places where age had attacked it, shiny in others where it had been recently patched. She turned to wave her thanks to the man who had driven her there, but could not see him.

A man stood on the other side of the fence, wearing a charcoal suit, open-collared white shirt and opaque sunglasses. There was something about the way he was staring at her that made her uneasy, something more than his obvious resemblance to the man she had been questioned by in prison. He walked towards the gate and was stopped by the ticket collector, who gestured for him to go to the ticket office.

Her knees felt like jelly.

Someone spoke close to Christine's ear. 'Excuse me, love. The train is leaving, you need to get aboard.' Christine turned around in a panic and saw a man in a uniform with 'guard' embroidered over his heart. He was smiling, looked kind. In a whisper, he continued, 'We can't stop that Agency man from buying a ticket and getting on the train, but we are due to leave soon enough, and we may accidentally leave earlier before he can finish buying a ticket.'

'What?'

'Hopefully, the ticket office can dither a bit, give you more time.'

'What?'

The train guard bustled her towards the train. 'It's okay. We know where you are from. We were told there was a passenger coming from that place, going to the city to look for someone. I don't know why that Agency man is interested in you, it doesn't matter to me. All that matters is that he doesn't get you. You need to get on the train now.'

A drone flew overhead as fast as she had ever seen one move. Christine allowed herself to be nudged towards the door of the train just as the sound of a quadcopter invaded her ears.

'Get in, sit down,' the train guard said, pushing her on. He spoke on a device that looked like a bulky phone with an antenna and somewhere a bell chimed. Christine sat down in the mostly empty carriage, the seat more comfortable than she expected, and stared out the window towards the tin and rust ticket office. The Agency man emerged, walking towards the ticket collector, who seemed to not be paying attention to anything but the train.

The Agency man thrust his ticket at the man with excessive aggression, his arms twitching like he was resisting the urge to raise a fist. The ticket collector took his sweet time, handing the ticket back just as the train started moving, just as a rushing copter became visible in the distance, growing larger. The Agency man fought to the gate but it was closed, a red warning light flashing above it; he beat against it.

The train built up speed and the copter turned to chase it. Christine knew they could never outrun a copter, knew it would catch up, stop the train and drag her off. Whatever happened after that would not be good. She quivered in fear. All she had gone through would be for nothing if that copter caught the train.

The acceleration of the train pushed her back against the chair, pushed her stomach contents up towards her mouth.

The sky went out.

For a long, breathless moment, Christine found herself surrounded by absolute darkness, even darker than the nights in the ruins, the nights in the forest thickets; darker than hiding under the covers as a child from imagined monsters outside the Wall. Her mind unhinged. She must be dead.

Then down the carriage, yellow lights flickered on and filled the train, almost blinding after such absolute darkness.

On the other side of the aisle, an old woman leaned over towards Christine. 'First time on the train, dear?' she asked with a tone that suggested she already knew the answer.

Christine just nodded.

'We are underground now, heading for the tube, a steel tube in the water. I wonder why they didn't make it glass or clear plastic so we could see out, but they say that's impossible. That's why it's so dark.'

'Thank you,' Christine said.

'Was that copter chasing after you?'

She didn't know how to lie about that. 'I think so.'

The other woman looked concerned, not for herself but for Christine. She shook her head faintly then spoke again. 'Well, I don't think they will get ahead of the train with that machine of theirs. The trains are too fast. You are safe now, I imagine.'

Christine leaned back in her seat and let her slow, measured breaths free her locked-in tears. She cried for Mother, who she both loved and hated but who she would never see again, for Father's love which she knew was gone, for all the women in Safetown in gilded cages; for Jack.

But not for herself; she was on her way to somewhere else, somewhere she hoped Sienna would be.

The train re-emerged into the light, slowed and stopped. She looked out to a windswept grass-green island, a station that was no more than a concrete slab and a weather shelter the size of a double garage painted chroma key blue. A couple of people were waiting impassively for the train, none of them frightening, none of them in suits. Silence stalked inside the train and she held her breath until they started moving again. She saw, but could not hear, the copter approaching as the train rolled away from the station.

She could not relax until they were back in the tube.

Another island, another station, a longer time in the tube. She felt trapped in there, terrified by the inevitable arrival of Agency men. They might be waiting for her when the train broke through to the surface. They might already be on the train, waiting for the right moment to make their move. She felt sure she was already caught, wished she understood why they were pursuing her when she was no longer around to shame her parents.

After an eternity, they were on the surface, then they were in the sky, the train travelling on a viaduct over a treed, rocky coast. On one side, a vast rough sea; on the other side, a forested spur of hills and ridges. Christine breathed more freely, realised from the relief in her chest how frightened she had been. The sky outside the train was wide and hot blue. She could hear the air conditioning in the train screaming, but could neither see nor hear a copter.

Forests, wooded hills, farmland, rolling pastures, small towns, all went by so fast she could barely make sense of them. The train slowed along the edge of a town and came to a stop at yet another station. There was nobody waiting to get on. The train paused only briefly before rolling on.

It was then she saw it. A quadcopter landed and charcoal suits poured out, running through the heat haze onto the concrete platform of the station just as it flowed out of sight.

More hills, more towns, more pastures, surprised cows and terrified sheep, idling cars at crossings. They crossed rivers and verdant valleys on viaducts, dived in and out of short, dark tunnels. Trees blasted past, merging at speed into a green-brown blur, golden grassland between them. Small bodies of water threw sparks of reflected sunlight at her eyes.

The train started slowing. There was no sign of a town, only a heavily wooded hill, glossy and green, almost glowing in the light. Small clouds chased each other across the sky, played games, teased the sun. The highway was not far away from the train, on the sunny side of the track. Christine had never seen such a wide road, three lanes, what looked like a long streak of forest. Then more road that played peekaboo between the trees.

There was a loud noise and a copter rose overhead, racing along the top of the train. Christine was not sure which machine was faster.

The copter would have her when they stopped at the next station.

The green hill, which was more of a mountain, got closer, poking jauntily out of a forest, wearing a green overcoat. The copter overflew the train, forcing it to escape vertically. Metal and stone glowed in the mountain of green in the distance, then the train dived into a tunnel of grey concrete lit with yellow lights.

The train stopped. They were at an underground station. Christine had no idea what to do.

'Welcome to Melbourne. This is our last station. Change here for metropolitan trains,' a voice crackled over hidden speakers.

Christine stood up, shouldered her bag, checked everything that mattered was in her pockets and stepped out onto a platform enclosed by concrete. Everything looked old, tan tiles, chipped paint. The train on which she had come lay lightly on its tracks.

The woman from across the aisle stood beside Christine. It took her a moment to realise she was speaking.

'It's okay, dear. You have to get off here,' the woman said. 'This train goes to the freight depot now. We need to go through there.' She pointed to a rectangular opening in the nearest wall that everyone else on the train was already making their way to. 'You can get a train there. Do you know where you are going?'

'No,' Christine sobbed. 'I don't know anyone. I don't even know where I am or why I am here.'

'Ah, you are from that place then. Is that why the Agency men were chasing you?'

Christine stared at her with shock, and a little fear.

'Oh, don't be afraid. I catch this train once a fortnight. You are not the first person from that place I have met. The first time I didn't know what to say, how to help. I worried about that poor boy, so I found out what I needed to know.'

Christine looked at her expectantly.

'You get the train into the city, get off when it ends, leave the station and there's an office across the road for . . . I think they are called Refugee and Exile Services. They will help you.'

Christine just stood there.

'Are you okay, dear?'

'I don't have a ticket from here to the city. I don't have any money to get a ticket, I don't have a credit card, I have nothing to eat.' She stopped to take in a hacking breath. 'I don't have anything.'

'Don't worry,' said the older woman, steering her towards the train, 'the trains are free, everywhere in the city. Keeps cars off the road. We are doing our bit. Not long now until cars become completely unnecessary.'

Christine had no idea what she was talking about. They walked together and she lacked the energy to resist. As they popped out of the tunnel and into the crowded open space, the woman disappeared.

Slipping her hand into her pocket, Christine felt the rubbed-soft piece of paper folded up safely. Sienna's number was on there if she could still read it, if she could find a phone; if Sienna wanted to see her. Standing lost in the crowd, she wept, unable to stop herself.

Suddenly the woman from the train was in front of her again, holding a small cardboard box, a wooden fork and a pile of brown paper napkins.

'Here,' she said, handing it all to Christine. 'I suppose you are starving. I don't know what you like to eat but I assume you're not vego or vegan. I imagine if you have made it this far alive, you would have stopped worrying about what you ate a long time ago. Welcome to civilisation.'

Then she was gone again.

Christine walked over to the train platform, nauseous with fear, weak from hunger. The food in the box smelled delicious but she felt too sick to eat it. Yet she was starved.

The doors of the train were open and she stepped in. The seats were in pairs on each side, each pair facing a matching set. Christine sat down, facing the direction she hoped would be forward when the train started moving. She had no idea how long a trip it would be.

Opening the box of food, she let the smell waft over her. She poked her fork into it. There was melted cheese on top of chips, and on top of the cheese was shaved meat of some sort topped with sticky sauces.

The confusing gloop in the cardboard box was one of the most delicious things she could remember ever having tasted. Taking the meat, sauce, cheese and chips into her mouth at once was better than breathing. She ate it too fast and sheepishly wiped sticky sauce off her face with one of the napkins.

The train moved fast through leafy suburbs, some of them so packed with plants, the houses so overwhelmed with life, they looked like forests rather than places where people could live. Yet there were happy faces everywhere.

The train dropped in and out of tunnels, trenches, under bridges overflowing with verdancy. More than once they passed mounts of green. Christine thought they were hills the first time, then realised they were clusters of buildings, covered so completely with vines and plants they looked like cloud forests; large glass panels glistening on any free spaces, reflecting the sky.

Crowds flowed on and off the train like the tide. An array of people rotated on the seats before her, nobody staying long, each dressed nothing at all like the person who had sat there before them, hair of colours she could not have imagined. A tattooed teenager offered Christine a banana from a sack. Nobody had tattoos except criminals she had seen on the news on Safetynet. There was no sign of Agency men, there was no sound of copters or drones. Nothing but the insulated rattle of steel wheels on tracks, the hum of electric motors and the burr of air conditioning and the murmur of people talking quietly.

They stopped at a station. The sign outside said 'Flinders Street'. A couple of minutes later she realised the train was not moving on. Maybe this was her stop. Gathering her bag and the empty box from her meal, she rushed out the door and stood on the crowded platform in confusion.

The train moved off before Christine did.

There was a track on the other side of the platform she stood on and then another track and then another platform. There were stairs going up and an escalator like the ones in the shopping malls back home. The roof was tin and what looked like wrought iron, old-looking, like the university. But there was an authenticity to it that she had not seen back home.

She had no home.

She needed to get out of the station, to find what help she could. Yet she could not move. There was a metal bench behind her in the middle of the platform. She moved over and sat on it.

Trains rattled in, hissed to a stop, rattled away, people came and stood in front of her, sat down beside her. Her buttock muscles began to hurt. Someone stopped to stare at her. Still she could not move.

A train pulled away with the whirr of electric motors and before her, across two tracks on the next platform, was a man staring at her. He wore a charcoal suit, white shirt, black tie. He kept staring at her until a train pulled into Christine's platform, blocking her view of him. Catalysed into movement she picked up her bag and allowed herself to flow up the escalator with the crowd.

The suited man was coming down the escalator only two feet away. He snatched at Christine and she half fell onto the random person next to her. She started climbing her way up, shoving through the crowd, saying, 'Excuse me, sorry, sorry, excuse me.' The man turned, tried to go up the down-escalator, but there were too many people going down, holding him in place. He stared at Christine balefully.

She reached the top of the escalator and knew the man had probably reached the bottom and was heading up again. He could push through the crowds, move faster than the machine would take him, just like Christine had. She had only moments.

Across the crowd was a roofed space that opened up into the wide streets in two directions, bright blue sky and harsh light. She could see hundreds of people, thousands; more people than she had imagined there being in the world. She could lose herself in that crowd but it was too obvious a way to run. The Agency man would follow and catch her.

She turned right, headed deeper into the station, moving as fast as she could to the third in a line of escalators, stepped onto it before turning around to see if she was being followed. It did not look like she had been seen.

At the bottom she strode down the left side of the platform, blending into the hordes of people, all the way to the end. There was no escalator on that side, only a short ramp leading to an ancient, tiled tunnel. She turned left, hoping she would not get lost, but hoping even more that she had confounded those following her.

Walking swiftly down the tunnel towards the light, she found herself climbing a short flight of stairs onto the stone-paved bank of a wide brown river. The sun looked to her like a killer, desiccating and dangerous, but in her jeans and t-shirt she had more hope of surviving it than the Agency man in his suit. She turned left again, heading for the shade under a road bridge. There, she caught what breath she had left and leaned against the cool damp concrete.

This was not what she had expected to see outside of her hometown. The opposite bank of the river was bisected by the shadow of the bridge, the left side verdant, a vast park with a few buildings scattered along the edge. The right side was built up and packed with people, like a giant breathing creature.

Buildings, glass, steel, concrete, rooftop gardens, plants escaping in cascades down walls – and light, so much light. Everywhere it could fit there was green, trees packed wherever there was soil, smaller trees in planters where there was not.

It was like a fever dream of a civic heaven, all light and beauty and people in connection with the natural world, which appeared to have been invited into all human spaces. Birds flew and roosted, ate seeds from feeders positioned where, in Safetown, there would have been cameras.

And everywhere there were people, men, women, people she could not determine either way, every spectrum of skin colour from darker than Sienna to lighter than her. Thoughts of Sienna made her shake.

There was a column of glass to her left, the buttons suggesting an elevator. She walked in and pushed the up button, the doors closed. They opened on the other side and she stepped out onto a footpath near some kind of public square: stone, sloping ground and steps. It looked like the train station was on the other side of the wide road.

Christine walked briskly up a stone-paved hill, down some stairs, across a road and up an alley painted in a riot of colour and smelling of spray paint.

She could almost feel the breath of the Agency man on her neck. She kept walking, fast.

ZOOM – MELBOURNE

THE CITY BREATHES like a living thing, like all great cities, but in the case of Melbourne that is not just a metaphor. No city is more green, more dedicated to fighting global warming through the growth of biomass; sometimes it has more in common with a rainforested mountain than a city, forever wet, the walls of the buildings dripping green life, taking advantage of vertical space to grow life, to grow food, to create a green utopia. It is home to ten million people yet has a carbon footprint of close to zero.

Melbourne was the fastest of the world's cities to change, the citizens there fought for their city, providing free services, bringing nature to the urban landscape, ending poverty and creating a type of utopia.

In certain light Melbourne sparkles like a water droplet, the small areas of roof that are not garden, too sloped, too old, too weak-structured to support soil or even hydroponics, are covered in photovoltaics. They reflect what light they cannot use back into the sky.

WEDNESDAY

THE DAY WAS warm, the air summer-clammy. The alleyway stank of piss, ancient beer and bins. Roofs, balconies and signs hung overhead, making the thin arrow of sky above appear even narrower. Christine sat on a low step before a doorway with her bag on her knees. She could not see the street; the laneway ended with more alleys on each end, more trash, the sort of graffiti she knew from Safetynet was used by gangs to mark their territory, like animals.

Up ahead, a door opened and a spiky-haired man in a white cook's uniform stepped out and threw a bag of trash into a huge rectangular bin, the hollow clink of glass bottles echoing off the hard surface. Stopping in the middle of the stone-paved alley between two buildings of blue-grey stone, in the shade of high-up rooftop gardens, he pulled out a small device, put it to his mouth, took it away and blew smoke into the sky. It dispersed almost immediately like fog.

He turned to her, waved a hand with a gesture that could have been half of a tentative wave. She flinched, tried to burrow backwards through the door, pulled her knees tight against her chest and hugged them as her bag flopped to the flagstones. He shrugged, blew more smoke out of his mouth, put the device in his pocket and went back inside, closing the steel door splattered with gang tags behind him.

Christine watched the door for a while, but it did not reopen. She was alone in the alley. Letting go of her legs, she stretched out. Her stomach hurt; she had not had anything to eat for at least twenty-four hours. The memory of her last meal made her stomach flip. The smell of rot and piss, the sticky flagstones, made her sick.

She was confused, frightened.

Keeping an eye out for anyone watching, she walked over to the huge bin. The bag the man had thrown in was atop a huge mound of other bags. Poking her finger into the plastic, she pulled. It tore easily. Kitchen waste, bottles and food scraps spilled out. She could see a half-eaten burger, still partially together; half a steak, bloodily rare; other scatterings that looked like they might be edible.

She had eaten worse.

Hearing the faint creaking of the door opening behind her, she grabbed the half-burger with one hand and the piece of steak with the other, hooked her bag with her arm and ran for it.

Out on the street, Christine nearly collided with a stranger, bumped into another one, ran into a narrow road, barely dodged a car that honked angrily, and fled into another alleyway where she hid behind a bin. There was a narrow doorway, slightly inset, the door ornately panelled like something from another age. She sat on the step and leaned against the wooden door, the angles of the panelling massaging her angry back.

The sun overhead kicked a hole through the clouds to paint the alleyway with a terrifying brilliance. The blue-grey flagstones glowed as if they were internally lit. There was a fairytale brightness to everything Christine could see; in that canyon of stone, brick, graffiti and steel it disturbed the status quo.

Maybe it was the hunger, but the cold second-hand burger was delicious, the meat, sauce and salad still moist. She consumed the steak so fast she barely chewed, almost choking on the meat. Only when the animal urge to feed herself had been assuaged did she look around properly and realise that the place was not as secure as the last one.

People walked past at the end of the alleyway in both directions, a rainbow of hair colour, a spectrum of skin tone, a riot of dress. Someone stopped on the street and looked at her. He was a dark man, darker than anybody she had ever seen; staring at her from the end of the alley. She hoped he would go away. He didn't.

He walked towards her, and as he got closer she could see he was tall, his face angular, his head shaved; he was so lanky he was almost a skeleton. Walking slowly, he held his hands in front, palms facing her. Christine stood, the flutter of her heart shaking her entire self.

She backed away, tripping over her own feet, staggered until she could get them under herself again. Her lungs hurt, her vision blurred. She felt like a rat in a wire snare.

She turned and ran out of the alley, away from the man.

Finding another doorway, she sat to catch her breath. Her ribs were grinding into her heart, compressing her lungs; her breath was a trapped bird, fluttering in her mouth. She tried to rest but the steel door was cold and hard, the step was even colder.

When the door behind her opened, she tumbled backwards into a hallway, stared at yellowed plaster, specks of mould and plastic conduit, and the white oval of a scared face. Christine rolled and fell back into the alley. Getting her feet under her, she stumbled and bounced off the side of a slow-moving van. She stood again and ran.

Later she sat on a deconstructed cardboard box, hugging her bag with one arm through the strap, watching the sun collapse. Night came to the city, working into the alleys and overhangs first, then moving onto the narrower streets, fighting the last of the sun on the battlefields of high walls. Lights flickered on in the streets but their glow did not quite reach where Christine sat. The people walking past the end of the alley were silhouettes, wrapped in a penumbra where cool fog caught the light.

The glow of the city reflected off low-lying clouds, making a lie of the night-time dark. The faint sound of music and laughter could be heard somewhere. Electric cars and larger trucks passed the end of the alley, casting light before them with their headlights, adding their notes to the song of the city. Christine flinched when a siren started, when a blue flashing light joined the yell of a siren as it passed. She would have run if she was not so scared, if she was not so tired.

She shivered, not sure if it was the cold or fear that shook her bones. She feared to sleep there in the city, wondered how she could get a ticket out, back to the island, back to the wasteland, where she understood the dangers. Her heart was racing, her limbs were leaden, her demons came at her out of the shadows.

THURSDAY

IT HAD BEEN a mistake to fall asleep seated in a doorway. Christine's head, bones, muscles, even her skin ached. She had only woken when the sun slapped her.

She had no idea where she was.

She had to find a way to somewhere safer. Even that town near the train must be better than here, this nightmare place, where every evil she feared lived. The people she had seen on the Safetynet news, killing, robbing, hating, rioting, dominated her imagination. She could not be safe as long as she was in this place.

Christine knew of only one place to find something to eat. In desperation, she returned to the alley from which she had run earlier. Or was it the day before? Or the day before that? She was losing track of time. Back to the alley where it had all started going wrong.

Everything not green was made of that blue-grey stone; it was between the cascading plants on the buildings, it threw into contrast the floor of the alleys, where nothing green grew, where the only thing besides stone was thickets of bins and explosions of spray paint. In the street, whirring, near-silent electric cars and clacking bicycles chased each other up and down, their combined song the dominant tone of the city. People's breaths combined into a new being that breathed like a great monster, a creature of stone, steel and flesh.

She found the not-quite-unfamiliar stench of the alley comforting. It reminded her of other places: the car park below the apartment that was to be hers, of the bin in which she had hidden in fear. It reminded her too of the wasteland, of the rot of human refuse and human skin, of the damp of broken stone, mouldering concrete and rotting dead. None of these were good memories, but they were all she had; they were familiar and familiar made her comfortable.

Her bag was secure on her back, her coat pulled around her and buttoned tight, even though the air was just a little too warm for it. She walked over to the bin, hoping there would be another bag of food in there, forgetting that it was not the same time of day. The heavy steel lid creaked.

The bin had been emptied since she had been there last. There was only one bag sitting in an inch-deep film of rot. She leaned against the side of the bin and tipped herself in, trying to reach for the bag, then heard the kitchen door to the cafe opening. She swung back onto her feet and started to run before halting suddenly. The pressure on her shoulders was making her feel like they were being ripped off. She pulled her arms out of the straps of her backpack and continued running.

Christine came to a rest in a covered tunnel down another alley, not remembering what paths she had taken or what corners she had turned to get there. She felt keenly the lack of weight on her back. Better to be caught than to lose her backpack; if only she had realised that before.

It was a challenge retracing steps that she could not consciously remember having taken. She had run further than she had thought. No sense of time. No sense of distance. Her mind struggled to hold a thought. She feared that soon she would start talking to herself, that even if she recovered her bag and left the city, found some other place, some other way to contact Sienna, it would be too late. She had seen madness out in the wastelands, knew the signs; there might soon be none of herself left to care about the parts she had lost.

She kept to the shadows, close to the dripping, green-draped buildings. Cars whirred past her in the street as she forced herself calm. A pigeon, healthier than the ones she had killed and eaten in the ruins, fluttered past; she thought of drones, she thought of snares. Somewhere above, a falcon screamed.

The smell of food flipped her stomach, came from corners, from doorways, from containers in strangers' hands; she toyed with the idea of snatching a container of food, knew that would be foolish, but was not sure she could stop herself.

She feared she would go mad.

She reached the alley where she had left her bag and approached the bin. Of course her backpack was not there. Whoever had come through the door had stolen it, or handed it to the authorities. It didn't matter which, she was doomed either way.

She had to think, but her head was not quite working right. Turning, she walked towards the doorway where only yesterday she had taken refuge. Stopping, she took stock of where she was. There was the doorway she had sat on, there on the step was her backpack. She approached the step. It could not be there, yet there it was.

On top of her backpack was a paper bag that was not hers. She was scared. What if it was something placed there to trap her? A bomb? Reaching down, she picked up the paper bag. Then shrugging to herself, she opened it. Inside wrapped in more paper was a bread roll with meat and salad.

She feared it was poisoned but was too hungry to throw it away. Sitting down on the step, she ate and waited to die.

FRIDAY

THERE WAS A sign on the door, 'Refugee and Exile Services'. She stood before it in a choked panic, fearful of the unknown, of the consequences should she step through that portal. It had not been hard to find once she pulled her head together and started looking. Despite the fear stealing her breath, everybody in the square had been helpful when she had asked for directions. In the end a large man covered in tattoos, with a shaved head, had walked her to the door, as if he was worried she would get lost.

She didn't even think of thanking him; hated herself for that.

Now she was there, she could not muster the courage to reach for the door handle.

It had been another long cold night sleeping on the streets. Then, in the morning, as the light of day assaulted her tired eyes, she had seen an Agency man at the end of the alleyway and run for it. She wove through alleys, into and out of buildings, as drones buzzed overhead; she hid under trees, climbed the stairs inside a building to the roof, ready to jump. They knew she was in the streets; she was not safe.

There was nothing else to do. She had no money, she was hungry, she was tired and dirty. The Agency men were out there searching for her. She could almost see them questioning everybody they could find, searching every alley she might have visited. There might be a hidden camera in that place where she had slept, that place where someone had left her a sandwich.

Remembering the kindness implicit in the bag that had been left for her on the step, she felt bolder. Perhaps the people at the Refugee and Exile Services could help her get away from the Agency men. Or at least give her a ticket to get back to the place where she had caught the train.

She felt the worn piece of paper in her pocket. Perhaps they could call Sienna. If she could speak to Sienna or, even more unlikely, if she could find Jack, she didn't care what happened to her after that.

She opened the door.

A waiting room. She could smell coffee. A stunning woman with eggshell blue hair and black eyes was seated behind a desk made of dark wood, smiling warmly.

'Can I help you?' Her voice matched her smile.

'I . . .' – Christine stumbled – 'I have been sleeping in the street. I, I came by train from the wastelands, the wastes around the walled town. I don't even know what you people out here call it. Safetown. I was exiled, I have nothing. I think the Agency are looking for me. I don't know why they are looking for me.' She felt faint. 'Somebody, somebody on the train, I don't know how many days ago, three maybe, told me I could come here for help.'

'Of course,' Eggshell Hair said, 'that's what we are here for. Nobody new has come in for a few weeks at least, but we will be here as long as those places still exist. There's a coffee machine over there' – she gestured to a corner – 'biscuits and stuff. You are welcome to eat the food on the table and in the fridge. Local people drop off stuff from time to time, so help yourself. It's okay, make yourself a coffee and take a seat. Someone will be with you soon. Don't worry about those Agency men. They know better than to come here.'

The machine pumped out coffee and she took a small choc-olate from the table; she could not bear the thought of biscuits. Collecting her beverage, she sat down and finished it quickly. She could feel the coffee doing her good, soon she might actually become human again.

Nobody stopped her when she went for another cup and she resisted an inexplicable caffeinated desire to dance to the beat of the machine. Grabbing some sort of mystery sandwich, she sat down again, sipped her coffee more slowly this time and ate carefully. Half the mug remained to be drunk and not a crumb of food was left when someone came out of a back room and stood before her.

'Hi, I'm Karl. If you come with me, we can work out how we can help you.'

She stared at him, desperate to see something in him she could trust. He was shorter than average, his head shaved bald like a criminal on Safetynet; his face was so closely shaved she could see no shadow or sign of facial hair. His voice and mannerisms reminded her a bit of Jack. That inclined her to trust him despite her almost unshakable fear.

He gestured for her to stand. 'You can bring your drink,' he said. 'You look like you need it.' He laughed. It was a sweet sound. 'I would not even try to take something off someone holding it so tight their knuckles are white.'

Christine followed him down a lifeless corridor; the carpet institutional sandpaper, the walls a colour so nondescript that she knew she would not be able to describe it later.

The room they entered had pleasant pictures of beaches and forest-edged lakes on the walls, a coffee table and a couple of armchairs. Christine sat down in one of the armchairs and put her mug on the table with only the faintest clunk. The seat was probably not comfortable, but it was to someone who had barely had anything padded to sit on for months. She worried she might fall asleep.

'It would be easier if I knew your name,' Karl said.

'Oh, sorry.' Her breath caught at the thought of what she had become. 'Christine.'

'Well, Christine, this office is to help the people who arrive here as refugees or as exiles from any of the private corporate, religious or political enclaves. Is that why you are here?'

'Corporate, religious or political enclaves.' Her tone made it a question.

'Several organisations have established walled enclaves where only the people they consider the right type are allowed to live. Government policies and laws at the time made it possible. Some of them are planned gated suburbs, others are religious and cult compounds.'

'I came from a walled city,' Christine said after a moment of confusion. 'My dad was a banker or something.'

'What was your town called, Christine?'

'We mostly just called it "Home" or "Town", but it was officially known as Safetown.'

Karl nodded. 'Safetown is an economic and sociopolitical enclave. It was started by people who were both extremely wealthy and scared of people they considered to be different. They believed a homogeneous society was a healthy society. We get a lot of exiles from there, people the founders of the town consider undesirable.'

That was her.

'We were established so there would be somewhere for refugees and exiles from those places to go,' Karl explained. 'The people of this city want it that way. Besides, they kick their best and brightest out. Every exile makes them weaker and the world better off.'

Karl pulled out a tablet and typed some information into it. 'Okay, Christine,' he started, 'we can help you with accommodation and food vouchers, enough to be okay for a time. Can you answer some questions so that we can get an idea of the sort of issues that are bringing people here?'

Christine nodded.

'Okay, do you know why you were exiled?'

Christine nodded again, struggled for words, opened her mouth and closed it again. 'The Agency caught me kissing a servant, a woman. They told Father and he cut off my income and kicked me out of the house. Security picked me up for having no income and nowhere to live.'

Karl simply nodded.

It was so quiet. Christine realised she could not hear a television, air conditioning, the sound of phones, or even the ubiquitous buzzing of currents through wires. The hum of the city was almost inaudible. Her heartbeat began to throb in her ears, her breath caught on her throat before grinding out, her blood washed, washed – fast tiny waves – through her veins.

Suddenly she realised Karl was talking to her. 'I'm so sorry,' she breathed shamefully. 'What did you say?'

He smiled. 'We can provide you with a temporary apartment, some grocery vouchers. And this.' He handed her what looked like a phone-shaped piece of transparent plastic.

Christine didn't bother trying to hide her confusion.

'It's a phone,' said Karl. 'It's a little more advanced than what you had available in that place. I don't think they can find a way to completely secure this kind of phone so they don't let them in. You long tap here to turn it on.' He held his finger on a point in the top left corner and glowing icons appeared in the clear plastic.

'There's a charger panel in the apartment. Just leave the phone on it and it will charge. The apartment is temporary, the phone is yours. We have put credit on it but once that runs out you will have to put more on. A volunteer will show you to your apartment, help you get some groceries. If you need anything else, feel free to come back, but there will only be a skeleton staff on tomorrow.'

Christine did not realise at first that she was being dismissed. She grabbed her bag and her new phone and left the room.

SATURDAY

THE MORNING SUN was already heating the road, reflecting off the glass and metal the pink stone of the cluster of buildings and terraced stone fields across the road.

Pulling a chair over to the balcony door, she sat facing the window to eat. From the height of the sun she knew she had slept in; it looked to be nearly noon. The crowds outside were a riot of colour and unfathomably large, surging and flowing, getting on and off public transport, gathering in small groups to talk. Christine thought at first there was some event bringing them together then realised there was no pattern to the movement.

The thought it might always be that crowded on the street was terrifying; she had never imagined there being so many people in the world. She watched the watery movement of the crowd, ebbing and flowing. It was beautiful, colour and light, a particle flow, a dance. She thought she could like it there, in the city called Melbourne.

Then a pattern appeared. She was good at seeing patterns.

A man in a charcoal suit stood on the corner, then another, and another. One left, crossed the road to the diagonally opposite corner. Another appeared beside the two together. They stood there for a few breaths then scattered, walking robotically and purposefully. A drone hovered over the square. At that distance, it was silent. Another one passed by close enough to her window for her to hear it.

Her coffee was suddenly so bitter she wanted to spit the taste of it away, her sandwich like dust and ashes in her mouth. The top of her stomach, the bottom of her lungs, felt like it had been stabbed; the knife in her gut made of ice. The surveillance machines must be controlled from somewhere: a person in the street with a phone, a van full of Agency men, monitors and machines.

A white van, POLICE on the side in blue, the sort of van she had seen countless times on Safetynet chasing criminals, stopped on the side of the road. Someone got out of the passenger side, dressed in blue; they might have been looking at a hovering drone. They raised some sort of weapon.

The machines scattered. She could no longer see any charcoal suits. If there were Agency men looking for her, she could no longer identify them. They could be anywhere. But why did they appear to run from the police? That didn't make sense.

Christine realised she had been holding her breath, exhaled and took in a shuddering inhalation. Time flooded back into the world. By the sun, she realised hours had passed.

Lumbering to the couch, she grabbed the over-complicated remote control and turned on the television. Eventually finding the right button, she flicked through the channels; there were too many to make sense of. She settled on a news channel. It was nothing like the news back at home. There were no riots, no theft, no violence.

Most of the news was positive; new technologies to fight global warming, whatever that was, emission reductions making everybody safer, new medical technologies to add even more years to people's lives. She gasped when she heard that life expectancy in Australia, wherever that was, had reached a hundred and fifty years; where she came from, eighty was the limit.

How could this place outside, that she had been taught was hell, be better than Safetown? All her life she had believed the Wall, the city she lived in, had been there to keep her safe.

Flicking channels again, she watched a show where people competed to make extravagant, brightly coloured cakes. It was hypnotic and batshit insane; entertaining, relaxing mental floss. She was as tight as a piano string, and a chord had been struck an indeterminate time ago, leaving her thrumming. She lay back on the not-too-soft couch and wished she could sleep forever.

Memories of her family kept her from sleeping properly, their betrayal like hand sanitiser in a paper cut. She had not even had the chance to talk to Brandon, to ask what he thought of her being disowned. She doubted he would care but she would liked to have known. She doubted she really cared what he thought if she was honest with herself.

Christine suddenly remembered what she had done to earn her exile and sat bolt upright. It hit her at the bottom of her stomach when she thought of Sienna and the feeling flushed downwards in a wash of heat. She wanted to blame someone other than herself for her being out there, but she couldn't. Her head said wanting Sienna that way was wrong, yet her body knew it was the only right thing in her world.

The phone! The number!

Christine reached into her bag and could not find it. She emptied the bag onto the table, shook it out, checked every item in case the paper was stuck to something. She nearly screamed, turned the backpack inside out, and there it was. A folded piece of paper tangled in a fold of fabric on the seam. Worn by age and weather, darkened by the oil from her hands, the writing was barely legible.

That strange phone had credit on it. She took it out, fumbled for a time with the slick plastic, trying to turn it on. It lit up, the glowing icons for apps embedded inside the plastic. The time was onscreen: 11 p.m.

It was too late to call.

Sienna might be dead. Sienna might hate her. Sienna might not want to talk to her. It was the middle of the night.

She could not bear to be hung up on, yelled at, hated. In the end she decided to send a text message: 'Sienna, a lady serving soup in the wasteland gave me this number. I hope it's really yours. I have made it to Melbourne. This is the number to the phone Refugee and Exile Services gave me. You can reach me here. I hope they haven't done anything to hurt you. It's all my fault, I'm so sorry. I will understand if you don't ever want to hear from me again – Christine.'

She felt better after sending the message and settled down to sleep on the couch, watching cupcakes bake, watching people panic at their cakes not rising. For a moment, there was nothing in her life more terrible than a stranger on television dropping a cake on the floor.

MONDAY

CHRISTINE WOKE STARVING. She had not eaten anywhere near enough the day before. Her egg salad sandwich was on a plate on the floor near the balcony door, barely touched. The top slice of bread was stale, the egg salad somehow both congealed and melting, the bottom slice of bread so soggy bits of it fell off when she picked it up. She took it to the kitchenette, scraped the foul mess into the bin.

There was nothing in particular to do, she vibrated like a phone receiving a call. All she could do was wait.

She wished she had bought more food. She would have to go to the shops again and remember this time that she had places to store whatever she purchased, that she could buy more than a meal or a day's worth. She stuck her plain white mug under the nozzle of the machine and pushed a button. The sound of beans grinding was louder than a passing train in the otherwise near-total silence; the smell was exactly what she needed.

Halfway though her second cup, a loud buzz sounded from near the door. Immediately she thought of drones, the noise that dogged her footsteps, that haunted her sleep. Investigating, she found a monitor next to the door, the face of the volunteer who had helped her find her apartment the other day in the middle of the screen.

The speaker buzzed again.

The face in the screen turned as if the woman was planning to walk away. Christine searched desperately for the door lock button, found a key-shaped icon on the screen and tapped it. The woman disappeared from the screen.

Christine opened the door on the first knock, the second landing on thin air. The volunteer from Refugees and Exiles stumbled through the door, looking sheepish.

'I've come to collect you for your meeting,' the woman said, 'just in case you get lost.'

Christine heard words escape out of her mouth. 'I think there were Agency men out there yesterday.'

'I have heard of them but I've never seen any of them here. You are safe in the city,' the nice woman said in a tone that suggested she doubted Christine's sanity. 'They can't legally do anything to you here. It's against the law.'

'Yeah,' snorted Christine. 'I don't think they care about your laws.'

'Don't worry' – there was a 'you lunatic' tone to her voice – 'I will keep a lookout. Nobody will take you away on my watch.'

Christine grabbed her phone and stuck it in her bag.

At the entrance of the building, Christine refused to go outside until the woman had checked there were no Agency men around. She could do nothing but trust the all-clear she was given and stepped tentatively outside. Crowds bustled, crows dug into bins, a seagull flew overhead squawking, pigeons ate birdseed from a feeder. The sun shot rays from the open blue sky and attacked the street that fought back with radiant heat.

Christine wished she had thinner, looser clothes than the unwashed jeans and sticky t-shirt she was wearing. She had no idea where she was going to get those things and less idea where she would get the money for them. She hoped Karl would be able to help.

'Have you eaten?' the woman asked.

Christine shook her head.

'I will buy you breakfast,' the woman said, waving a credit card. 'Any requests?'

Christine stopped as crowds flowed around her like water around a rock. 'I had something on the train. Someone bought it for me, I don't know what it was.'

The other woman grinned. 'Describe it to me and I will try and guess. It's Melbourne, it could be anything.'

Christine described what she had eaten on the train, her stomach rumbling at the thought of the chips, cheese, meat and goop.

'That was an HSP,' the woman said. 'A halal snack pack, from a kebab shop, one of the pillars of Melbourne's famous food culture. We just happen to be right near a great place to get one.'

Christine stood in place as if nailed down, too frightened to move. The woman noticed, returned to her, looking perplexed.

Something like understanding dawned on her face.

'Are they still saying awful things about halal in that place?' She looked disgusted. 'Those monsters. There's no reason for that. I wish they would grow up, it's sickening. There's nothing wrong with halal food. Nothing wrong with it at all. In fact it's delicious.'

Christine had no reason to trust this woman, but no reason not to trust her either. Everything else she had learned all her life had been proven false. She shrugged her assent.

The woman led her to a narrow shop. The signs were in neon; the ones in English said 'HSP', 'Kebab' and 'Open 24 Hours', the others were in a curly script she could not read. There was a brown man in the shop, his beard and hair perfectly groomed. The woman ordered HSPs for both of them and they took the food and sat at a white laminate table.

It was even better the second time around.

'My wife loves the food here. We come here sometimes after the theatre,' the woman said. 'I keep telling her there are better places, but no, she has to come here.'

The idea that women could marry women was so improbable that Christine was unable to process it. She froze with her fork halfway to her mouth, shook the clouds from her brain then kept eating.

@

Christine did not have to wait long in the waiting room, but she took the opportunity to make a cuppa anyway. Her cup was still full when she sat down in Karl's office.

'So I need some more information before I can establish how we can help you start a new life in the real world,' Karl started. 'I know many people where you came from were simply idle. Did you have an occupation before you were exiled?'

'Student,' Christine said.

Karl looked at her expectantly.

'Postgraduate student in pure mathematics, specialising in calculus. I haven't started my master's yet, but I enrolled.'

Karl tapped on his tablet, read for a moment and nodded. 'That's fortunate for you,' he said. 'You can continue your studies if you'd like. Most students from your university don't fare too well out here. Safetown University is one of the most backward in the world. In most disciplines of academia, Safetown is far behind even the poorest nations in the world. In many sciences, especially.'

Christine could not stop the shock showing on her face. She could feel a gorge rising in her throat.

'But mathematics,' Karl continued, 'particularly pure maths and applied maths, for accounting and economics, for manipulating stock markets, is one area where Safetown excels. It also does well in classical literature.'

Karl suddenly sounded angry. 'It's all they do in there, find ways to manipulate the world's economies, to fuck with the banking, the interest rates, the stock market, rip off the rest of the country, the rest of the world. We are not even sure why and how they do it. We have never had anyone who works in their Agency, or the trust, or a business graduate from in there end up outside. I suspect they would shoot a business graduate or an Agency man before exiling them, or make them disappear at least.'

Christine was not even sure what a country was. She had been taught it was an old-fashioned concept. Karl's laboured breathing slowed down.

'Sorry,' Karl said, eventually. 'I shouldn't have blown up at you like that. You are far more their victim than I am. Anyway, we can help you get back into university. That should keep you out of trouble, keep you occupied, make the people who pay my wages happy.'

Christine shook her head. Karl raised his eyebrow.

'I can't afford school,' she said. 'I had to drop out because my father cut off his payments to the university. I have no money, no way to pay. I don't know how to make money, I've never worked.' She felt tears stinging her eyes.

Karl laughed.

Christine stiffened, ready to get angry. How dare he laugh at her.

He collected himself and raised his hand, became serious. 'You don't have to worry about that,' he said. 'Education is free at all levels right up to and including a PhD. The economy is strong and we, as a country, like it that way. Only private universities, like where you went, charge fees. Which is a travesty really when you consider how poor an education they provide.'

Christine sat for a time staring at the wall, fighting her disbelief and confusion, while Karl typed on his screen. He pulled out another tablet and handed it to her. 'There are forms on here you need to fill out. I have already remotely loaded them. Just fill them in and we can get you sorted out.'

When she looked perplexed, Karl spoke again. 'Some forms are to get you an ID on our system. These are tailored to people like you who were born in closed enclaves, who have no identity papers or even an identity we would recognise. Another is for your universal income.'

'Pardon,' Christine interrupted, 'my what?'

'Your universal income. Everybody gets a guaranteed income. It stops people from going hungry when things go wrong. Once you fill in the forms it will be paid into a bank account, which you also have to set up, but we can deal with that next. Once your income form has been sorted out, it's easy to connect an account to it. The other form is a university application. I know you don't have your academic transcripts, that's fine, they have dealt with that before. They will give you a series of exams to determine the level of education to start you at. Hopefully, after some bridging courses, you can get back into your master's.'

She looked at the tablet. It was visibly old. There were cracks in the casing and deep scratches on the touch screen, yet it seemed much more advanced than those she had used growing up.

'That place you come from,' Karl added, 'they teach you that it's hell outside the Wall, out here. To us, we know where you come from is the bad place. We've worked hard to make our world better.'

Christine's head spun, she was no longer sure she was breathing.

Someone brought her and Karl food as they filled out her paperwork. Her identity papers were processed. Soon after, her registration for a universal basic income was completed but delayed pending her getting a bank account. And there was eventually an email from one of the city's universities saying they would be delighted to test her aptitude at her convenience to determine her level of education. Then another email from another university. Then another.

She felt sick, but whether it was from the challenge of setting it all up or because it was so easy, she could not answer.

Christine applied for an online bank account, set it up on her government account, and was informed her first income payment would arrive within days.

She left Karl's office only a couple of hours after she walked in, rather than the days it felt like. She was exhausted. When she stepped out onto the street, the sunlight brightened everything, the city a benign living thing, more green than a garden, with more life than some of the thickets and forests she had seen. Random people smiled at the world, at each other, at her.

She had the best coffee she had ever tasted in one hand and the best salami sandwich she had ever experienced in the other.

Then looking around absently, she saw a charcoal suit watching her. She could not let him see where she was living. She ran.

Christine pounded down the street, outpacing the Agency man effortlessly, but aware more would be coming. Seeing what looked like a train in the middle of the road, she jumped on it.

She watched the scenery flow past to the sound of electric motors, a suit walking briskly along the footpath almost as fast as the vehicle she was on. Then he stopped, halted by a man in a blue uniform. Another Agency man appeared and walked past him, following Christine's tram. He pulled out a phone, held it to his ear.

At an intersection, she jumped off the vehicle and immediately jumped back on another travelling perpendicular to it. Then again, and again, before losing count. She got off the last one, not knowing where she was.

The buildings around her were green and glass, glossy dark leaves billowed from planters down gleaming walls. Luxurious electric cars slid past silently, people on foot and on bicycles passing in both directions. Nobody looked poor, nobody looked angry or sad or lost. Faces held a lightness she had never seen before; she didn't know how to read it.

People were too happy, too content. It began to worry her. Yet she could see no Agency men.

She found a restaurant in an alley, with comfortable-looking chairs and white-clothed tables. The cascading plants were in flower, white to match the tables. She sat down and waited for service, the warm air embracing her like a lover. Looking at the wine list, she ordered one that was described as a local shiraz. She tasted it. Fireworks went off.

She wondered why they did not have it in Safetown, where only one boring red was available. There were more than twenty varieties of red on the wine list in front of her. And they weren't even expensive.

Nothing on the dinner menu was recognisable so she asked the waiter to surprise her, and he did. Not one single thing she ate was something she had seen before, and not one single thing was anything but delicious.

Later, she walked through the city, delirious but still nervous. Finding a navigator app on her phone, she took as complicated a path as she could manage back to her apartment, enjoying the walk through what she could only see as an urban fairyland.

She saw no Agency men.

Tried to forget them. Almost could.

Unlocking the security door to her building, she ascended in the elevator, opened the locked door to her apartment, crawled into bed, fell into a restless haunted sleep.

The morning sun rose and she looked out from the balcony. Her breath caught. There was an army of Agency men moving quickly all over the square, quartering the crowds, seemingly unafraid to be seen looking for someone. Drones buzzed past her apartment, so close that she feared standing near the window in case they saw her through the glass.

She stared half-blindly at her phone as she had done a thousand times before back in that place. There was a tiny symbol in one corner she had not noticed. It was an envelope.

Breathless, she touched it.

It was a message from Sienna.

She broke into sobs.

Sienna wanted to see her, in two hours. Christine felt the tiny hairs on her arm stand at attention, felt again the knife of ice in her gut, felt the competing heat in her crotch. She replied with a 'yes, see you soon' when she wanted to type 'oh god yes'.

She could not leave. They were looking for her, with all their force they were seeking her.

She had to leave. No matter the risk.

@

The footpaths were packed full of people, anyone could be among them – thieves, liars, criminals rapists, even Agency men in disguise – but she too could use those crowds to disappear. She tried her best to blend in. Not wanting to be conspicuous, not wanting to look lost, she took her phone out to memorise the next few directions then put it back, then checked again. People bumped into her repeatedly. She could not quite understand this landscape of people, could feel bruises blooming on her skin. Feeling for her phone, she confirmed it was in her pocket, unable to shake the fear.

What if someone in the crowd had a gun, or a knife, or a bomb? What if a knife entered her kidney before she even knew she was under attack? All her life Safetynet had told her she was unsafe here. She could not quite put that thought away.

Christine began to shake. She stepped into a narrow alley and leaned against a paint-slicked wall. There was a cafe in the laneway, so she sat down and ordered a coffee. Normally there was no such thing as too much caffeine, but she was already anxious and it tapped into her nerves like a live wire.

According to the navigation app, the place where Sienna wanted to meet was five minutes away. She had about half an hour to get there, effortless even in that traffic jam of humans. She tried to relax but it was futile, her mind and soul too raggy. It felt like she had been put back together with her skin inside out, her nerves clear for all to see.

She wanted to stop there, in the shade of an umbrella, with a coffee in her hand and hope in her soul, watching the crowds pass by the end of the lane, letting the breeze desiccate her exposed nerves to leather. For a moment she felt almost safe, almost home.

Instead, she walked out onto the street again, fought the desire to run, took out her phone and checked the directions. An alleyway so thick with plant life it was impossible not to brush against it, a shopping mall connecting two streets, a skywalk over to another. Then, a quiet food hall high up in a multistorey shopping centre.

There were windows on two sides. They possessed a glow, as if some tech was projecting something within the glass. A pattern in light moved across the windows, a work of art, a moving decoration. It flowed down one glass wall, turned a corner, then down the other. Turned coloured then colourless, opaque, transparent, clear. She could not understand or follow it, but it left her shaken. Did they have the technology to turn entire windows into screens? She walked over and looked closer. The window looked like it was the same as her phone; technology used for beauty.

In Safetown it would have been used to project the news into people's faces, to drive them insane with fear. Or for advertising. There was always room for more advertising.

Through the window the city was green and sparkled. Every rooftop had solar panels, every wall had plants cascading down it. The patterns in the glass wall danced across utopia. She turned to look for Sienna.

A strong, warm-skinned woman dressed in black, not quite right. Someone of a gender so ambiguous it might have been

Sienna, but wasn't. A tall, thin woman smiling at her; no, she was too white.

Then.

Sienna. As perfect in Christine's eyes as a person could ever be. Nobody should be allowed to be that beautiful, like sunlight on gold, a cool breeze on hot skin. Christine couldn't remember how to breathe. She stepped forward, did not know what she would do once she closed the gap between them.

Could she touch this woman whose life she might have ruined? Should she touch this woman whose beauty had ruined her? Could she not?

Would she want to live if that gap that separated them could not be closed?

People avoided them like water around a rock, as if knowing somehow that this moment was too important to risk breaking it.

She took another step. Sienna turned her head to its side in a voiceless question.

'I'm sorry,' Christine breathed.

'What for?' Sienna raised an eyebrow. She did not look angry. 'You must have been fired and exiled,' Christine said, with blood in her voice. 'I am so sorry. I am so sorry if I overstepped the boundaries. I could not control my feelings, could not control myself and I . . . I'm sorry.'

'So,' Sienna said deadpan. Her voice lacked all inflection it may as well have been the computer voice of a screen reader. 'I didn't send you a train ticket and give you my number for you to come all this way, come to me, and apologise.'

'Then why?'

'I was really worried about you. I knew they might kick you out once they checked the cameras. The moment I was fired I knew they would remove you. I didn't think your father would be forgiving even if they gave him a choice. I sent you the ticket and the note, because I wanted you to have a chance to get here.'

'Is that all? Just a chance.'

'You're special. I knew that place would chew you up and spit you out. It was only a matter of time.' Sienna's eyes were glossy and screwed up like someone holding back tears. 'I admired you. I kept my eye on you. A part of me felt something for you long before you even noticed me.' She shrugged. 'I think I loved you before you noticed me.'

Christine felt like she could fall, felt like she could fly. She took another step closer until she could reach out and touch Sienna's skin.

'I noticed you. I couldn't stop thinking about you. I didn't even stop to think that it was wrong. And it was. My feelings for you were taboo. That's what they made me think. That's the world I was from. In prison my mind went everywhere but where it should have. I blamed you, I blamed myself. I should have hated Father, and that place.'

Somehow the sun was still shining outside the window, somehow the world did not end, somehow Christine did not die.

'It took me too long to work that out. I couldn't really blame you, and I couldn't stop thinking about you.'

Sienna stared at her, her left hand twitching. Christine could not imagine what she was thinking, what would happen next. She itched to bridge the gap between them.

Lunch rush began and suddenly there were people every-where, buying food, looking for tables, ignoring the two women who were clearly tied up in their thoughts and each other.

'I am not sure what you mean,' Sienna said, 'and why once you were here you messaged me and came here. Why did you come here?' There was an edge to her voice, to the question that Christine couldn't quite make sense of. It scared her.

'I . . .' Christine said. 'I am not sure what love is. I was never allowed to love, or I was allowed but I didn't want what I would be allowed to have. All I know is, if you were sad, I would be sad; if you cried, I would cry. I know not knowing what you are feeling right now is killing me. If you walk away from me, I think I will die. I think that might be love.'

'Good enough,' Sienna breathed. She bridged the gap between them, sweeping Christine's thoughts away, sweeping Christine into her arms.

It felt like dying. It felt like being born. It felt like coming home.

THURSDAY

IN SILENCE SHE was home; breathing, in love with the air itself. She was home where she belonged, held in those arms, holding that body in hers. If that was love, she was in love.

'Chris,' Sienna breathed in her ear.

Christine just wanted to lie there, breathe in that whisper, soak in that breath through her skin. She wanted to hear Sienna call her 'Chris' again. Coming from that mouth the name suited her, it stirred her. It was her name now; for in those arms she was home. She melted like a grub in a chrysalis, preparing to be remade again in the arms of love.

'Chris?'

'Yes?'

Sienna was silent but for her measured breathing. It was reassuring, comforting; Chris basked in it.

'I was spying on you. Not at first, I was spying on your family, but I got interested in you eventually.'

'What, why?' Chris wormed her way out of Sienna's arms and sat up on the bed.

'Well, for a start, I'm a spy. I spy on the people in your town, your people, though I don't want to call them that.'

Chris shook her head. 'You are my people now.'

'Your father is a shareholder in what the city calls the Fund, a corporation that controls everything that goes on there. They are represented by the Agency. They control housing, land, service, goods, every contract that place has with the world outside. They also control your news, communications, everything. You only get to know what they want you to know, every word of news, of media, is censored or created by them. I was spying on your father, and I worried about you. You are the kind of person unsuited to that place, the kind who gets kicked out.'

'What? What sort of person?'

'Any child who associates with the servants too much, who isn't a fucking racist, who's gay, is kicked out and ends up in the wasteland. Some people end up in the wasteland just because the family can't afford two kids. Once I was fired, I knew you would end up there, it was just a question of when. I had watched you. I thought you were gay, and you have a brother who can carry on the family line. When your father found out who you are, you were going to be a goner. Unlike your mum, you don't have an innate instinct for fakeness.'

'What about Mother?'

There was a hum somewhere, a fridge or a switched-off

television. Chris could feel it with her gut more than she could hear it. She wanted it to stop.

'Your mum did what most women who love women do in that place, she married anyway and got up to shit with women on the side. We have been watching her for a long time too. Those women she spends all the time with, those wives of senior men in the Fund, they are her lovers.'

Chris didn't know whether to feel furious at Mother for letting Father kick her out, or pity for her for the world of pain and self-hate she must live in. It had never occurred to her that Mother could be sleeping with those women, those empty-faced women, those women who lunched. It was never really lunch, she suddenly understood.

'It's probably why your parents only had a couple of kids. I don't know how she managed to force herself to fuck your father enough times to get pregnant twice. But that's not why I told you about my watching you, although I imagine you must be angry with me right now. I know you lost someone, your best friend, Jack. We were watching you both well before' – Sienna paused – 'he disappeared.'

There was a long silence. Chris manoeuvred until she could better see the expression on Sienna's face but it remained unreadable. 'I know where to find your friend Jack if you are interested.'

Chris jumped out of bed, grabbed her clothes and started getting dressed.

'I guess that's a yes.'

@

'I work in a theatre,' Sienna said as they rushed down crowded streets. Sienna's hand was warm and soft in hers. She liked that a lot, maybe more than she wanted to admit. 'It's not the best work, no, that's not true, it's the best work, I love it, but it wasn't enough, I felt like I needed to do something. I knew too much about that place, saw the damage they were doing to any queer kids in there. It was easy to get a job there because of this.' Her hand made a sweeping gesture down the bronze skin of her arm.

Chris let the confusion show on her face.

'My skin,' Sienna said, irritated. 'Did you never notice that every servant was black or brown? We were paid well, but we were all aware that your people, your old people, your family, demanded only people of colour as staff.'

Chris shuddered.

'We are not sure whether it's because they are racist or so they can tell the difference between us and them easier. I suspect it's racism. Fuck it. I am not going to mince words with you even if it makes you hate me. It is racism. Your town, everyone in it, is fucking racist. Your parents are fucking racist. You are probably a fucking racist deep down and eventually it will bite me on the fucking arse.'

'I'm sorry,' Chris said. 'I don't think I am racist and I don't want to be.'

Chris could feel the tension in the hand she was holding.

'Well, it's too late to not love you,' Sienna breathed. 'Anyway, my real work, when I am not taking your Enclave down, is in a theatre, directing. Jack showed up one day – must have been not long after those bastards threw him out – with a play for us to produce. We took it, of course. It was brilliant. Um, he is brilliant.'

Chris's legs had turned to rubber; it was like trying to walk on licorice ropes, on string cheese. Of course Jack was brilliant.

They strolled hand in hand down a corridor of green that looked like a path in a thick forest covered with planters, tangling dragging, climbing vines, dripping with moisture. A glass and steel wall they passed reflected their image. All of the people walking in the opposite direction looked happy, looked different. If they had ever had plastic surgery, it had not homogenised them.

'We are rehearsing the play,' Sienna said. 'Everybody is at work today, the entire company. I want them all to meet you, to finally meet you.'

Chris stopped, her mind unable to cope with what was going on. She could not parse this world, could not compute, could not zero the equation. She knew she was in love, but did not know precisely what that meant, did not know if she wanted anybody to know of her love.

She opened her mouth and no words came out. She did not think Sienna was giving her a choice.

Sienna opened a door with 'stage door' written on it and dragged Chris through. A harried-looking woman, her white hair in a bedraggled ponytail, met them. She hugged Sienna who introduced Chris, her hand on her arm with a possessive air. Chris was surprised by the warm feeling this gave her.

The white-haired woman stepped over and hugged Chris too.

They moved through the building, where posters of what Chris could only assume were theatre shows hung on white walls.

She had been to the theatre only twice in her youth. One of those times was to see an amateur theatre group of housewives; Shakespeare performed half-mockingly, half-self-mockingly. The second time had been a show by a travelling troupe of servants. She corrected her thought: a travelling troupe of *outsiders*. She had been consumed by the performance, although she had not really understood what was going on.

A labyrinth of halls and rooms and doors and chairs, posters and books and misplaced furniture. Sienna dragged a confused Chris by the hand.

Another person appeared, a young woman with a boy's haircut, dressed in loose black pants and a purple t-shirt. Another introduction, another hug. Chris could feel her lithe muscle, her fierce strength; she was maybe a little younger than Chris, but far stronger than the Chris before the exile. Chris knew she was stronger now; the time in the wasteland had turned her into steel.

Again and again, through the corridors and small rooms, the open spaces filled with flimsy-looking furniture and functionless items that must have been props. The light so changeable it was impossible to adjust. Everybody they met greeted Sienna with a hug, then embraced Chris when introduced.

'We are workshopping the script in the lunch room,' Sienna said after the tenth meeting, the tenth warm embrace. They walked down one last corridor, the walls plastered with torn pieces of paper that were covered with what might have been cartoons or jokes. Chris could not be sure, they were moving too fast.

Through an open doorway was one of the most cluttered rooms Chris had ever seen. It was like every person who had ever stepped foot in there had left their mark. Every surface, but the table in the centre, was covered in mugs and small items, phones, toys, unidentifiable things, a hat here, a spirit bottle there, shot glasses, pens, tablets, hairbrushes, make-up, books, things Chris could not identify. All that was on the table in the centre was a pile of paper in front of each chair, a forest of glasses and a couple of water jugs.

A tall, slender woman stood at the sink, poking buttons on the coffee machine. She turned, her face familiar. Her eyes widened when she looked at Chris. The expression on her face was Jack's shocked face.

Chris stared at the woman who was staring back at her, perplexed.

'Christine?'

The voice was Jack's. Almost. It was higher and breathier, more self-assured.

'Sienna, where did you find her? Oh my god, where the fuck did you find her?'

There was a pregnant silence, breeding more silence.

'Please tell me you told her.'

'You were best friends,' Sienna said, her voice expressionless. 'Are you telling me you never said a word about this?'

'Jack?' Every moment Chris had spent with Jack rushed before her eyes. So much of their life had been spent together. She loved him more than she loved the world; not more than she loved Sienna, but that was a different kind of love.

Her head swam like it did when she drank too much.

Someone came through the door behind her. She did not see them but could hear their flustered breathing.

'My name isn't Jack anymore,' said Jack's voice. 'I'm Jenny.'

'Chris,' she choked out somehow.

'Pleased to meet you, Chris,' said Jack's voice – said Jenny – looking frightened.

Sienna took a step towards her. Chris's head shook; she could not focus her mind on anything. She worried about Jack, Jenny, Jack, she worried about her friend. The concern on Sienna's face made her cry.

'Fucking hell, Sienna, what did you do?' asked the voice behind her. A kind hand was suddenly on her back holding her up.

'You should have warned her,' said Jack . . . Jenny. He . . . she was crying, mascara blackening those familiar tears.

'Fuck,' said Sienna.

'I'll deal with her,' said the voice. 'You stay here, look after Jenny. Stupid kids.'

Chris could see that Jack, Jenny, her friend looked distressed. That wasn't right. She did not want to see distress on that once-familiar face, did not want to be the cause of that pain.

She was confused and broken.

A gentle pressure on her back drove her out the door, down the narrow corridor and into another room. Everything was carpeted in crimson, even the walls; the overstuffed couch was a slightly darker red. The only thing not red was the armchair, which was a dark green with a mysterious sheen of gold.

She dropped onto the couch and looked up at the woman who had helped her get there. The woman had short, spiked hair that was black and grey, her skin the blackest Chris had ever seen. She was about the age of Mother, she guessed, although she was bad at reading faces that had never had a facelift.

Chris wondered if every woman in Melbourne was uniquely beautiful.

'I'm Gabbie,' the woman said. 'I am the producer, but I seem to spend most my time stopping Sienna doing anything stupid. I assume you are the girl who Sienna likes, Jenny's friend. Sienna told me about the girl who got her in trouble in that place, who she got into trouble too. I should thank you for that, getting her fired. She's here a bit more now. We just need to find a way for her to keep gathering information to take down that shithole you come from.'

Chris's mouth fell open, her throat choking on a wordless stutter.

Someone walked in with a mug, handed it to Gabbie, who handed it over to Chris. 'Drink, and don't even ask how I know how you like your coffee. Just know that that stupid girl can't stop talking about you. She was talking about you even when you were in that shithole of a place, when she was spying on your family.' She rolled her eyes theatrically.

Chris put the cup to her lips. The kindness inherent in that delivery shook her. She blinked away what tears she could.

'I can't believe Sienna did something so stupid. This is epic by even her high standards. She should have guessed that seeing Jenny would be a shock, with you already feeling so messed up. She has always been impulsive.'

Chris just sat there.

'Drink. I will go talk to those stupid kids.'

Her thoughts chased each other across her mind, getting lost in the tangled thicket of her unconscious. She drank her coffee, holding it under her nose as she swallowed. The smell was comforting. It reminded her of home. It reminded her of Mother, of that place, where she could never go again. She wondered if coffee would ever stop reminding her of Mother, didn't know if she wanted the memories.

If Safetown was comforting she was not sure she wanted to be comfortable.

Her back hurt, her chest hurt. Wriggling, she tried to find a more comfortable position on the couch. Finally, she put her elbows on her knees and rested her head in her hands.

Someone said her name. Chris looked up.

It was Sienna, standing in the doorway, the expression on her face speaking louder than words. She looked like she hated herself. She looked like she had risked too much. She looked like she wanted to cry.

Chris didn't want Sienna to cry, that would be worse than crying herself. The sobs caught in her throat, mugged any words that were trying to escape.

'Chris,' she said. 'I am sorry. I don't know why I avoided telling you before we came here. I must have been afraid I would fuck it up if I tried to explain. I probably seriously fucked it up anyway, and now I have pissed both of you off. I'm going to lose you, aren't I? You must hate me now.'

Chris looked down at the red carpet. If she bled out there, nobody would notice before it dried. A tiny sound, like the word 'no', came out of her mouth.

Sienna crouched in front of her. 'Jenny asked me to explain. I will do as she asked then I will understand if you never want to speak to me again after that.' She sat down cross-legged on the floor and chased words in her mouth for a moment.

'Jack came to us right away after arriving on the train. He stayed in an apartment like yours for two days, I think. We don't know what he must have gone through to get to us. We didn't ask. I am sure you can imagine what she went through better than we can.'

Chris nodded, tears in her eyes. She wished she could cauterise the memory, stop imagining Jack out there where she was. She imagined her friend having to live like she had, eating rats and pigeons, living on biscuits and occasional soup, sleeping in the dirt and filth, betrayed by loved ones.

Killing to survive.

'Your friend, your best friend, was thrown out of home when she told her parents she felt like she was supposed to be a woman. Even after a year, it's hard to get my head around that. Those fucking people in that fucking place, I wish I had done more to take them down. I don't know how she got here, what she went through to get here, but I am sure you can imagine. She must have walked to the train, somebody must have paid for her to get here. She gave us a piece of work, rewritten from memory in the town at the other end of the train line. All she had were memories.'

Chris was crying.

Sienna reached out and wiped her tears away, making her tears flow faster; the dam of her lover's hand could not hold them back.

'We helped her find the right doctors, helped her find her self. I should have told you,' Sienna said, 'not just brought you here like that. I should have broken it to you gently. Instead I was a coward. I am so sorry. I will understand if you never want to see me again.'

Sienna stood and turned.

'No,' Chris said.

Sienna nodded, started to walk away.

'No, don't leave me.' Chris's voice was frantic. 'I couldn't bear that.'

Sienna turned back with a startled expression on her face. Something else too; pain, maybe. The kind of pain that could only come from love lost, love unrequited. Chris would not let her lose it.

'You are my strength,' Chris said.

'I doubt that very much. You crossed the wastelands on foot, alone. You are so fucking strong, like Jenny. That fucking place you came from, they lose the strong ones, the smart ones, the best ones. They all end up dead or howling in the wasteland. Or if they are strong enough, they get here. Only the selfish, the stupid, the weak stay there.'

Chris shook her head. 'Even if I hated you right now, I would still love you. I know that doesn't make sense, but I can't help that. I need you with me when I talk to Jack, when I talk to Jenny. I have to talk to him, her, my best friend, and I can't do that alone. You are Jenny's friend too. It would be better for him, for her, if you are here too.'

Sienna only left her long enough to go get Jenny, but Chris wished she had not gone at all. She felt so alone, with no buffer between her and herself. Time had not yet faded her memories of the place before, the place where she was born, with Father and Mother and Jack. Without Sienna.

Jack was gone, she knew that. There was nothing of Jack to find, except Jenny.

Could Jenny replace Jack in her heart? Was it fair of Jenny, to expect to fill the Jack-shaped hole in her heart? Was it fair of Chris to not give Jenny the chance?

Her thoughts were interrupted by Sienna walking back through the door. Jack, no, Jenny followed.

'I am so sorry, Christine, Chris,' Jenny said, a Jack-like expression on her face.

Chris had so many questions but could only put one of them in words. 'Why didn't you tell me before you left?'

Jenny shook her head. 'I was going to. I thought my parents would understand. I was going to go straight to you after talking to them, but I couldn't. My dad called Security, had me removed straight away. I didn't even have a chance to get a message to you, nobody would let me. They took me straight to the gates and turfed me out.'

Chris was furious. 'Why didn't you try to call, email, leave me a message once you were safe here?'

'There's no communication into Safetown from outside. I couldn't even get a message into Safetynet. They don't want people inside to know how great it is out here. It's impossible without a phone from inside.'

Sienna was nodding her agreement. 'We have tried to hack into your town's so-called Safetynet for over a decade,' she said. 'It's impossible without the hardware encryption chips from one of the phones inside. None of us have ever managed to steal one. Security always find it. They confiscate the phones from exiles without fail.'

Something was niggling at the edge of her consciousness, some distant thought was hammering on the walls deep in her brain looking for a way out.

Chris froze. 'I have a phone.'

'What?'

'I threw my phone off the Wall when I was being chased by Security. I searched for it because I hoped' – she gestured to Jenny – 'I hoped I could use it to talk to you. It's useless. It won't connect. I have no account.'

Sienna looked shocked, then took out her phone, so superior to the one from inside, tapped it and said, 'My girlfriend made it to Melbourne and she has a phone from Safetown in her possession.'

The words 'holy shit' emitted tinnily.

Jenny looked as confused as Chris felt, but what hit Chris in the gut was being called Sienna's 'girlfriend'.

'Girlfriend?' Jenny asked, mirroring Chris's confusion.

'Shut up,' Sienna replied with a smile.

THE NEXT DAY

CHRIS, SIENNA AND Jenny stopped in front of a wall of planter pots dripping with ripe strawberries. Sienna hulled one, threw the green bit in a composter next to the recycling bin on the street, and pushed it into Chris's barely opened mouth. Then she hulled another and ate it herself.

'I fucking love strawberries,' she breathed, her tone nudging on the sexual.

Jenny shrugged, took one and smooshed it in Sienna's mouth.

Sienna poked at a number pad in front of a door, and waited.

'What?' said a voice from the speaker grate. They sounded put out.

'It's Sienna, dumbarse. Fix your camera.'

'Oh,' crackled the speaker, 'come in.' The door buzzed.

The building was a maze of small studios and apartments. Chris was soon completely lost, could only follow Sienna to the door and through it.

The room through the door could not be more different to the tidy minimalism of the corridor outside. Every surface was covered. Half-dismantled tablets and computers sat on cracked dinner plates, a monitor was knocked over on a desk, its screen down. Here an empty coffee cup, there a half-filled takeaway container, a film of mould furring the top of the unidentifiable slop. There were books teetering in mountainous piles. Tools and parts, screws and screwdrivers, wires and wire-cutters, more tools and other tools, other inexplicable bits everywhere.

Someone sat in the gaffa-tape repaired desk chair, a woman or a man; Chris wasn't sure it mattered.

They stood, hipped like a woman but standing like a man in shapeless mechanic's coveralls. Their skin was the most gorgeous colour Chris had ever seen, a dark mahogany. Their hair was dyed platinum white.

'This is Schtick,' said Sienna. 'They are the brains of the operation. Well, the technical brains anyway. They are the greatest hacker I have ever met, probably the greatest hacker in Melbourne.'

Schtick grinned cheekily, and when they looked at Chris their grin got wider. 'Why hello,' they said.

Sienna stepped between them. 'Back off, you,' Sienna said with both venom and humour. 'This white girl's mine.'

They laughed and returned to their desk chair. A scattering of tiny parts lay in front of them, along with a coffee cup so filthy even the people living just outside the gates of Safetown would have refused to use it.

'Grow a sense of humour, sis,' Schtick laughed.

'Fucking hell, sib,' Sienna said, throwing some newspapers off the couch and sitting down. 'What's with the fucking mess?'

Chris sat down next to Sienna and leaned back against the couch, hoping there was nothing filthy soaked into the cushions. She leaned into Sienna with a contented smile.

'How adorable,' Schtick said, 'finally found a woman to make an honest woman out of you I see.'

Schtick stood in the middle of the room with their arms crossed across their chest, grinning.

'Don't think I haven't noticed you,' Schtick said, looking at Jenny. 'I prefer tall babes, but hitting on you was not going to piss off Si so much. We will talk, have the pronouns and preferences chat later. Maybe over drinks or dinner. So Si, what do you have?'

@

Chris was in the green room of the theatre on her favourite couch, papers scattered all around her. She was accustomed to the red-carpeted walls and appreciated the implicit irony that nobody talked about.

She had passed the aptitude test and had come close to passing the exam to enrol in a master's; she was now undertaking self-directed bridging studies with relish.

The actors, the set-builders, theatre techs, assistant directors, people whose jobs she could not understand, had stopped taking the piss out of her for studying in their green room. Sienna had assured her they would not need it until dress rehearsals at least.

Chris was beginning to find the muttered sounds of the theatre relaxing; the hammering and drilling of sets being built, voices raised in argument, people walking across the creaking wooden floors, the drumming resonance of the stage above.

A buzzer sounded, alerting people that the stage door had opened. She wondered who it was. Sienna was working, Jenny was on a date with Schtick.

She heard raised voices. That was not unusual.

Then the crack of a gunshot. That was.

Papers and books slid off Chris's lap onto the floor as she stood, her tablet thudding on the carpet. There was screaming, then a masculine voice shouting her name – the name her parents had given her – and the word 'phone'.

She ran out of the green room. If what was happening had something to do with her, she had to do something about it. It was likely all she could do was take the next bullet. Better her than someone else getting hurt trying to protect her.

Chris saw the back of the charcoal suit of an Agency man. It looked like he had his arm around someone. He turned abruptly and she could see Sienna peering out from the bend of his elbow, a gun pointed at her head. She looked terrified and Chris felt it in her gut like a stabbing.

Behind them, Gabbie lay in a pool of blood.

'Hello, Christine,' the Agency man said, grinning like a carnivore. She was suddenly struck by how artificial he sounded, not like a person at all. He spoke like engine grease, like a bleeding wound. His voice made her sick.

'Give me the phone you took and I will not shoot your friend. I have seen the security camera footage. We had quite a few movie nights watching you, especially the footage from the hidden cam in your bedroom. You didn't know we had a camera in your bedroom? I think you would be a bit put out if I splatter this lesbo slut's brains over the walls. I personally would see it as a privilege to pull the trigger. That would be a story to tell the guys.'

Chris stood frozen, afraid he would shoot if she made any sudden movements. She would not hesitate to give him the phone if she had it. She wanted the gun away from Sienna, would rather have it pointed at herself.

'How dare you talk about her like that,' she said. 'You coward. Can't even intimidate women without a gun.'

The Agency man flinched, almost pulled the gun away, then grinned. His teeth were too white.

'Oh you're good. Nice try. Phone. Now.'

'You are nothing,' Chris said. 'You are a fool, working for the Agency who will never make you a full partner in the Fund.' She noted the slightest change in his blank expression.

Chris concentrated. It was just a problem to solve. There must be a solution, a way out of this. There is always a solution, she just had to work it out. If she was smarter than this Agency man, too smart to stay inside the Wall, this was time to prove it. She had survived outside, now was the time to find out how tough it had made her.

'I am reaching for my phone. I am unarmed,' she said.

She did have her phone in her pocket, but it was not the phone he was looking for. Chris put her left hand in her back pocket, held her right hand out in a 'stop' gesture.

The Agency man smiled and she wanted to kick his teeth in. Sienna looked terrified. Chris wanted to kill him for that.

There was a faint movement behind the Agency man. Someone else was going to get themselves killed. She prayed it was not Jenny, prayed it was not anybody. The Agency man started to turn around.

'Here, take it,' Chris barked, pulling out her old-fashioned paper notebook, black and vaguely phone shaped, hoping the Agency man was as stupid as he looked.

She needed his attention entirely on her, maybe she would be the only one he would hurt.

He looked perplexed, didn't know how to take the notebook. Chris stepped towards him with it. He reached out with his left hand, releasing the pressure on Sienna's neck.

Sienna dropped loose-legged to the ground as the Agency man pulled the trigger. A bullet hole appeared on the wall, spattered with droplets of blood, cracks radiating out from it. Sienna was flung sideways, slumped into the wall and slid down. Chris stepped forward, punched the Agency man in the face and he staggered backwards. She punched him again, and he almost fell then stiffened. There was another crack and a bullet embedded itself in the floor. The Agency man's legs buckled and he collapsed onto Sienna.

Jenny was standing there with something phone-shaped in her hand. She dropped it, pulled out her phone, started dialling.

Chris threw the unconscious Agency man off her lover like a rag doll and dropped to her knees.

'Ambulance and Police' – Jenny was talking into her phone – 'we have two gunshot victims. The gunman is down. An Agent from Safetown.'

Jenny covered her phone and whispered. 'We knew they would come here one day, come for me, come for a spy, for someone we were protecting. The police believed us and gave us a special licence for a stun gun.'

Chris scooted closer to Sienna, who lay unmoving on the floor. Blood had formed a halo, a thought bubble, around her head, matting her short hair. She could feel the tears, though she could not hear them through the keening in her mind. She looked over and saw that Jenny had a first-aid kit by her knees and was tending to Gabbie.

'Gabbie,' Jenny said, 'stay with me. Gabbie, the ambulance is coming. Hurry, please, I think she's dying.'

Chris did not know if Sienna was breathing.

PART 3

THE FALCON CANNOT
SEE THE FALCONER

SUCH A PERFECT DAY

CHRIS RELAXED ON the train even though she was heading in the direction she least wanted to travel; the direction she most needed to be going. When she had been on the train last she could not have imagined ever returning or how different it would be on the way back. Nestling her head into Sienna's neck, she took comfort in the warmth of her, the smell of her skin. She ran her finger over the raised scar and gave silent thanks to the hospital that Sienna was still alive. It was frightening to return to Tasmania, but Sienna made it possible, made her stronger.

After surviving the wasteland, she knew she could face anything with Sienna beside her.

There were servants all around them. She corrected her brain, wondered how long she would have to do that. They were people dressed in staff uniform, to differentiate and identify them where she had grown up. They were her people now. She looked down at the engagement ring on her finger. Her people, all around her, they would not let anything happen to her.

Chris knew that many of them were spies working to take down the Enclave; the place she once thought was her home. All the spies had worked to ensure they would be on shift when she and Sienna, her future wife, would be there.

She was heading towards the most danger she had ever been in yet felt the safest she ever had.

She worried that she had become incapable of fear. She worried that life had damaged her in some way. She worried about falling in love. She worried more about falling in love with the first woman she had kissed, that it was first-kiss, first-lovemaking afterglow that masqueraded as love. But all she could do was stay on the ride and see where it went.

Opening her eyes, she looked over and saw Jenny grinning at her. 'Oh shut up, Jenny,' she said.

'I didn't say anything.'

'You were thinking something.'

Jenny kept grinning. Chris closed her eyes.

Her best friend was still her best friend. It was weird, it was different, but she was still her best friend. Maybe now they could be even closer; now that Jenny was happier, now that Jenny had found herself. Now that she was happier herself.

They had both found themselves on separate but similar paths.

Jenny sat, drinking from a steel bottle of water.

'Will you be my bridesmaid?' Chris asked abruptly.

Jenny spluttered, choking on her water. Chris fought hard not to laugh. 'Got ya.'

'I, I,' Jenny stuttered. 'I . . . of course.'

Chris grinned when she felt a slender form drop onto her, squishing her into a comfortably smothering hug.

Sienna was less impressed and squeaked. 'Get the fuck off me, Jenny.' She laughed, shoving Jenny's legs off her lap. 'You are skinny but not that skinny.'

@

'Are you sure you want to do this?' Sienna said as the bus rolled to a stop.

'Yes,' Chris replied, though her tone was not convincing. 'There are other kids in there, queer kids, smart kids, who deserve the truth, deserve the chance to see the world outside, the chance to be as happy as us.'

The staff in the bus stood and filed to the front. Chris followed Sienna, hating the memories invoked by seeing her in a servant's uniform. She was in a staff uniform too, wearing a curly wig and glasses in a pathetic attempt at disguise.

Outside the bus they milled in the crowd, Chris deeply aware that her skin colour might make the cameras home in and identify her. She had no choice. Schtick had informed them that the autocannons disabled only when staff passed through the gates.

Chris didn't want to know how they had tested that.

They edged forward with the movement of the crowd, letting the flow sweep them towards the Wall.

Right on schedule, there was a scream at the edge of the bus park and someone ran towards the bottlenecked staff. A volunteer, dressed in rags, grabbed a servant and tried to drag them away. Theirs was perhaps the most dangerous role in the mission; there was a chance they could be killed. The staff surged towards Security, and Chris and Sienna moved with them, getting closer to the Wall, trying to reach the gates where Security were mostly occupied.

'Schtick's toy had better work.' Chris could barely hear Sienna's whisper as the crowd pushed them against a guard.

Chris's hand was in her pocket. She pushed the button on 'the Thing'. She could hear shouting and screaming, the people Sienna had arranged to make a commotion. The Thing vibrated. She took her hand out of her pocket in the arranged signal.

Sienna waved her fake ID at the guard, who bipped it with his now compromised scanner. He waved her through.

Chris followed after her.

Then they separated. Chris headed for a bus, Sienna disappeared into the shadows. She had broken into the Security enclave before and promised she would be okay.

Chris suppressed the fluttering in her stomach. No matter what went wrong, Jenny would be waiting for them in the ruins. She would take them home.

TIME COME AT LAST

CHRIS WAS ON the couch in the maths postgrad lounge in the pitch black. Security were not patrolling. They had been kept away somehow. She suspected Sienna had something to do with it. She was not aware of having been asleep until a hand touched her shoulder. It was a girl, only a few years younger than herself, but innocent. She gestured for Chris to follow.

Down the dark halls, they found their way by the glow of mobile phones to a lab full of fidgeting students.

'We have made a decision,' said a boy so young she thought he should be in high school, not university. 'We want out.'

The other students, most of them just as young, nodded; some more vigorously than others.

'Are you sure?' Chris said. 'I don't know what will happen. Your parents might withhold your trust funds. The Agency will almost certainly freeze all your accounts. You might get your freedom but will have to start again.'

'We used the tunnel through the firewall you helped us make and now we know,' one of the students said.

The whole room breathed in near unison, frightened and nearly manic.

'They lied,' another said. 'Our parents. We checked what you told us about the world outside, used the technology you gave us, the software your friend hacked for us. We drilled out through the firewalls and piggybacked on the Agency's network to have a look at what we are not being told.'

'It really is better out there,' someone added.

'Yes it is,' Chris said.

'I would rather succeed or fail on my wits outside where I can be free than live on a trust fund here where the Agency controls everything.'

Chris nodded.

'They told us this is a perfect town, but it's a shithole.'

'Yes,' Chris agreed.

'They will shoot us if we just try to leave.'

'They might,' Chris said.

'So,' asked the first boy, 'what do we do?'

Chris was sure she looked as exhausted as she felt. She was not a hacker, though she was no slouch with machines. It had been discovered early in the night that the encryption protecting the firewalls around the security system was built around mind-bogglingly difficult mathematical solutions. None of the undergrad comp-sci students could solve it, so she buckled down and gave the code-kiddies a lesson.

It was calming to have a problem to solve.

A friend of Sienna's from the outside snuck into the university from their job at a late-night cafe and brought mind-boggling skills. The other cafe workers were covering for them, but it was still dangerous. Like many of the rebels and spies working hard that night, they were queer, this rebel in particular only pretending to be male while inside the Wall.

There were others who deserved to be free. That was why she was there, to free people like her, like Jenny, like Mother. She didn't even care if she took the place down as long as people had the chance to be free.

When her mathematical solution slotted into the hack and worked, everybody was too tired to cheer and it was nearly dawn. Light was sneaking into the outside world, security were starting to move around. She grabbed her stuff, hoped Sienna would forgive her for taking an unnecessary risk.

She had something, probably stupid, she needed to do.

Chris stood, loose-limbed and falsely calm, in front of the house where she had grown up, where she had spent more time than in any other place. It was beautiful, a mansion, a house of privilege.

Behind her, the security camera lay in bits on the road, broken; the steel bar she had used to take care of it nearby.

The sun was rising, casting its stark light on the front of the house, Chris's long shadow oppressing the building. That faint blue glow, the first light of the day, was clean, honest.

She could see the house for what it really was.

Built of ticky-tacky, as thin as paper, it had warped in places, cracked in others, been painted over again and again. She could see where the thin walls had pulled away from the corners and been filled with something rubbery, where the corners were crooked; there was not a vertical or a horizontal that was not off true. No life grew on it; even the plants in the garden, while still photosynthesising, had been carved into lifeless regularity.

The whole neighbourhood was lifeless; the clinker-built boxes people lived in cooked by the heat, the gardens so manicured they may as well have been plastic. It was not hot yet, but sprinklers came on yard by yard, misting the air and wetting the ground, the topiary, the grasses.

There were motion detectors and spying lenses everywhere, on the corners of the buildings, under the eaves, on lampposts. The eyes of cameras everywhere made sure all was under control, ensured that the people who thought it was all for them controlled nothing.

She did not want to be there, but she had something she had to do.

She took out her new phone, an engagement gift from Sienna, even better than the one Refugee and Exile Services had given her, and marvelled at its superiority to what she had before when she lived inside, when she believed their lies. She now knew the people in Safetown had a reduced quality of life compared to what they had cut themselves off from.

She was not supposed to be freeing her mother. It was a risk and Sienna would be furious at her. But it was Sienna who told her that Mother was almost certainly a lesbian. She deserved a shot at getting out, a chance at freedom, at peace and love. Chris just hoped she would take it.

The mission to break down the firewalls, let the citizens see the truth of the outside, to get as many young people out as possible, was going well. Chris had done what she could. Now it was time to see if she could do what she felt she needed to do.

She had hoped to confront Father in the confused moment when he was leaving the house and heading for his car.

He hadn't emerged. Maybe he was not even at home, maybe he was away, leaving the house to the dust and to Mother. She had to do something. Security would come if she just stayed there, watching the house. Alerts would have sounded the moment her face was identified by the Security AI, the moment before she smashed the camera.

She waited for a parent to step out the door so she could confront them. They didn't.

Maybe they were scared. She should not have been surprised they wouldn't want to confront her.

As if her thoughts had summoned them, security vans appeared at each end of the street. The door of the house suddenly opened and she saw a black silhouette, as bulky as a sack of grain, head tipped quizzically to one side. Father. He must have seen her. She was disgusted at the coward who would rather call Security than confront her. She could not understand why she had ever feared him.

With all the time she had spent on foot lately, she knew she could outrun Security easily. Her time in the wasteland had made her stronger. She need not fear them either. The last

Agency man to fuck with her was nursing his broken nose in a jail cell in Melbourne.

He was lucky Jenny had zapped him unconscious before she had a chance to kick his face in. Chris was lucky too, she would have gone to jail for murder.

She typed on her phone one-handed as she dashed down the street and then to a path between fences, just too narrow for Security to follow in their vans. The fences leaned into each other, creaking and crackling, threatening to close the gap. The path ended at a park, as she knew it would, grass so trimmed it looked like plastic. It was plastic, she realised. Through the soles of her shoes, she could feel there was no soil under it; instead it squished like memory foam. Stopping, she leaned against a tree in the middle of the park.

She could hear the drones coming for her. From the sound, she knew there would be more than she had ever seen in one place. Her phone chimed and she pulled it out. There was a message with a map coordinate on it. She quickly memorised the directions. She might make it. In the enclosed space of the park the noise of an approaching copter shook her resolve. The path she needed was out of the cover of the tree.

She did not imagine they would just exile her now, did not want to imagine what they thought they could get away with. Their law was not absolute. If they hurt an outsider intentionally, there would be consequences.

She and Sienna had argued for a long time over whether the Agency would care about the potential consequences. In the end, she had decided that her ID card from the outside and the fact that Sienna would tear the world apart to get her out would be enough to protect her. She hoped that was true.

If it wasn't, she would have to fight her way out.

She ran for the path she needed to follow as Security swarmed the park from the direction she had come from. Drones skittered and swooped into her airspace from all sides. The quadcopter was so close she could feel the hammering of the wind off its blades in her stomach.

Taking a length of strong, thin bead chain, weighted at both ends, from her pocket, she spun it and flung it into the air. A couple of drones, their blades tangled, clattered to the ground. The other drones backed away. She would have to remember to thank Schtick for teaching her that trick.

Sweat stuck her t-shirt to her back, ran out of her short-cropped hair, dripped into her eyes, but she knew she could keep up the pace easily. She was almost where she needed to be. Her phone chimed again, but she had no time to pull it out of her pocket.

A white quadcopter flew overhead. Drones swarmed towards it and it exploded with a whump. In the flash, debris and broken drones rained down as Chris covered her head with her arms.

Fuck, that was close. Not that she would complain to whoever was controlling that thing.

She heard the pursuing Security quadcopter peeling away.

There was the roar of an engine and the squeal of brakes as a car stopped in front of her. The back door swung open. She prepared to run again, but there was too much stuff falling from the sky.

'Fuck it, Chris. Get in,' a voice yelled.

She looked through the window and saw a stranger beckoning. She had nowhere to go. Security vans cornered into the street and the hovering copter moved towards them as she slid into the car.

'I can get you to the gates,' the driver said. 'I have been watching the net. Safetynet is claiming there's been a terrorist attack on the city. It's time for me to try for the gates before they start questioning people.'

'No, not the gates. Not yet. I have something to do.'

@

That house, that off-white, too-tall edifice was across the road again. Chris assumed Father and Mother, even Brandon, were in there. Maybe they were watching her again, maybe they were on the phone to Security, to the Agency, to whoever else they might call for help.

Hopefully, they were panicking. Hopefully, she had even made Security nervous. She had never felt so calm.

Chris almost swaggered across the road, looking at the lounge-room window, wondered if Father was in there, watching her. She was sick of messing around. When she made it to the garden, she reached down and picked up a fist-sized rock, stretched back and threw it at the window with all the force she could muster. She had never been a good throw, had been mocked for it at school, but at that range she could not have missed. The glass of the window splashed inwards.

'Mother,' she hollered, 'you don't belong here. Come with me!'

It was Father who was first out the door. He was holding a small handgun, and Mother was sheltering behind him staring at her with disgust and fear. Father raised the gun. Chris pulled out the telescoping baton she had hoped not to need and readied it with a flick of her wrist and backed away.

'Father, we don't have to do this,' Chris said calmly, 'Mother, you can come with me, you can be free.'

Mother just shook her head.

Sirens were screaming, copters and drones were coming.

The car pulled up just before Chris had reached the middle of the road, just as the drones appeared, travelling as fast as she had ever seen drones fly.

Oh well, she tried. Not worth getting shot over. Not worth killing Father over if he missed.

'Are you fucking nuts?' the driver asked.

Chris climbed in and the car accelerated, blowing smoke from its wheels. She looked back. Father, Mother and Brandon were waving down a security van behind them. Just before the car turned a corner, she could see Father climb in.

'Possibly, but I don't think so,' said Chris, hoping she was right and they would follow. Maybe she could still set Mother free.

THE LAST DAY

THE GATES GROANED open just as Chris reached them on foot, her driver pounding the ground at her side. The hackers must have won their fight; for now, at least. Security were still in their guard houses, having relied on the gates and auto defences for too long. Drones scattered wildly, returned and scattered again, like a murmuration of small birds, before stopping dead in the sky and falling.

She owed someone a drink for that.

Somewhere techs would be trying to reverse the hacks that had overwhelmed Safetynet all at once. Once the students had burrowed through the firewalls, Schtick's mysterious hacker friends would have come through the other way. There was no way to close the firewall.

Hackers had taken control of the Safetynet news feeds and were showing the real news for the first time. The truth about that place was out, the people in the city were being told what was really happening outside, what the rest of the world thought of them. The hackers, their families, their friends, would be piling into cars that were arriving for them and heading for the gates.

She did not know how many people would believe what they saw on the news, but she doubted the Agency would ever be completely trusted again.

Chris ran out the gates. Sienna was already across the car park among a knot of Security. More security, who had been waiting to scan in the staff, turned and ran after Chris. They suddenly stopped, looked at their phones, turned again and ran back through the gates. It was probably best that they ran away. Chris was not in the mood to be polite.

Buses were unloading the servants, who could tell there was something wrong. There was no Security to greet them with scanners, batons and guns; only broken-winged corpses of drones all over the ground. Some buses stopped on the road, the drivers refusing to go further. The servants forced the bus doors open and headed for the hardstand.

Father and Mother stepped through the gates and stopped. Brandon stood near them. Security showed no genuine desire to stop them from coming out. Behind them, staff flooded out, not waiting to be scanned.

Chris dashed across the no man's land of the car park and into Sienna's arms. They kissed like they had not seen each other for years.

'You take too many risks, Chris,' Sienna said.

Father and Mother just stood there, mere metres past the gates, glaring at the gathering crowds. Someone brushed past Father, nearly knocking him over.

Sienna's hand was warm and comforting in hers. Chris gave it a squeeze then let go, walked the fifty metres that separated the two groups.

'Mother,' she said, ignoring Father and Brandon, 'the world outside is better than inside.'

'Really,' Mother said. Her voice was stuck somewhere between curious and venomous. 'Then why were you so desperate to get back in?'

Chris could not fathom Mother's attitude. She thought she would want to be free, as free as Chris and Sienna. She turned, held out a beckoning hand at Sienna, who walked over and took it.

'I had my reasons,' she said. 'I wanted you to meet Sienna. We are engaged to be married.'

Mother looked ready to be sick.

'I know what you are, Mother. You don't belong in there, you belong outside where you can be yourself. It will never be the same in there again. You and Father, the other parents in there, you chose to lock yourselves in. The children didn't. A lot of them, maybe most of them, seeing what you did will try and leave.'

'Christine,' Mother said tensely.

'It's over, Mother, but not for you. You can come out and find a new life, maybe even find happiness.'

Father's left hand clenched and unclenched like he wanted to punch her. The little gun in his left was almost forgotten.

'How dare you,' he snarled, his eyes black and glistening. 'I gave you everything, you dirty little bitch. All I have done my entire life has been for my family.'

Chris stared at her father's empty face and hollow eyes, his clichéd suit and money – so much money, he stank of it.

'Mother,' she said, 'he wants to be here. There is much for him here, for him and Brandon. They got what they want. Come with us.'

Father growled and raised his gun, Chris struck out fast and her baton struck his wrist with a sickening crack. He dropped the gun and involuntarily stepped back, bracing himself. Chris thought he was going to lurch at her, but she was wrong. He dived at Sienna with his fist out. She bent like a blade of grass in the wind and he missed. As Father stood up, Sienna swung her fist, opened her hand and slapped him across the cheek.

Father looked embarrassed, enraged, confused. Chris smiled faintly and stepped between them.

'Don't make me kill him,' Chris said. 'If he touches you, I will'

'You don't deserve her,' Sienna snapped.

'Father,' Chris said. 'I can't believe I was once so scared of you I didn't even know it was fear. I never even knew your name.'

A Security guard picked up his fallen gun.

Father stood up as if steeling himself to strike at Chris. She held out her hand, palm towards him. He stopped.

'You don't scare me anymore,' Chris said. 'You kicked me out of here and I survived things you would not even be able to imagine. What I had to do to survive, I don't think you can do worse than that to me. I would kill you if you hurt Sienna. I would not hesitate and you would not be able to stop me. But it's over now, so none of that matters.

'I know why you kept the fake news going. You wanted people scared so they would stay in the city, leaving you and the rest of the Agency, the Fund, in control of their money. It's all hidden in your computers, everything that happens in there. The Agency skims a bit off the top of every transaction. It's made you rich. Well, by now, hackers have cut through the firewall in both directions and the people inside are seeing the truth of what's outside the Wall, what's past the wasteland. The people here can see how you have manipulated them to keep control.'

Father signalled to a security guard. 'Arrest her, lock her up!'

Security ignored him.

He turned to a security guard in a supervisor's uniform. 'Arrest her!'

'Sorry, sir,' the guard said. 'It has come to my attention that you have lied to me, to us. I don't work for you anymore.' He walked away across the tarmac. One by one, the other security guards did the same, some across to where the servants were gathered, others back into the city.

'The problem is,' Sienna said, 'you kept Security in their own little enclave just outside your wall. You lied to them, fed them the same bullshit you fed your own people, told them they needed you and the walled suburb you gave them, to stay safe. Generations of them, training their kids to be your security so they could stay safe. They now know the truth. They know they can have better lives. Every one of them will be resigning when they see what we have for them.'

First a trickle of people, then a flood.

A group of hackers, computer science students, stepped out the gates. Next, the families of the Security staff.

Steadily, much of the population of the walled town walked out, some of them curious, some of them probably looking for opportunities. Not all, but enough. Soon there were so many young people, students, hipsters and rebels accumulated on the edge of the car park that there must have only been shareholders left inside.

The people who had worked as servants watched. Chris and Sienna walked back to join them, the servants nodding at them in respect.

The hackers, code kids and students from inside joined the crowds from the buses, shook hands, hugged strangers.

From around the ruins, vagabonds, tramps and thieves emerged; dirty and ragged, mind-broken and tired. They stepped out from the shadows, from the tumbledown buildings, dressed in their tatters, carrying bars, poles, rocks. People in servant's uniforms, their neat braids undone, stepped in as if to stop that ragtag army, but instead handed out food, clothes and water, led some of the ragged and damaged to an empty bus.

The people from the Enclave milled about then collected together as if all thinking the same thing at once. There were whispers and talking. Father walked away and went back inside the gates, Mother stayed where she was. Brandon walked over to a group of business students and huddled with them.

A white quadcopter with a cross on the side landed in the middle of the hardstand and unloaded paramedics. Soup kitchen vans arrived from the road carrying food, aid workers brought buses full of help. Jenny appeared with the aid workers and walked over to join Chris and Sienna.

Chris saw Brandon walking towards her, dragging a knot of business students behind him.

'We have spoken and made a decision,' he said with artificial authority in his voice. 'We are coming outside and will take what's out here. We are meant to be in control. We can buy everything.'

A voice in the crowd that had followed him shouted 'yeah'. Others echoed. The cluster of confused gatherers, huddled near the gates, approached Brandon's mob, murmuring their assent.

'If I remember rightly, we, the shareholders in the Fund and the Agency, own this place, most of this island. I want you people to bring us all we have missed out on. We will buy it, we will buy everything. We will buy you.'

'Not this time,' Sienna growled. 'You, fucking dumb shits who let a company lock you in a town, are the richest people on the continent, but I don't care. We don't care. You have a ton of money and own shitloads of land but have used that money to imprison yourselves. You can't buy what we have, not anymore. We have moved on. We, and our stuff, are not for sale.'

Chris looked at Brandon like he was a petulant child. 'Your money does not mean anything anymore.'

Chris looked to her brother, to Jenny, to Sienna, back to Jenny.

Jenny stood silent, just breathing. Chris knew that stance, the danger in it; all their lives it had been a sign of foolishness to come. It was then she was sure Jenny had not changed all that much, was still her best friend, always would be.

Jenny looked down, stooped and picked up a half-brick. She weighed it in her hand, looked at her parents in the front of the crowd. They were sneering at her.

The half-brick flew from her hand towards the crowd of empty-eyed suits, of identical women in sundresses. The servants and free people, as though waiting for an excuse, roared and ran at the crowd from the Enclave, who did the only thing they could possibly do.

They ran.

They did not get the gates closed in time.

Nothing added up, nothing ever had. Nothing mattered, nothing ever could. Only one thing mattered.

She reached out and took Sienna by the hand.

ACKNOWLEDGEMENTS

FIRST, I WOULD like to thank my Noongar ancestors who did whatever they needed to do to survive when the colony wanted us dead. This novel was written mostly on the stolen unceded lands of the Wurundjeri, Woi Wurrung people of the Kulin nations. I acknowledge their elders who fought for their people for generations, the elders who now keep culture alive and the young ones learning culture to become the elders of the future. I also acknowledge all Aboriginal and Torres Strait islander people across the continent now called Australia, we are strong.

Thank you also to all the great First Nations writers who have showed me what is possible.

I would like to thank Robert Watkins who, while at Hachette, started the development and editing of this work. Thank you Robert for always believing in me.

I would like to thank Hachette who have now published three of my novels. Thank you to Vanessa Radnidge, who took over where Robert left off, taking on the difficult challenge of organising me and my novel. Thank you to Camha Pham for the edit and Emily Stewart for the proofread. Thanks also to Karen Ward, Chrysoula Aiello, Jenny Topham, Isabel Staas, Fiona Hazard, Madison Garratt, Eliza Thompson, Lillian Kovats, Chris Sims, Kelly Gaudry, Louise Stark, Alysha Farry, Eve Le Gall and everybody else at Hachette Australia.

Thanks again Grace West for the incredible cover, you always make my books look so good.

Thank you Lily for being there again, as always, you give me purpose and strength. I couldn't do it without you.

Finally thank you to my readers and fans for your ongoing support. Writers are nothing without readers.

Claire G. Coleman is a Noongar writer, born in Western Australia and now based in Naarm. Her family have been from the area around Ravensthorpe and Hopetoun on the south coast of WA since before time started being recorded. She wrote her black&write! Fellowship-winning book *Terra Nullius* while travelling around Australia in a caravan. The *Old Lie* (2019) was her second novel and in 2021 her acclaimed non-fiction book *Lies, Damned Lies* was published by Ultimo Press. *Enclave* is her third novel.

hachette
AUSTRALIA

If you would like to find out more about Hachette Australia,
our authors, upcoming events and new releases, you can visit
our website or our social media channels:

hachette.com.au

 HachetteAustralia

 HachetteAus